With Full Malice

WITH FULL MALICE

BRENDA HILL

FIVE STAR

A part of Gale, Cengage Learning

GALE
CENGAGE Learning·

Detroit • New York • San Francisco • New Haven, Conn • Waterville, Maine • London

GALE
CENGAGE Learning·

LIBRARY OF CONGRESS CATALOGING-IN-PUBLICATION DATA

Hill, Brenda.
    With full malice / Brenda Hill. — 1st ed.
    p. cm.
    ISBN 978-1-4328-2572-0 (hardcover) — ISBN 1-4328-2572-0 (hardcover) 1. Murder—Investigation—Fiction. 2. California—Fiction. I. Title.
PS3608.I4266W58 2012
813'.6—dc23   2011045589

First Edition. First Printing: March 2012.
Published in 2012 in conjunction with Tekno Books and Ed Gorman.

Printed in the United States of America
1 2 3 4 5 6 7 16 15 14 13 12

ACKNOWLEDGMENTS

To the following, I extend my deep appreciation for sharing your time and expertise. Thank you.

To Robert Dearmore, Sergeant (Ret.) Los Angeles County Sheriff's Department, and his patient wife, Sheila.; D. J. (Don) Stephens, nearly ten years military service, Airborne Ranger, Sniper and Small Arms; Claire Marie Teeters, Editor, *Yucaipa/Calimesa News Mirror;* Debi Faris, Founder, Garden of Angels Safe Surrender for Newborns; the staff of Desert Lawn Memorial Park & Funeral Home, Calimesa, CA; the paramedics and EMTs in Calimesa and Yucaipa, CA, who allowed me to interrupt their off-time to ask questions; Wayne Hall, Legal Dept., Denny's Corporation, Spartanburg, SC; Patti Wollerton, General Manager, Denny's, in Yucaipa, CA, and her wonderful staff; Southwest Airlines Customer Relations; Yuma Community Food Bank, Yuma, AZ; Chelle Cordero, Stony Point Ambulance Corps, New York State Emergency Medical Technician; Brandon G. Cole, D.C., and his wife, Rosa Cole; Diane Mierzwik, Yucaipa Writers' Gallery; John McLeod, Yucaipa; Carolynn & Catie and the crew, Postal Annex, Yucaipa. And to Maxine Piotrowski. Thanks, everyone. All the errors are mine.

To our wonderful law enforcement officers in Yucaipa. You've worked hard to keep our community safe. Thank you.

To First Readers Ginny Lewon, Joyce Hunt, Earl C. Baker, Cheryl McDaniel.

To authors M. Jean Pike, Victoria Howard, Michael Prescott.

Acknowledgments

To my patient editor, Alice Duncan. And to Tracey L. Matthews, Content Project Editor, Five Star, and to Tiffany Schofield, Acquisitions Editor, Five Star. You're the best!

And always, my love and thanks to Roger & Debbie Bowman, who dropped everything countless times to respond to my SOS calls. And to Amanda, Kyle, and Sean, the lights in my life.

CHAPTER ONE

If that scumbag deserved anything, it was to die.

She had planned it to the smallest detail, but anything could go wrong. If her timing was off a split-second, if a customer appeared at the wrong time, if, if, if. She had to do everything she could to make sure nothing unexpected happened.

She turned into the restaurant parking lot, pleased to note only two vehicles besides his. If her luck held, the steakhouse would stay dead for another fifteen minutes or so.

Jeff Hawley's rusty red pickup faced south, with the driver's door opposite the restaurant's windows.

It couldn't have been better.

"All systems go," she murmured, using dialogue from an old movie she'd recently watched.

She had chosen a dark blue Chevy Aveo that at dusk might appear blue, dark green, or black. After leaving the rental agency, she'd taken Sand Canyon Road over the hill from Yucaipa to the orange groves and had smudged dirt on the California plates.

At the steakhouse, she parked so she could keep watch on the front door. Hawley was inside, enjoying his dinner. If she were successful, it would be the last thing he'd enjoy.

She placed the wide-brimmed straw hat on her head, dug in the shopper's tote for the surgical gloves and tugged them on, then retrieved the oversized man's long-sleeved shirt and draped it over her blouse. She checked the washcloth in the plastic bag.

7

Good. It still had enough moisture to wipe away any splattered blood.

Next came the gun. She snapped the case open and lifted the black Glock 26 9mm from its egg-crate-foam bed. She screwed the titanium silencer onto the threaded barrel, but before loading the magazine, she paused. Did she really want the extra weight and length of a silencer on the gun? How would she be able to conceal it when she approached Hawley?

She glanced around the parking lot. Still dead, so deciding to take her chances, she unscrewed the silencer and loaded the magazine containing hollow-point bullets.

Even though the G-26 was a powerful subcompact, it felt good in her hand. From the back of the slide to the tip of the barrel, it was about six inches long. Loaded, it was heavier than the small-caliber revolvers she'd fired as a teenager when target shooting in Wyoming with her father, but last week she'd ventured into the woods for some practice just to get the feel of the gun. The low bore axis design helped reduce muzzle rise in recoil, so hitting him quickly in the targeted areas should be no problem.

Once more she went over the plan: he'd leave through the front door, and she would approach him as he walked to his pickup. Then, if her luck held, he'd turn his back to her and she would have the perfect excuse to trail after him.

Then she'd nail him.

It sounded simple enough, but the timing was critical. She had to shoot after he passed the restaurant windows and just before he entered his pickup. And she would have to fire before he saw the gun. If he overpowered her and called the cops, they'd come, even for him. Then what would she do?

She couldn't allow that to happen.

She picked up the engraved envelope she'd received in the mail. Inside, a note-sized sheet of paper had today's date stamped below an elaborately scripted header, The Ruby Red Society. There was no signature or return address. She folded the note and slid it back into its envelope to dispose of along with the tote.

Beads of sweat rolled under her bra. Sweat slicked her hands. No matter how determined she was to kill him, she felt moments of doubt.

Was she doing the right thing?

She had gone over her decision many times, debating first one issue then the other, but she always reached the same conclusion.

He had to die.

Behind her, rush hour traffic on Yucaipa Boulevard was thinning out. To the west, the amber sun slid behind the San Bernardino Mountains, and the first stars sparkled in the coral and indigo sky.

She went over the plan once more, making sure she remembered every step. Did she have it down? Would she make some simple mistake like forgetting to pick up the casings?

The straw hat scratched her tender scalp. She squirmed in her seat. What on earth was he doing? He'd had time to eat three meals.

A minivan pulled into the lot and headed for a parking spot by the restaurant door.

No, no, no! She didn't want witnesses! Maybe, if he stayed inside for a while longer, it would be okay. Tracking the car's progress, she caught a glimpse of children in the back seat.

She went cold. Not children. She might chance adult witnesses if other circumstances were right, but she'd scrap the plan before risking trauma to a child.

She checked the restaurant door.

"Not now," she whispered, "don't leave now."

The minivan doors slid open and two boys around twelve

years of age jumped out. A man and woman followed, both dressed in jeans and gold T-shirts with large blue numbers on the back.

Hurry inside, she urged. Hurry!

Only when they had made it safely inside did she breathe. Immediately after, the door swung open again and Hawley stepped out. His lean figure passed the restaurant windows and she tightened her grip on the gun. She scanned the lot behind to make sure no one was pulling in.

This was it.

Now! Go now!

She grabbed the shopper's tote and slipped out of the car. Sliding the gun inside her pocket, she headed straight for him.

Hawley shuffled toward his pickup with his shoulders hunched and head down as if he didn't want anyone to notice him. She hoped he was ashamed, but he probably wasn't. His type seldom was.

Just as she got within ten feet of him, he raised his head and looked directly at her. For just a second, she was taken aback by his handsome face, the green eyes, slim nose, full mouth. No one would have guessed how rotten he was inside simply by looking at him.

Like Satan, she thought. Beautiful on the outside.

She flashed her winning smile and tried to look helpless. "Excuse me, could you help me? I'm so scatterbrained that I've lost my—"

"Go away," he mumbled, brushing by her.

Perfect, she thought, trailing slightly behind. Just ignore me, keep your back to me.

Suddenly, as though alerted something was wrong, he began to walk faster toward the red pickup and reached for the driver's door handle.

Now!

So fast it was almost one movement, she dropped the tote, pulled out the gun, and lifted it with both hands. He must have heard the tote hit the ground, because he spun around and saw the gun.

"No!"

She aimed for his heart and pulled the trigger. Blood sprayed from a blackened hole in his shirt and he staggered backward. The pistol recoiled, but she stepped forward and fired a second time, knocking him off his feet. Bending over his sprawled form, she fired again, putting a round through his temple. Blood splattered, chunks of skull flew, and he was still.

From behind her, someone shouted and she heard footsteps pounding toward them. She dropped the gun into the tote, snatched the warm casings from the pavement and pulled off the gloves, dropping them all into the tote. A man about thirty, wearing a baseball cap, pushed her down beside the pickup.

"What happened?" Crouching beside her, he glanced wildly in all directions.

"He's dead, he's dead!" she screamed. "Somebody killed him!" Staring in horror at Hawley's body, she rose.

"Get down!" He tugged her arm to pull her back down, but she didn't budge.

"Are you hit? Did you see who shot him?"

"A man . . . shot him and ran . . ." She dropped her voice to a whisper as if she were going into shock.

"Which direction?"

She simply stared at him.

"Which way did he go?"

She blinked several times before pointing to the empty field next to the restaurant.

"He must be gone." He patted his shirt pocket. "Damn, must've left my cell phone inside. You got one?"

She forced herself to remain expressionless.

"It's okay," he told her in a soothing voice. "My wife will call the cops. Just please, lady, get down and stay down until they get here." Crouching, he crab-walked to the victim. "Who is he?"

When she said nothing, he turned his attention to Hawley. Crossing himself, he began CPR. Only then did she ease back a few steps.

Confident it was too late to save the dirtbag, she turned and, carefully pacing her steps, headed for the Chevy. Just walk. Don't draw attention to yourself.

A woman behind her screamed and someone shouted something about an ambulance, but she didn't look back. Keeping her measured pace as she approached the car, she yanked off her hat and oversized shirt and stuffed them into the tote. Then she wiped her blood-splattered face and neck with the rag and dropped it with the other things.

It wasn't until she reached her car that she risked a quick glance backward. Several people were gathering around the pickup. Pole-mounted floodlights flipped on, illuminating the entire parking lot.

Time for her escape, but she didn't have to rush.

No one suspected her; no one was even looking her way. Even if someone saw her, her feigned innocence shone brightly, like a golden halo.

Now all she had to do was unload the tote and she'd be home free.

CHAPTER TWO

He lay face up on the pavement outside of Jimmy's Steakhouse, arms and legs spread. Like a snow angel, Madison thought, only this angel had chunks of his skull blown away.

Blood pooled around his head and torso, staining his plaid shirt, the pavement, and splattering the pickup beside the body. Madison caught a glimpse before the medics surrounded him and hoped she wouldn't disgrace herself by passing out.

Revolving lights from the fire truck and two San Bernardino County Sheriff's Department patrol cars threw a kaleidoscope of reds and blues on the restaurant and the gathering crowd. Sirens wailed in the distance, growing louder as more teams responded to the *Shots Fired* alert.

"Grab the BVM!" A female paramedic bent over the victim. An EMT slapped a ventilator mask into her hands. "Start compressions!"

No matter how they tried to resuscitate, Madison doubted anyone could live after such a massive head wound. What were his last thoughts? she wondered. Had he known he was going to die?

"Miss! Miss!" a deputy shouted, pushing her back with the gathering crowd. "Please step back."

She stumbled back about ten feet, and with trembling hands, retrieved her camera from the briefcase slung over her shoulder. She took deep breaths as her therapist had taught her and snapped photos of the scene, trying to maintain a professional demeanor, wishing she were anywhere but here. This was her first crime scene as a reporter, and it was certainly going to be her last.

An ambulance pulled into the parking lot, followed by several other vehicles. Cutting its siren and flashing lights, it cruised toward the victim, the crowd parting to make a path as if they were a living Red Sea. The crew unloaded a gurney and pushed it toward the victim.

Madison stepped to the side and punched Marie's number on her cell phone.

"Where are you?" She tried to keep her voice below a shriek. "What's taking so long?"

"Traffic snarl on the 605," Marie Campbell, the *Yucaipa Tribune*'s editor told her. "Sorry to do this to you, kid, but it looks like it'll be at least an hour before I can get there. Talk to witnesses and hang in there. You're doing good."

"Yeah, sure," Madison said to a dead line. She wished she'd never called Marie in the first place. Of all the times she could have picked to do a review of the steakhouse, it had to have been that night. And of course it was one of those rare nights when not one of the three news reporters was available.

If she ever saw emergency lights at a review site again, she'd simply turn her car around and leave.

A collective moan came from the gathering crowd and Madison moved to get a better view. The EMTs had halted their efforts and were gazing at the navy-clad paramedic.

"Call it," she said, rising and pulling off her latex gloves.

An EMT disconnected monitor leads, while another pulled an IV tube from the needle. A deputy stepped forward, glanced at the body, then spoke into the microphone on his shoulder. Another deputy began cordoning off the immediate area with yellow tape.

He's dead, Madison thought, staring at the victim before

they covered him with a tarp. She hadn't known him, but she felt like weeping.

A deputy took notes from the paramedics, and a few moments later, the fire truck's diesel engine revved up several degrees to a loud clatter. When it pulled out, followed by the ambulance, most of the waiting crowd broke up and headed for their cars.

What now? Madison wondered. Talk to witnesses, Marie had said. Oh, Lord, she didn't have any training as a reporter and didn't want any. Her nice, safe, restaurant review job was just right for her, as far away from violence as she could get.

But Marie was depending on her, so she turned her camera to a sheriff's patrol car, its front doors open, splitting the black and gold logo along the side. A deputy sat inside, writing on a clipboard and talking to a man in civilian clothes. A witness, Madison thought, wondering if she should approach him, what she'd ask if she got the opportunity, all the while praying Marie would hurry up and get there so she could go home to her quiet apartment and well-ordered life.

About six feet from the open patrol car, another deputy stood talking to a young family who looked as if they'd just come from a Little League game. She hoped, for the kids' sake, they hadn't seen the shooting.

Madison exchanged her camera for her notebook and thought of the mantra she'd overheard from the reporters: Get the five Ws: who, what, when, where, why, and how. Okay, six.

She jotted down her impressions of the victim. Late thirties, perhaps. Shorter than her ex-husband, so probably around five-nine or less. Hair color? Difficult to tell with all that blood. His eyes? She'd never forget how they looked, half open and staring, as if accusing his tormentor—or begging for his life as she imagined her parents had done.

"You from the paper?" the fortyish man standing next to her

asked. "Can't believe this. Me and the wife here"—he tugged the arm of a straggly haired blonde next to him—"just stopped to have a bite."

Determined to stay focused, Madison flipped to a new page. "Did you see what happened?" she asked, then remembered to ask their names.

"Middleton," he told her. "That's M-I-D-D-L-E-T-O-N." He paused long enough to make sure she got it, then recited his phone number. "Me and Candy got here just ahead of the fire truck, but that guy saw it all," he added, jerking his head toward the sheriff's car. "He was there."

"Did you talk to him?"

"Nah, he was doing that CPR-thing until the medics took over, but I heard him talking to the cops."

Although Madison avoided looking at the body, she was aware of him lying there, covered in his own blood. Had he known they were trying to save him? Had her parents known? Her legs wobbled. Locking her knees, she tried to concentrate.

"Did he see who did the shooting?"

"I don't think so, but the woman with him might know something."

"What woman? Where? With the witness or the victim?"

Middleton shrugged. "Wasn't no woman when me and Candy got here, but that's what he said. Older woman, he told them. Before I could hear anything else, the cops pulled him to the car."

"Older? How old?"

"I don't know. Old."

Madison added *senior woman* to her notes.

Just then two more patrol cars arrived and a county CSI van pulled into the site. Doors flew open and the crew unloaded boxes of lights and equipment.

Madison imagined them finding a chunk of bloody skull and

all her reserve crumbled. The ground swayed.

"Lady, you all right?" Middleton grabbed her arm.

"Maddy!" a male voice boomed from several feet away.

No one but her grandmother and San Bernardino County Homicide Detective Dexter Quinn called her by that name. She tolerated it from Grandma Ella, and under different circumstances, she would've berated Dexter for it, but now his voice was the most beautiful sound she had ever heard.

"Dex."

He was standing behind the tape, a notepad in hand, talking to a deputy. At six-four, his white hair in the same flattop he'd worn as a college football player thirty years ago, he was a mountain of a man. How had she missed his arrival?

Sliding his notebook into his pocket, he strode toward her, his linebacker's bulk expertly cutting through the crowd. She felt the strength of his supporting arms, and his familiar scent of soap and aftershave offered a safe haven.

"Can you walk?"

Head down, she nodded, too embarrassed by her weakness to show her face. Dexter kept an arm around her and led her to his Tahoe.

She should have protested, should have questioned more people, but her wobbly knees desperately needed a moment's rest. Besides, few people argued with Dexter Quinn. Once again he was rescuing her, just as he'd done when she was six.

He helped her into his eleven-year-old SUV and retrieved a bottle of water from the rear floorboard. She took a long drink and leaned her head against the soft gray leather. She sighed. Safe again.

Her teeth began to chatter.

Dexter must have noticed because he snatched a fuzzy blanket from the back seat and spread it over her.

"You could use a shot of whiskey. Got anything stronger than iced tea at home?"

"Diet cola," she said, attempting a joke. The warmth from the blanket was seeping into her bones.

"You look like hell," he said. "What in God's name are you doing here? Of all the people I know, you shouldn't be at a crime scene."

"Marie—"

"You're not bucking for a reporter's job, are you? That would be the worst mismatch since your sorry attempt at marriage."

"You're incorrigible, but I love you anyway." Keeping a watchful eye for Marie, she explained why she was there. "I wonder who he is . . . was."

"Hey, listen to me. Don't worry about him, you hear? There's nothing you can do for the guy now, and it's you I'm concerned about."

"I'm a big girl now."

"Take a look at your face and tell me how big you are. You still look as if you're going to pass out."

"Marie's not here yet, and she's depending on me."

"Dammit, you don't need this shit. Go home, Maddy. I'll square it with Marie."

Dexter had a decision to make. Loyalty to the dead or concern for the living?

In all of his thirty years on the job, his first consideration had been for the citizens he'd sworn to serve and justice for the dead, but when he saw Maddy's face, there was no question.

From the time he'd carried her out of the carnage at her home when she was six, he had been committed to her safety and well-being. He'd never forgotten how she had looked then, her silky blonde curls tangled, her big blue eyes wide with shock, so traumatized that all she could do was scream when anyone tried to get her out of that house.

But when he'd called her Maddy and reached for her, she had wrapped her arms around his neck, lain her head against his cheek, and held on. In the twenty-odd years since, he couldn't have been more concerned for her welfare if she were his own daughter.

But Maddy on a violent crime scene? Christ-all-Friday, no matter how much progress she'd made, that was enough to send her back to the shrink. What the hell was Marie thinking? She knew Madison's past. If Dexter didn't have a job to do, he'd personally drive Maddy home, put her to bed, and stay with her in case of nightmares.

But he did owe the dead, so, arranging for a deputy to drive her car home, he watched the white Saab disappear up the boulevard. Muttering a curse, he turned to the crime scene.

CHAPTER THREE

Dexter's new partner, Detective Felipe Rodrigo, a forty-five-year-old Latino whom Dex had dubbed *Rico*, had questioned the restaurant personnel, and of course, no one had seen anything. Now he was talking to Deputy Hesketh, the first responding officer, and even from several feet away, Dexter could see that the deputy was more than a little irritated.

Shorter than most detectives, Rico had perfected a certain swagger, reminding Dexter of a strutting peacock he'd seen years ago at a theme park. Instead of fanning iridescent feathers, Rico wore tailored suits and spouted procedure to any poor fool he happened to catch unaware. No one liked him. How he'd advanced through the ranks, Dexter couldn't guess. More than once, he'd been tempted to knock the little prig on his ass.

The crime scene techs were taking photos, and the coroner would be arriving soon to declare the cause of death.

Dexter snapped on his latex gloves and crouched down for a closer look at the body.

Male. Caucasian. Late thirties. Blond. Two gunshot wounds to the chest, one to the right temple, all front entrance wounds. Powder burns indicated the perp's close proximity to the victim. Needles, cotton swabs, and the medics' latex gloves still lay where they had left them. Forensics would examine each one for trace evidence. Tattoos covered the victim's knuckles and his black lace-up ankle shoes were prison-issue. The pager under his shirt and the GPS ankle bracelet, Global Positioning System, confirmed it.

Interesting.

Since 2005, when a nine-year-old girl had been raped and murdered in Florida by a convicted sex offender who, it was later revealed, lived across the street, a number of states had passed laws requiring or allowing GPS tracking. Perhaps it wasn't foolproof, Dexter thought, but it was damned close.

"You see the ankle bracelet?" Rico asked Hesketh.

"High-risk offender," Hesketh said with a slight rolling of eyes.

Dexter held in a sigh. Rico was still playing his game of one-upmanship. As a rookie detective, he had a lot to learn. He just didn't realize it.

"One witness," Hesketh continued, "Brandon Searl, Yucaipa, was having dinner with his wife. When he heard shots, he ran outside, saw the victim down, and administered CPR until paramedics arrived."

His notes were detailed and precise, Dexter observed, and if called to testify, the defense would have a difficult time finding holes in his story.

"You make your notifications?" Dexter asked.

"Yes sir. The coroner is en route, and I let the mayor and city council know what we have."

Dexter hated all the unofficial protocol, but Yucaipa was a growing community of over fifty thousand in the San Bernardino foothills below Big Bear Lake, and the mayor was active in city affairs. He attended city functions, and it didn't matter if it was a ribbon-cutting ceremony for a new market or a fund-raiser for a school activity. While Yucaipa hadn't suffered from many violent crimes, the newly elected mayor made it known he'd be unhappy if someone asked about a murder and he hadn't been prepped.

Dexter had learned early in his career that it wasn't good to have an unhappy mayor.

The coroner's van pulled into the lot, and a deputy waved him through the yellow tape.

About five-ten, slightly balding, and even in his neatly pressed jumpsuit, San Bernardino County Coroner Julian Goertzen resembled Mikhail Gorbachev and was twice as sharp.

After logging in the time, Dexter joined him and briefed the coroner on what they had so far.

Goertzen opened his evidence collection kit and took photos of the body, the blood splatter on the pavement, the pickup, and the surrounding area. After making a few notes, he knelt, and with Dexter beside him, began his preliminary examination of the body.

"What do you think, Jules?" Dexter asked.

"Two entrance wounds to the left anterior chest may have penetrated the heart. From the size of the wounds, I'd say the perp used a 9mm, possibly hollow-point ammo. Surrounding area is clean, no casings, so I'll have to open him up to be sure."

"A drive-by?"

"The shots were deliberate, Dex, especially the one to the temporal lobe." He pointed to the victim's right temple. "That one was a hard contact discharge, up close and personal. See the gunpowder stippling?"

Rico joined Dexter to observe the pinpoint skin abrasions surrounding the wound. They resembled tiny black pimples.

"Those marks tell me the muzzle was within two feet of the body," Goertzen said for Rico's benefit. "The eccentric margin of abrasion, this area here," he added, pointing to a ring of scraped skin with the abrasion thicker in one area, like a lopsided circle, "tells me the bullet penetrated the skin at an angle. I'd say the assailant discharged two shots at the victim's chest, and then leaned down and fired directly to the temple.

Someone wanted him dead."

"Can you estimate the time of death?"

"Rigor's just starting, so I'd say in the last three hours."

Dexter nodded. The timing fit.

"The witness says the perp escaped in the field," Rico told them. All three men gazed at the scrub grass field next to the steakhouse and beyond to the newly paved hillside road and housing tract in various stages of completion.

"Could've gone anywhere," Dexter mused.

"We'll check the area for footprints," Goertzen said, "but it'll take a while."

"Any thoughts about the blood splatter on the pickup?"

"I need time, Dex. You know that."

"Your best guess?"

Goertzen's heavy brows furrowed, and Dexter knew from experience the coroner was already working out the scenario.

"Wrong angle to be from the field. I'd say the shots were fired from the parking lot. Shoes look like Chino's, heels good condition, so I'd guess he got them within the last couple months. Skin's peeling on the knuckles, so the tattoos are recent, perhaps a week. Based on that plus the standard issue shoes, I'd say he's recently released."

Dexter made a note to contact the prison for the exact date.

The victim's pockets yielded a plastic wallet with a California driver's license issued two months earlier to a Jeffrey Hawley, thirty-seven, Calimesa.

After Goertzen wrapped Hawley's head and hands in unlined paper bags and secured them with tape, he nodded at the forensic team. They worked in unison under the floodlights, taking photographs and swabs of the victim's blood, laying tape for a grid search of the parking lot and the dirt field on the west side of the restaurant. They placed tent markers at blood drops and measured the splatter on the pickup to determine the bullets' trajectories.

Dexter wanted to run a search on the victim, so he headed for his Tahoe. A cold breeze blew through the parking lot, ruffling papers and the yellow tape.

Hurrying to catch up, Rico hunched into his suit jacket. "Must've dropped twenty degrees. A suit looks sharp, but it's not as warm as a uniform."

For the first time, Dexter felt a speck of camaraderie for the new detective. "Still spring, Rico, and it gets cold around here in the evenings."

A black SUV pulled into the parking lot and Dexter, recognizing Marie Campbell's 4Runner, paused. She bolted out of the vehicle and rushed over to him, her white-streaked hair bouncing off her shoulders.

"God, what traffic. Where's Madison? I can't reach her on her cell." Marie's sharp eyes took in the scene, darting from the glaring floodlights to the CSI techs. "He died?"

As much as Dexter wanted to let loose with a string of curses, he remembered he was a gentleman. And after working with Marie for over twenty years, hassling the city council for improvements, co-sponsoring activities with underprivileged children, he'd never berate her for anything, even if he detested certain aspects of her job.

"I sent her home where she should be," he said after describing her condition. "Here's her camera and notes."

"I need details—"

"You'll get them when I know them," he told her. "As of now, it's the standard fatal shooting in Jimmy's parking lot, assailant unknown, investigation ongoing."

"But—"

"Good night, Marie." He firmly dismissed her and continued to his car. Rico ran to catch up.

"That woman's hanging around, taking photos," he said,

checking over his shoulder, his voice incredulous.

"She's a newspaper editor and a professional," Dexter told him, swallowing a snarl, remembering his vow to the captain to get along. "She's done a lot of good for this community and gives her free time whenever someone's in need. She's dedicated and will get this news in the morning's edition even if she has to stay up all night and print it herself. So knock off the attitude."

With Rico in the passenger seat beside him, Dexter ran the ID on his mobile data terminal, and CLETS—the California Law Enforcement Telecommunication System—pulled up a criminal file. Clicking through, Dexter discovered Hawley had a sealed juvenile file and had served seven years for the rape and murder of an eleven-year-old Yucaipa girl before being released from CIM, the California Institution for Men at Chino, a month ago. Presently, he was living with his mother in a mobile home park in Calimesa.

Pedophile. Child murderer.

"So the innocent victim wasn't so innocent after all," Rico said.

Dexter had seen it all before, some victim's boyfriend or father going off half-cocked and taking revenge. While he could understand it, he couldn't condone citizens taking control of the law. That would throw civilization back to the Old West days when people shot each other for a wrong look.

After a quick word to the deputy, he and Rico slid into the back seat of the patrol car. The witness clutched his red cap. The skin around his mouth was white, and Dexter knew the man had reached his limit for tonight. He'd keep the questions brief.

"I know it's been a long night, Mr. Searl," he said after introducing Rico and himself, "but tell me what you saw."

"I already told him everything I know." Searl nodded wearily in the deputy's direction. "Twice."

"You were there?"

"Like I said, the wife and I were inside, having dinner. I heard what I thought was backfire. After all, we're close to the boulevard. Who'd expect gunshots?"

"I understand. How many shots did you hear?"

"Didn't count them, but maybe three, four. That's when I went outside to look. I told my wife to stay inside."

"And? What did you see?"

"At first I didn't see nothing. Then I see this screaming woman bending over something. This guy, he was all shot up."

"You didn't actually witness the shooting?"

"He was down when I got there."

"Did you see anyone running from the scene?"

Searl shook his head. "I didn't see nothing except this guy all shot up, so I pulled the woman down and started CPR. Poor sonofabitch."

"Did you know him?"

"I just saw him inside the restaurant."

"Was the woman with him?"

"I guess. I wasn't paying attention. No reason to, you know?"

"When you pulled her down, did she say anything?"

"She was hysterical, didn't make much sense. You can imagine how she'd be."

"Did she see who shot him?"

"Just that they were talking and someone came running up to them and shot him. Just like that. Then he ran off into the field."

"She said he escaped in the field?"

Searl nodded.

"Who was she?"

"Didn't ask."

"Is she around here now?"

Searl's gaze swept the parking lot. "She's not here, and I haven't seen her since. I was trying to keep the guy alive."

"Can you describe her for me?"

"Can't remember much about her except a big straw hat like ladies wear outside to garden and stuff."

"Was she older or younger than the victim?"

He shrugged. "Older."

"Old enough to be his mother?"

He shrugged again. "I don't know. Older than him. That's all."

After taking Searl's name and number, Dexter released him to go home.

"Let's call it a night, Rico. I'll make the next-of-kin call."

On the way to Calimesa, Dexter thought about the older woman. Was she Hawley's mother? If so, why had she left the scene? Had she panicked at the sound of gunfire and run? Had she felt threatened herself, threatened enough to leave her son behind?

He wanted some answers and he wanted them now, before the trail grew cold.

CHAPTER FOUR

The farther Madison got from the crime scene, the stronger she felt. She dropped off the deputy at the station and headed home. Once in her driveway, instead of shutting off the engine, she sat behind the wheel and stared bleakly at her middle unit in the stucco triplex.

Light from the living room lamps glowed through the closed sage drapes, and even though one couldn't tell from the front, a light shone in every room—including the bathroom—and her radio softly played New Age music. By all appearances, someone was home.

Pathetic, Madison knew, absolutely pitiful that a grown woman had to keep her home staged in order to enter it, let alone sleep there. She'd even chosen a middle unit so she wouldn't have to worry about side windows.

Tonight, however, even a fully lit condo didn't give her the sense of security she needed, so she headed for the one place where she felt safe—her grandmother's home, an older two-story frame house nestled in the foothills overlooking the city. It even had a wrap-around porch that her grandfather built because Grandma Ella loved to sit with Maddy at night and watch the lights glimmer in the valley. Fairy lights, Gran would tell her, weaving magical stories about fairy godmothers who watched over their charges.

But it was Ella's big, homey kitchen with its yellow walls, butcher block counters holding glass jars full of cookies, homemade pastas, and spices that Madison loved best. An oak table large enough to seat twelve stood right in the middle of the room, and it was there, during Madison's growing up years, that she'd help her grandmother roll out dough for noodles, bread, cookies, cakes, and pies. That kitchen was a room full of love and warmth as well as good food, a sanctuary where her grandmother had nurtured her back from the hell in which she'd been thrown at age six.

Madison desperately needed that comfort now.

The hillside home was ablaze with lights and Madison felt a prickling of alarm. Although active in the Women's Club and several charitable organizations, evenings usually found her grandmother tucked on the sofa watching her favorite TV programs.

Then Madison spotted the familiar 1980 Mercedes W126 parked behind Ella's Hyundai. Cora, Ella's best friend for nearly thirty years. No doubt the two women were inside, munching popcorn, "For the fiber, you know," debating the evening's programs. Ella loved a good tearjerker while practical, down-to-earth Cora usually argued for a documentary.

Still, even with Cora visiting, it was unusual for the house to be so bright.

Inside, the Tiffany lamps were lit, the TV dark, and through the archway into the dining room, Madison could see, under the chandelier, the carved dining table set for four with dessert plates, cups, saucers, and even her grandmother's Royal Doulton teapot.

So Gran had been entertaining? Madison felt relief, but why hadn't she known? Since her grandfather's death when she was seventeen, she'd stepped in and helped Ella with most of her activities.

Cora's authoritative voice sounded from the kitchen along with one Madison had never heard. Curious, she walked through and found her grandmother, dressed in a linen pant-suit, taking a can of whipped cream from the fridge. Two pies from the local bakery sat on the oak table.

A woman she didn't know was chatting with Cora and her sister, Clara. Madison was surprised, not only because of the other woman, but because Clara, opposite in every way from her stern sister, preferred evenings at home. Tonight must be special, but again, why hadn't she known?

"This is Adelle Parkins," Ella said, "my best friend from high school. She called this afternoon . . . late. I was so surprised . . ." She seemed to prattle, which was unusual for her. Of course one never had much chance to talk when Cora was present.

Madison offered her hand to a woman quite different from her grandmother. Ella loved her salt and pepper hair, telling anyone who asked that she'd never consider coloring it, that she finally had a frost job for free. Adelle wore heavy makeup and her hair was jet black. Or was that a wig?

Ella was soft and round, and about an inch shorter than Madison's five-six. Even sitting, Adelle appeared much taller.

"Your grandmother and I haven't seen each other in years," Adelle explained, "but my son just moved to Riverside and I flew out to see him. I'm so glad I caught Ella at home and not off gallivanting to some exotic place."

"Ella's idea of exotic is the occasional trip to the casino with Sis and me for the seafood buffet," Cora sniffed, sounding even more sharp-tongued than usual.

A bit of jealousy? Madison wondered, sliding onto a wooden chair. Maybe she didn't like the thought of sharing her best friend with a stranger.

"Perhaps next time you visit our area, you can join us." Clara spoke in her usual, barely audible voice.

Life was funny, Madison thought. Gran and Cora, although so different, got along better than either did with Clara, who was so passive and sweet-looking that she was like a living Kewpie doll. But appearances could be deceiving. Clara was a widow, and although the sisters descended from an orange baron in Old San Bernardino and had never needed to support themselves, Clara spent her adult life teaching English and literature. Cora, on the other hand, was exactly as she appeared. Tall, rail-thin, with metal-frame bifocals, she'd been a secretary at the Marine base, and with her commanding demeanor, she could have been a general.

"Want some pie, honey?" Gran asked, her voice higher pitched than usual. Tighter, as if she were on edge.

"No thanks. I just wanted to see you before I went to bed."

Ella frowned. "What's wrong? You look pale. Did something happen during the review?" She explained to Adelle about Madison's job at the newspaper, her voice filled with pride.

"The three of us often visit the places Madison recommends," Cora said. "Not that we always agree, mind you, but quite often I do." She said it with authority, as if Madison should be flattered. And she was.

"Normally I love it," Madison said with a sigh, "but tonight was something else. Guess you didn't hear that someone was murdered in the parking lot. Marie asked me to cover it until she could get there."

"Murdered?" Both sisters echoed. Everyone looked horrified. "At that Japanese place in Redlands?"

"That's next week. I was at Jimmy's."

Ella dropped the whipped cream. "You were there?"

Madison rose to pick up the can. "I didn't actually see it happen," she said. "When I got there, the paramedics were working on him."

Her grandmother slid into a chair.

"You okay?" Madison filled a glass with water and gave it to her.

Ella struggled to speak, but it was as if all the air in her lungs had been forced out. "What happened?" she finally managed.

"A man was shot." Madison briefly described what happened and about Marie needing her. "I tried to do what she asked, but I didn't get much. I let her down."

"Nonsense," Cora stated. "You're no reporter, and it was preposterous that your editor asked you to stay. At least Detective Quinn had the good sense to send you home."

"Are you okay, Madison?" Clara asked. "You look so pale. Have some tea and pie with us."

"I'm better now, but I'm concerned about Gran."

"It's just been a long evening with her friend unexpectedly showing up." Cora threw a disapproving frown at Adelle. "I'll make sure she gets some rest, so don't worry about that, and I'll drive Adelle to Riverside."

"No!" Ella said, and when everyone looked at her, she blushed. "I'm sorry, Cora. I appreciate the offer, but I might want to spend some time there, meet Adelle's son."

"But Ella—"

"No, it's okay. I'll be fine by morning."

Cora's sharp features settled into resignation. "Who was murdered?"

Madison didn't want to talk about the evening, especially since it made her grandmother uneasy. But Cora wasn't one to let a subject drop, and, even though Adelle couldn't possibly be interested in local matters, she was paying close attention.

"I don't know who he was, Cora. He didn't look familiar—at least from what I could tell, and Dexter didn't say anything about knowing the guy. But I saw him lying there, and . . ."

Ella took her granddaughter's hand. "After all you've been through, and now this."

Madison's cell rang, and it was Dexter. "I'm okay," she told him. "I'm at Gran's." They spoke briefly. "He worries about me as if I were still a child," she said after hanging up. "I'm fortunate to have him."

"Why don't you stay over, Maddy? You shouldn't be by yourself tonight."

"Thanks, Gran, but I'll head on home. I have to face Marie in the morning, and all my clothes are at my apartment. I'll pick you up tomorrow afternoon."

"Are you sure you're up to it after what happened tonight?"

"Of course. We don't often get the opportunity to see him."

"If you don't mind me asking," Cora said, "where are you going?"

"To see Senator Stone. He's home from Washington on sick leave. Exhaustion, according to the news, but he still made time for Maddy and me."

"Senator Logan Stone?" Adelle asked, her eyes wide. "You know a United States senator? I'm impressed."

"Don't be, I'm not that important. Years ago when he was the district attorney, he prosecuted that, that—"

"Degenerate," Cora offered.

"Thanks. He worked like a madman to get that degenerate who murdered Madison's parents locked up."

"I heard about that," Adelle said, "and I'm so sorry. It was your daughter, wasn't it?"

"And her husband, but I'd rather not talk about it."

A brown wood-spider made its way across the kitchen. All the ladies, including Madison, silently stared as if it were an invader from another planet.

Cora rose and stomped on it.

"One less undesirable to worry about." She wiped her shoe with a paper towel. "Too bad we can't do the same with Bates."

At Adelle's questioning frown, she explained. "Michael Bates, the man who murdered Ella's daughter and son-in-law. Although he's supposed to serve a life sentence, they just may release him one day. You never know what the courts will do."

"Cora! Drop it," Ella said with the sharpest tone Madison had ever heard. For once, Cora went silent.

Release Bates? Just the thought of him getting out of prison made Madison's heart skip a beat. But she didn't want to worry her grandmother, so she managed to portray a calmness she didn't feel and kissed Ella goodnight.

Was it possible that her worst nightmare could come true?

CHAPTER FIVE

Deputy Sheriff Hector Gonzales followed Dexter to the senior mobile home park. Most of the yards were brown and overgrown with dandelions, although he noticed an occasional attempt at a flower garden. Even they looked wilted. A dark streetlamp marked a left turn, and only one trailer had outside lights.

"See any numbers?" Dexter radioed, slowly cruising the dim narrow lanes.

"Too dark," the deputy replied, "but I think that's it ahead. That faded pink trailer."

The Hawley place, which, in his headlights, looked at least forty years old, had no flowers, just a brown patch that hadn't been trimmed in years. No gardener there, Dexter thought. But that didn't mean she didn't own a straw hat.

She wasn't truly a suspect, at least not yet. Most mothers didn't kill their offspring—once past the teenage years, he thought wryly. Dexter knew of several times his sister was furious enough at her teenage son to smite him into the next galaxy, but the kid had survived so far. He doubted that a mother, no matter how angry, would accompany her grown son to a restaurant and kill him there. She could've shot him at home. From the looks of the place, he doubted anyone would even notice—or care.

But Mrs. Hawley might know the woman with her son.

He knocked on the torn screen door. The woman who answered appeared to be about sixty, her gray hair a patch of fuzzy corkscrews. She wore pants several sizes too big for her thin frame and a bulky blouse that didn't hide the absence of a bra.

"What now?"

"Detective Dexter Quinn, ma'am." He flashed his shield. "And this is Deputy Sheriff Hector Gonzales. Are you Mrs. Hawley?"

"What's it to you?"

"We'd like to speak to you about your son."

"Jeff's not here, and I don't want to talk to no cops." She backed up and slammed the door shut.

Dexter knocked again. "Please, ma'am, we need to talk."

She cracked open the door. "Look, quit hassling us. Jeff checks in with his parole officer and does everything he's supposed to. I told him he had to or he'd have to leave. He's trying, so why don't you people leave him alone?"

"There's been an incident involving your son."

A long moment passed, and she finally opened the door to a tiny, closed room. Cigarette smoke and the stench of dirty cat litter hung in the air.

"Please sit down, Mrs. Hawley." Dexter spoke quietly. "I'm sorry to tell you—"

"He's dead, isn't he?" At Dexter's nod, her hostility crumbled. Her eyes filled and overflowed.

Dexter dismissed her as a possible suspect. Unless his instincts from years on the job were dead wrong, he'd swear she knew nothing about the murder. But if she hadn't been the woman with the straw hat, who had it been?

It never got easier, so Dexter and Gonzales waited awkwardly while she wept.

"How did he die?" It was little more than a whisper.

"He was shot—" Dexter began.

"It was that poor little girl's father, wasn't it? Jeff was my son,

36

but he was . . . cruel. What he did to that girl's body just wasn't decent." She shook her head as if it was all beyond her. "I tried to raise him right, but somewhere, he went wrong."

According to the notes Dexter had taken about Jeff Hawley's conviction, he had tortured and murdered Angela Jordan, an eleven-year-old local girl. And he'd only spent nine years in the Chino Institution for Men. Nine years. Dexter wasn't sure he wouldn't want to kill him too.

"Did Mr. Jordan threaten your son?" he asked Hawley's mother now.

"Said he'd kill him."

"When was that?"

"When Jeff's lawyer did that thing to get him a lighter sentence."

"Plea bargain?"

She shrugged.

"There was a woman, an older woman according to witnesses, with your son when he left the restaurant. Do you have any idea who it could be?"

"A woman? Jeffrey didn't have any friends. Someone got his story wrong."

"Did he attend any social functions where he could've met someone?"

"He didn't go nowhere," she told him. "About drove me nuts. I couldn't get him out of the house except to go to that steakhouse. He loved it there, went most every night. Said for once, he could eat all he wanted."

"Did he talk about meeting a woman there?"

"He didn't talk to me, wouldn't even look at me most of the time. Ever since he was released last month, we don't talk. It was like he blamed me for everything. What did I do? Maybe I smacked him too much, but I tried to raise him right. It's not easy being all alone."

37

"Is there someone who can identify your son for you?"

"No one." She sounded so dejected that Dexter wished he could help. Everyone should have at least one person to love— and who loved them. He wondered if he'd wind up like her, unloved and alone.

"If you'll get your things," he said gently, "Deputy Gonzales will take you to your son."

Dexter drove out of the court and took a deep breath of the cool, evening air.

His next stop was the Spencer Jordan residence in Yucaipa. Dexter gave a moment's thought to calling Rico, but he was too tired to tolerate the dickhead. He might have to suffer some hand-slapping for not doing so, but he'd face it in the morning.

After calling to make sure her grandmother was okay, Madison turned off the radio, and, leaving most of the lights on, slid into bed.

She tried to sleep, but the night sounds seemed louder than normal. A nest of birds chirped in the lemon tree outside her back window. Great. If she didn't get some sleep, she'd be a zombie at work tomorrow. Her head pounded. She felt like throwing a can at the tree. Who ever heard of birds singing at night?

Suddenly, all noises stopped. Even the fridge went silent. Listening intently, Madison sat up. A creak sounding just like someone walking in the living room made her mouth go dry.

Someone was in the house!

She almost bolted for the closet as she'd done all those years ago, peeking through the louvered doors, watching, heart pounding, trying not to make a sound as he had searched for her, throwing back the covers, stooping to peer under her bed.

He straightened and looked around the room. His eyes caught hers. He smiled, a creepy, skin-shivering smile.

"Gotcha," he'd whispered, moving toward her . . .

She wet the floor.

Distant sirens wailed, growing louder as they moved closer. He stopped to listen.

"I'll be back." He flashed that sly smile and disappeared through the door.

Panic pushed the memory aside. If he were here and had broken in, she needed to think, to stay alive. Pulling open the nightstand drawer, she took out the handgun Dexter's former partner had helped her to buy. Holding the .38 revolver in front of her, she waited, then after hearing nothing more, she crept through the hallway and into the living room.

Nothing had been moved. Magazines were still neatly stacked on the coffee table, wing chairs angled just so, the lamps exactly in the middle of end tables. The front door was closed and locked, dead bolts in place.

Just to make sure no one was there, she made her way through the condo, still holding her weapon, checking every corner, throwing open every closet door, flipping on every light. She checked the sliding glass doors leading from the kitchen to the courtyard in back and found them closed and locked, the steel rod still in the track. In order to get in, an intruder would've broken through, and she would have heard the crash.

Feeling a little foolish, she poured a glass of water from the polished fridge door and began to think rationally. Even if someone had broken in, it couldn't have been Bates. He was still in prison, locked up so he couldn't hurt anyone else. The talk about his release was just that. Wasn't it?

Back in bed, she couldn't keep her eyes closed. The night noises came alive again, and she lay awake and guarded against the night.

Superior Court Judge Joseph Lewon didn't sound happy when Dexter called at two in the morning, but it was part of the job.

Dexter asked for and was issued a search warrant that included the house, vehicles, and the surrounding property such as detached garages, workshops, and the lawn itself. Too many defense attorneys shot down evidence obtained in a location that hadn't been listed on the document.

Warrant in hand, Dexter, accompanied by three deputies, knocked on the Jordon residence door, trying not to wake the neighbors in the upscale Chapman Heights home facing the golf course. When no one responded, he knocked louder. Inside, a large dog barked, then an upstairs light flipped on. The man who opened the door was in his early forties, his robe slung over pajama bottoms, dark hair sticking straight up in back like an errant cowlick. He glared at Dexter.

"Who the hell are you? Do you realize it's almost three in the morning?"

"Are you Spencer Jordan?" Dexter flashed his shield and identified himself.

"Homicide! What could you possibly want here?"

"I have a search warrant issued in the investigation of a homicide that occurred earlier this evening, and I'd like your cooperation. May we come in?"

"Search warrant? For me?"

"Afraid so."

"Homicide? Who was killed?"

"Jeffrey Hawley."

Jordon appeared stunned. His mouth actually dropped open. "Jeff Hawley," he repeated cautiously, "the scum who murdered my daughter? He's dead? Really dead?"

At Dexter's nod, Jordon broke out in a smile and threw open the door.

"Come in! I'll even open all the drawers and cabinets for you." He flipped on the living room lights and yelled upstairs. "Gerri! Come on down! Got wonderful news!"

Dexter had seen a myriad of reactions to a search warrant, but this one was a doozer. He wouldn't be surprised if Jordon did handsprings across the room.

He dismissed Jordan as a suspect. He'd follow through with the necessary questioning and weapon's search, but instinct told Dexter that Jordon was innocent.

However, when Mrs. Jordan glided down the stairs, her pale blonde hair only slightly disheveled, her floor-length blue robe shining like silk, he wondered if she were involved. Wives didn't always tell their husbands everything.

Seated in the living room large enough to hold his entire studio apartment, Dexter questioned the couple while the deputies searched the house.

"Mrs. Jordan, do you own one of those large straw hats that ladies wear outside?"

"I don't go outside in the daylight, Detective Quinn. I'm one of those unfortunates who are allergic to the sun." Dexter noticed her smooth skin. Not only was it flawless, but it was so light it was almost albino.

"May I ask your whereabouts around six this evening?"

"Detective—" Mr. Jordon began.

"It's okay, Spence." She patted his hand. "My husband and I were at a dinner party raising funds for a local benefit, Detective. If that's when that monster was killed, I have about three-hundred witnesses who can testify I was there." Her eyes filled, but she kept her gaze on Dexter. "I've often thought about killing him over the years, even fantasized about stabbing him in the heart and watching him die, but my belief system says murder is a sin. I may rejoice that he's dead and no longer a threat to anyone else, but I didn't kill him."

Dexter believed her.

But who killed Hawley? And why hadn't the woman with him come forward?

CHAPTER SIX

Madison braced herself before entering the office the next morning. Instead of looking forward to finding an obscure new restaurant to review, she dreaded facing Marie.

Even though her editor had been a fantastic mentor, patient and encouraging when instructing, overlooking foibles she didn't tolerate with her reporters, this morning Madison dragged her steps. Leaving a crime scene without all the information was a major sin at a newspaper, and a throbbing headache and scratchy eyes after only three hours sleep didn't help.

As usual, the office was noisy with ringing phones, clacking computer keys, conversations among the four reporters and the two ads-salespeople, and the accountants, as usual, nagging reporters for time sheets and expenses.

All work stopped when Madison entered, and everyone looked at her.

"What?" She looked down at her trousers. "Did I forget my skirt? Oh wait, I don't wear skirts. So what is it?"

Several co-workers grinned. "Good job," Madison heard. "Atta girl." "Madison Young, star reporter."

Making her way to her desk as quickly as her pounding head would allow, Madison flushed. "Oh, for heaven's sake, everyone go back to work."

"Oooh, touchy this morning, are we?" Sue, a red-haired accountant, said with a grin.

Madison made a face and Sue laughed. She dug in her drawer for aspirin; neatly filed below were copies of the year's previous reviews, new restaurants to check, and ones outside the area that looked interesting.

"Guess you had an exciting night." Steve, the senior reporter, slung one arm over the back of his desk chair and leaned back, ready to hear all the gory details.

Madison groaned. Divorced and single, Steve was the typical Latin ladies' man in his prime—at least according to him. He was also devoted to his job. Too bad he wasn't as devoted to child-support. Madison had heard him on the phone many times, making excuses why he hadn't sent a payment. This morning she was in no mood to spar with him.

Marie sat at her computer behind the inner office door, her corner desk messy as usual with scattered notes and a paper plate full of crumbles from her morning muffins. Pinned to the walls were drawings the local schoolchildren had made during outings she'd sponsored and attended as counselor, as well as plaques and scrolls from various organizations thanking her for her unending participation and service.

Madison slid to the chair beside her.

"I'm so sorry," she began.

"You did good, kid. Just look at this." Marie pushed the morning's paper at her, and Madison caught a glimpse of the fire truck and ambulance from last night.

"I don't want to see it."

"You're a natural, girl. Wish you'd reconsider training as a cub."

"No way. Not only do I want to stay as far away from that stuff as I can, but there are too many variables in that sort of reporting. At least at a review, I can control what happens."

"You change your mind, you let me know. And by the way, don't waste any sympathy on that guy. He was a pedophile just out of prison. Not only did he rape an eleven-year-old child, but he tortured her and dumped her body in the ravine off Highway 38 to Big Bear. She was found not far from your grandmother's property. I'd say he deserved what he got."

An hour later, just as Madison finished her research on a new seafood restaurant in Moreno Valley, her cell phone rang. The ID said it was Greg Wright, the man she'd dated a few times.

Should she answer it? He wanted to *step up their relationship*, and Madison wanted it to stay right where it was. After her short marriage ended in divorce three years earlier—her fault, she knew, because of her paranoia—she hadn't dated until Greg. Now she wasn't sure she wanted to see anyone. She had enough trouble living with herself.

After a few more rings and a questioning glance from Steve, she took the call.

"Madison, I just read what happened at Jimmy's last night. Are you all right?"

"Other than a sleepless night, I'm fine."

"How about I pick you up after work and we'll have a nice, relaxing dinner? I'll even let you pay."

He was teasing her, although it was true that she often insisted on going Dutch, just to make sure he remembered they were just friends.

"Thanks, Greg, but I've made plans with my grandmother this afternoon, then I'll probably grab some take-out and eat in front of the TV. I'm exhausted."

"Tell you what. Come on up and I'll prepare dinner, even make eggplant parmesan, and you can nap. I'll wake you when it's ready, and I'll even do the dishes. How's that for an offer you can't refuse?"

Madison wavered. It did sound tempting.

They'd met six months before when he'd opened a family-style restaurant in Oak Glen—a fourteen-acre apple-growing community in the foothills of the San Bernardino Mountains about six miles east of Yucaipa—and she wrote a glowing review. Since then, they'd seen each other occasionally, and while she'd enjoyed the outings and wasn't seeing anyone else, she wasn't ready for anything serious.

And she'd never invited Greg into her home, wouldn't allow anyone in except Dex and her grandmother.

"Thanks, Greg. I appreciate the offer, but maybe another time."

After she hung up, she felt disgusted with herself. She had just turned down a wonderful evening with a young man who seemed interested in her, all because she found it difficult to form an emotional bond with anyone other than Gran and Dexter. Her therapist had tried to help her reach out to people, to trust again, but she still hesitated. And now, instead of sharing a wonderful dinner with Greg, she'd stay home behind her locked doors and windows.

Safe, yes. But living? Madison didn't think so.

On his way to the station at ten that morning, Dexter picked up two cups of coffee from a drive-thru and loaded them with several packets of sugar and several containers of cream. After only an hour's sleep, he needed something rich in his blood to get it moving.

The scorching sun didn't help his scratchy eyes. The mercury had already hit ninety and was expected to top off near a hundred.

At the garage, he checked for Rico's sedan, hoping he'd come and gone. His body screamed with exhaustion and every muscle ached, and he simply didn't have enough energy to pacify hurt feelings.

In the squad room, dubbed the bullpen after the place where relievers on a pro baseball team waited to go into the game,

Detective Bob Tieche, an old-timer who'd mentored Dexter, sat with a phone to his ear, nibbling on a Danish. Tieche's partner of a year, Christine Swensen, a tall, slim, blonde, was a perfect contrast to pudgy, bald Tieche. The pair, dubbed Tish and Chris, looked comical together, but they were a top-notch team. True to his Taurus sign, Tish stubbornly hung on to an investigation, probing leads, checking tiny details from every possible angle, and when one played out, pursuing another.

Tish and Chris looked up and grinned.

"What?" Dexter asked. "Did I forget to zip my fly?"

Chris grinned and went back to her files. Tish rolled his eyes toward Rico, who, as usual, was at his desk. Even sitting, Rico looked rigid, his back straight as if he didn't want to wrinkle his finely tailored suit.

He glanced up when Dexter entered the room and scowled, his eyes so dark they were almost black. Points of red highlighted his olive skin, and his lips were slashed in anger. But instead of threatening, he looked as if something had his balls in a vice.

Ah, Christ, Dexter thought. Rico's got a hair up his ass. Guess he'd have to deal with it later, but not now when all he wanted to do was give his report to the captain, check Hawley's background for possible leads, and knock off early and get some rest. He was getting too old for all this shit. At least the captain would be reasonable.

Captain Jessie Silva was pouring steaming cocoa from a thermos when Dexter entered, and the room smelled like rich chocolate.

"Want some?" he asked, his voice as smooth as his Native American features.

"Got my coffee, thanks." Dexter dropped onto the chair.

"Good chocolate, fresh milk, sugar, some water. Next to pure water, it's the best thing you can drink. You might try it sometime. It'll do you good instead of that sludge you torture your guts with." Silva took a couple of small sips from his mug and sat back to listen while Dexter filled him in on last night's events.

"What now?" Silva asked when Dexter finished his report.

"I could knock on a few doors. Might try Hawley's parole officer, see if he has any insight."

Silva nodded, and Dexter was about to make his escape when the captain spoke in the deceptively calm voice that all the detectives dreaded.

"Detective Quinn," Silva said, bringing Dexter to a halt. "Do you have any idea what I've had to listen to this morning because of you? What tirade the entire station had to hear?"

Even irritated, Silva's voice was conversational. Like his Cahuilla ancestors, he made calm decisions after weighing all possibilities. Over the years Dexter had cooled his heels a number of times while waiting for the captain's okay in one matter or another, but the captain had earned his respect, an honor Dexter awarded to few men.

He knew Silva expected a response, although experience told him to run like hell. "What?"

"Rico," Silva said. "I'm sure, if you think about it, you can guess how it went."

"Captain—"

"I don't like tirades," Silva told him. "It upsets the balance of nature. Balance, Dexter. If someone cuts you off on the freeway, you get irritated, but now you add a certain amount of frustration because you can't pull the asshole out of the vehicle and beat the shit out of him. So what do you do to maintain balance? You cut someone else off. They, in turn, cut another poor soul off, and the cycle continues."

"Cap—"

"As it is on the freeway, so it is here in the bullpen. I have to listen to a tirade from your new partner, I get irritated at you.

When I get irritated at one of my detectives, although I try not to stoop to such levels, I sometimes seek revenge. I cancel vacations."

Dexter came to full alert.

"Aren't you scheduled for a vacation in the near future, Detective Quinn?"

"You wouldn't."

Silva leisurely sipped his cocoa. "Thirteen days from now, isn't it?"

Thirteen days until Dexter's vacation, and for the first time in years, he had plans. He was going back to his hometown, a small coal-mining town in southwestern West Virginia.

He'd only visited once since joining the Navy after high school. His parents had moved to California when the underground mines played out, and his grandfather had died years ago of black lung disease. Most of the buildings in the once-vibrant town were boarded up, and the two movie theaters were long gone. The hollow where he'd been born was inaccessible, gated at the mouth by another coal-mining company that had torn down the houses and taken over operations in the area. About the only things left were a few homes scattered along the highway leading into the ghost town.

But far beyond the decay was the tragedy of the mountaintop removal. His beloved Appalachian Mountains were being decimated in several states, the tops blown off because it was the fastest, cheapest way to extract coal, the rubble filling once-pristine streams. From the air, the barren area looked like a Martian landscape, and he hadn't been back.

But memories of his childhood had been pulling at him and he longed to walk the forests and rivers once more. Might be old age, a yearning for what had passed away, but he had to go, at least one last time. Maybe it was his growing need to connect to something, anything.

His marriage had only lasted four years, and his one serious relationship after that had dissolved after a few missed dinners, with him coming home, exhausted, at five in the morning. Most people thought doctors had strange hours; they had no clue about a homicide detective's life.

"Okay, Captain," he said wearily. "What's the problem with Rico?"

"He's unhappy that you left him out of the process last night."

Dexter opened his mouth to speak, but once again, Silva didn't give him the opportunity.

"I don't want to hear reasons or excuses. Just realize, like it or not, he's your new partner. I want him to learn from the best and that's you. Now get the hell out of here and fix the problem, Dexter. I don't want to be unhappy."

Golden light from wall sconces glowed on rich cherrywood paneling. Matching floor lamps illuminated the corners of the book-lined room. The soft chatter of light conversation came from seven men and women who sat around a highly polished table enjoying a buffet breakfast. All were dressed in tailored suits—except for an eighty-year-old man whose alias in the Ruby Red Society was Number Three. He wore jeans and a bottle-green smoking jacket with shawl lapels. Although he hadn't smoked his pipe in fifteen years, he told everyone he kept his favorite cherry-scented tobacco in his pocket—just in case.

A ruby red glass basket sat on the table within arms reach of the chairperson sitting at the head of the table. In front of each member lay a stack of four manila files.

A gray-haired man in a crisp white shirt and black trousers served coffee and cleared the dishes when the members were finished. Once he left the room, the chairperson—known as Jericho One or simply Jericho—picked up the top file. All conversation ceased.

"I'm pleased to announce the elimination of Jeffrey Hawley, case number four-eight-fifty-six, has been successfully completed."

Murmurs of congratulations wove around the table and Jericho smiled. "While we would have preferred a little less risk, we all know that due to circumstances, our plan for this particular target was the best possible course. Are there any comments?"

When no one spoke, the chairperson made a notation on the first file, placed it on the table, and picked up the next one.

"If you'll open the next file, you'll find the next case for consideration is that of William 'Willy Boy' Martin, age twenty-seven, Yuma, Arizona. Resided with his wife, Sharon, twenty-two, and infant daughter, Jennifer.

"On January thirteenth of this year, Martin was arrested for the murder of his wife and daughter. He told police his daughter had cried all day and he couldn't hear the TV, so he picked her up by her ankles and shook her as one would shake a towel. He then threw the body into the corner of the room. Mrs. Martin screamed and ran to the baby. The noise was too much for Martin, he told police, so he got his gun and shot her five times. Neighbors reported gunshots, and Mrs. Martin was pronounced dead at the scene. Mr. Martin was apprehended several blocks away."

"Well, I'm certainly glad to hear that," Number Six said. "But I have a feeling that's not the end of the story."

"You're right," Jericho told him. "Martin has a history of violence. At the age of eight, he was in counseling for setting a live dog on fire, 'just to see what it would do while burning,' and he spent four years in custody until the age of eighteen for the murder of his friend, James Roche. According to the records, the boys had been taking turns batting a softball. When James refused to give up the bat, Martin forcibly took it from him and beat James over the head with it until he was dead.

"The justice system has been very good to Mr. Martin." Jericho poured a cup of steaming coffee. "He served only four years as a juvenile for the murder of the young boy, and as an adult, was indicted on two counts of first-degree murder for the death of his wife and daughter. However, he later recanted his confession, and his defense attorney charged and proved to the court's satisfaction that forensics had mishandled the evidence. The charges were dropped and Mr. Martin was released from custody. He's now seeing a woman with a three-year-old daughter.

"Ladies and gentlemen, I'll pass the ruby bowl for your vote."

"You know what mine will be," Number Three said, taking his pipe from his jacket and inserting it, unlit, between his teeth.

"Yes, Three," Jericho replied with a smile. "None of us have any doubt."

"Damned right. I believe in the old saying, 'Turnabout is fair play.' In my opinion, Mr. Martin should have the opportunity to see what it feels like to burn to death."

Number Five spoke up. "You must remember we're not a malicious society. We're for justice, not revenge."

"Once a spoil-sport, always a spoil-sport," Number Three replied with good-natured grumbling. "You won't let me have any fun. But you're right. I suppose we must stick to our Code."

Jericho passed the ruby bowl to the member seated on the immediate right, and it made its way around the table to collect the votes.

Jericho tabulated the results and announced the planned extermination of the man who, in the opinion of everyone around the table, deserved to die.

"Thank you for your votes. We'll take a short break before we proceed to the next file."

CHAPTER SEVEN

Madison escorted her grandmother down the hillside stairs.

"Where's your friend?" she asked, helping the older woman into the Saab.

"I drove, uh, Adelle back to . . . to Riverside this morning."

She seemed unusually flustered, and Madison was concerned about her grandmother's sudden decline in health. Until the last couple of months, Ella had worked crossword puzzles in ink. Madison made a mental note to suggest a checkup.

She took the scenic route to Redlands over Sand Canyon Road that Ella liked, enjoying the green hills that would soon turn brown in the scorching summer sun. They passed the few remaining orange groves.

"How did it go this morning?" Ella asked. "Did you get some rest last night?"

"Marie told me the victim was a child murderer and pedophile, so I don't feel quite so sorry for him. But still, people shouldn't go around taking the law into their own hands."

"There are some I'd like to shoot," Ella said quietly, staring out the side window.

Madison glanced at her grandmother's strained face. She couldn't recall much about her parents' murder and the trial, only that it nearly put Ella into the hospital and left Madison with memory fragments and terrifying dreams. After a lifetime of therapy, she could still hear the sound of her mother's screams as clearly as she had that night.

But no amount of therapy had helped her remember her mother—a fugue state or selective amnesia due, her shrink believed, to not only the trauma, but also to Madison's feelings of guilt.

Michael Bates had been apprehended outside of the Youngs' home, bloody knife on his person, jewelry and cash from the home in a knapsack. He was serving life at San Quentin, and each time he'd been eligible for parole, Dexter, accompanied by Senator Stone when he could take the time, testified to the cruelty in which Madison's parents had been slaughtered.

Madison had never visited their graves.

Concerned about her grandmother, Madison said nothing more. She owed Ella so much and wanted nothing more than to care for her, to take her on the trips she'd sacrificed to raise Madison. She'd even suggested moving back in after her failed marriage, but Ella wouldn't hear of it.

"You have your own life, Maddy. Get out and live it."

Madison owned her own home, worked at a job she loved, and had begun dating again—if you could call three dates in two years dating. But she wasn't sure she was living.

Now, crossing Redlands Boulevard, Madison drove down a palm-and-oak-lined street housing older bungalows and Victorians, each home looking as if it had been freshly painted.

"How's your young man?" Ella asked. "Any good news yet?"

"Please. I don't have a young man and I don't want one."

"That young man you've been seeing. What's his name again?"

"Greg and I have only gone to dinner a few times," Madison said, not bothering to hide her exasperation. "Don't make it into something it's not. Okay?"

"Did I tell you he stopped by one afternoon to introduce himself? I thought that was a fine thing to do."

Madison jerked the wheel and almost drove onto the sidewalk.

"He did what?"

"Shall I drive, dear?" Ella asked innocently.

"Don't change the subject. When did Greg stop by? And what did you two discuss, as if I didn't know."

"We had cookies. Peanut butter is his favorite, you know. I'll give you the recipe."

"Oh, my, God. You two are cooking up something besides cookies. Gran, I love you, but stay out of my nonexistent love life. Please."

"He's a good man, Maddy. I could tell that right away."

"Gran—"

"You're young and beautiful, and you need to get out of that house and explore what life has to offer. Go out with Greg. Let him be part of your life."

"I'm not going to talk about it any longer, and if you insist, you can get out and walk."

Her grandmother laughed. "If there's one thing I know, Maddy dear, is that you'd never abandon me, and that's part of the problem. Quit worrying about me and concentrate on your own life. Get married and give me some great-grandchildren."

"No one could stand living with me." Madison's tone changed. Her voice was barely audible. "Ted walked out in less than a year, said I was too controlling, too much of a shrew if I couldn't run things the way I wanted. And he was right. The biggest fight we had was when he forgot to lock the bedroom window."

"Well, there is that. Have you considered going back into therapy?"

"Dr. King didn't cure me in all the years I went, so I'm not about to waste more time and money on a hopeless cause."

"I'm not sure I agree, Maddy. Even if it's—"

"Gran, I love you, but I don't want to talk about it. I just want to have a nice visit with the senator without a grilling about my personal life. Just a nice relaxing chat and something good to nibble on. Besides, I don't know if I could change even if I wanted to."

The senator's red-tiled rooftop was barely visible through the trees lining the iron fence set in concrete. At the security gate, Madison punched in the new code that had been telephoned to her grandmother the day before, and they wound through grounds shaded by maples, oaks, and sycamore trees.

A circular driveway led to the front of the L-shaped home, and outside the office wing, young cherry trees were in bloom. In the back, Madison knew, a swimming pool sparkled in front of tree-shaded guest quarters.

Mr. Chauncey opened the door.

"Nice to see you again," he said with a smile. Dressed in his usual navy-blue trousers, crisp white shirt, and blue vest, he'd served as a butler as long as Madison could remember.

"Are you sure he's up to a visit?" she asked. "I understand he's not well, and Gran and I wouldn't want to intrude."

"Oh no, Miss Young," he assured her, leading them through the massive living room to the cozy anteroom outside the senator's office. "The senator mentioned he was looking forward to seeing you both. He'll be with you shortly." He withdrew from the room.

When Ella settled into her favorite chair, a Queen Anne with a footstool, Madison took the upholstered sofa, and, as she'd always done, turned to look at the framed photo standing on the end table. The tender moment when a much-younger senator was holding his infant son and leaning toward his wife always intrigued her, no matter how many times she had seen it. The couple looked at each other with such love that she'd envied them. Even today, many years after an accident had tragically torn his family from him, the senator's eyes still reflected the pain of that loss whenever he spoke of them.

Would she ever experience such love?

"I hope I didn't keep you waiting." Senator Logan Stone walked into the room from his open office door, his long legs taking slower steps than normal. Instead of his usual suit, he wore pleated khakis and a polo shirt, the dark indigo shade setting off his perfectly groomed silver hair.

Madison thought he looked fantastic, especially for a man in his sixties whose doctor sent him home for some much-needed rest. He seldom wore short sleeves, she knew, preferring to cover the jagged six-inch scar on his right arm. He never discussed it, but his act of bravery in combat was well known.

During visits when she was a child, she'd long to climb onto his lap and loosen his collar as she'd once done for her father. And she had suffered through an adolescent crush when she was thirteen. Now she thought of him as a family friend, not as dear as Dexter, but as someone she trusted and admired.

After giving each woman a brief, informal hug, the senator settled into a large wing chair opposite the sofa.

"I'm so glad we had this opportunity to get together," he told them. "Ready for some tea?"

As was the custom, the housekeeper pushed a scrolled tea cart into the room, and Madison didn't realize how hungry she was until she saw the food.

The top tier held a teapot, cups and saucers, a tray with several blends of teas, silverware, and all the sides, including sliced lemon. A variety of finger sandwiches and scones occupied the second tier, and on the third, cookies, tarts, cakes, and other goodies sat alongside Madison's can of soda and a bowl of ice.

He never forgot.

The senator served the tea and Madison helped herself to her favorite, a cranberry scone with a heaping spoon of freshly made Devonshire cream.

"Just as wonderful as always, Senator. I don't know what I'd do if your cook ever retired."

"She'll never leave, Madison. I've bribed her into the next century. So tell me, how are you both?"

"Madison witnessed a murder last night," Ella told him. "At Jimmy's Steakhouse."

For a moment, the silence in the room was electrifying.

After completing the morning's paperwork, Dexter suggested grabbing a bite to eat. Rico had made a point of ignoring him, and while Dexter couldn't bring himself to apologize, a late lunch was the next thing. Even that didn't settle well, but he knew the captain meant every word of his threat if he didn't make nice to the asshole.

"I still have paperwork to complete," a sullen Rico said, "although obviously not as much as *you* do."

Tish and Chris snickered, but at Dexter's glare, they bent their heads to their own paperwork.

"Come on, Rico," Dexter said. "Give me a break. I spent a long time without a partner, and it'll take some getting used to."

Rico kept writing.

Damn. Dexter glanced up to see Silva, cup in hand, watching the drama through the inner-office window. Dexter shrugged helplessly, which was quite a feat. He'd never been helpless in his life and Silva knew it.

"Come on, buddy." He about choked on that one. "Let's grab a bite and then check with Hawley's parole officer."

"Well . . . if you make sure it doesn't happen again."

That did it. Vacation or no vacation, he wasn't going to grovel. He grabbed his jacket from the back of the chair and stormed out of the room.

"Where do you want to eat?" Rico asked, running after him.

An hour later at the state offices in San Bernardino, Dexter and Rico waited a few moments for Hawley's parole officer to finish an interview.

Mike Taggert's cubicle was one of several in the large room, and over the noise of conversations and phones ringing, Dexter and Rico introduced themselves and took seats.

His white shirt wrinkled and sleeves rolled to his elbows, Taggert presented the perfect picture of a harried government employee. He grabbed a red file with Hawley's name scribbled on the front.

"Sorry, detectives, I can't help you. I've only been assigned to Hawley a few weeks. And with this kind of backlog," he swept his hand over the stacks of files, "I've only talked to him once."

"Any clues to his social activities?" Dexter asked.

"GPS report showed no unusual actions, no attempts to approach restricted zones. Since he was high-risk, we tracked him with real-time monitoring for the first month, then downgraded him to a daily basis. Got the impression he was a loner. No friends, no activities."

"He had someone," Dexter said, and filled him in on the woman with the straw hat, careful to let Rico contribute to the conversation.

"Guess he was trying to readjust to civilian life," Taggert said.

"Someone made sure he didn't adjust to anything."

Back in the Tahoe, Dexter received a call from Josh Gidding on his cell phone and stepped out of the car. As a member of the Adult Parole Operations with California's Department of Corrections and Rehabilitation, Josh never called to pass the time of day.

"Bates' hearing got pushed up to tomorrow," he told Dexter. "This time it looks good."

Damn.

"Have to make a quick trip north," Dexter told Rico, fastening his seat belt. "You do what you can on the Hawley case, and I'll be back tomorrow evening or the next day."

"What's up?"

"A ghost from the past."

"I didn't actually witness the murder, Gran. I arrived afterward. Besides, Senator Stone doesn't want to hear about the shooting," If Madison had ever been exasperated with her grandmother, it was now. She felt better once she had eaten, but her temples still throbbed.

"I most certainly do, Madison. Anything that concerns your family is of interest to me. I'd heard about the incident, of course, but had no idea you were involved. Please tell me all about it."

There was no way Madison could refuse a request from such a longtime friend. When she finished telling him about last night, he seemed horrified.

"Good God, Madison. Your grandmother is right—you should not have been involved. I'm surprised at your editor."

Madison closed her eyes. "Once again, my editor had no other choice. It was a big story and if no one had been there at all, the paper would have been horribly embarrassed. After everything Marie has done for me, I wanted to help. So please, as a favor to me, let's just drop the subject."

"As you wish, my dear. Your grandmother and I have some catching up to do. As you know, my last bit of legislation is stalled again. Would you care to join us in the office?"

Normally, Madison loved to assist the senator, felt honored to contribute to drafting the senator's legislation. His previous one, HQEV5454, allowing the prosecution to submit the defendant's complete criminal record at trial, had died in committee, but he kept working, and she and Ella had been strong supporters, working with the senator when he was in town, keeping in touch with his staff by phone or mail when he was in Washington.

But not today. Even with the spectacular view of the cherry trees outside of the senator's office, Madison couldn't face spending the afternoon inside.

"If you don't mind, I'd rather stroll the grounds. It's beautiful outside, and I'll enjoy the fresh air." She didn't mention that she needed to be alone. Something was nagging at her and she had to try to figure out what was wrong. Ever since Ella mentioned the shooting at Jimmy's, she'd felt a tension in the air, a feeling unusual in the senator's home.

After getting the official okay from Captain Silva to attend the parole hearing at San Quentin, Dexter caught the next flight out of Ontario for Oakland. Even though it only took a couple of hours, he left early to make sure nothing came up to prevent him from attending.

He and the senator had testified to Bates' brutality at the hearing a year ago, and Dexter was surprised that another was scheduled so soon. But with the state's budget crisis and prison overcrowding, hearings were pushed up and prisoners released without serving their full terms.

He'd called Senator Stone to inform him of the hearing, but the senator felt too weak to make the trip.

Dexter watched the shifting cloud formations and thought back twenty years to the crime that still gave Madison nightmares.

She hadn't witnessed her parents' murder or been physically injured, thank God, but she was left with emotional scars that time and therapy hadn't lessened.

Instead of running to her mother when awakened by her screams, Madison had been so terrified by the sound that she hid in the closet. Not only did she have to cope with losing her parents, but she carried the burden that she hadn't tried to help, as if a six-year-old could've done anything except get herself killed. While her therapist had helped her to work through the logistics, she had never recovered from the guilt of that night. Or the fear.

And Dexter understood. Mrs. Young's screams must have been unbearable. He'd seen crime scenes before, but nothing that heinous, not in his county, not in his town.

Talk about nightmares.

Small burn marks on Mrs. Young's eyelids, face, and breasts indicated torture with a cigarette, then she'd been sexually assaulted and stabbed multiple times, the wounds so deep in her stomach that she'd almost been disemboweled.

Mr. Young had been bound and gagged on the floor next to the bed, his head propped against the wall, his legs drawn up. The medical examiner speculated that he died about a half hour after his wife and might have been forced to watch his wife's torture and murder. He'd bled out after his carotid artery had been severed, his throat slashed so savagely that only a few tendons kept his head attached.

The neighbor on the south side of the house had heard the screams and called the police. Dexter had been one of the responding officers, and during a search of the house, found Maddy in her closet, terrified, reeking of urine, unable to move. If there was anything to be thankful for, it was that she hadn't seen her parents' bodies.

When Bates had been apprehended, records proved he'd been arraigned on a burglary and murder charge two months before, but the case had been thrown out of court because of an illegal search of his premises.

But the pattern was there.

God help the citizens of California if that monster were allowed back on the streets.

"Gran, is there anything I can do for you?" Madison asked, back inside Ella's hillside home. "You look so pale, and you haven't said a word since leaving the senator's house. Would you like something to drink?"

Ella leaned her head against the back of the sofa and closed her eyes. "I'm fine, Maddy. Why don't you run along, now. I'm sure you have things to do."

"What's wrong, Gran? This isn't like you. Are you angry that I didn't help with the senator's bill?"

"No, dear. Of course not. I'd never be angry with you. It's just, uh, between Adelle showing up unexpectedly and visiting the senator today, I'm exhausted. And this sudden heat doesn't help."

Madison adjusted the air conditioner, then brought her grandmother a glass of iced tea.

"I hate to leave you alone, but I have some work to do. Maybe Cora can stay with you today. Just let me give her a call."

"I don't need a babysitter, Maddy, just some rest. Now quit fussing."

Twenty minutes later, Madison was driving Cora to stay with her grandmother.

"Is there anything going on that she won't talk to me about?"

"Not that I know of," Cora said, "but she's been too quiet to suit me. I'd suggested a checkup, but you know your grandmother. She won't go unless she's dying."

"I'm really worried about her. You're her best friend and she'd tell you things she wouldn't tell me. Can you think of anything we can do?"

"I have no clue what's wrong with her, but I'll pay closer attention." Cora angled the air conditioner vent to blow on her.

"This heat's a bit much this soon in the season, and that doesn't help."

They were heading east on Oak Glen Road toward Bryant Street, and already the green scrub on Crafton Hills was turning brown.

"I have an idea." Cora checked her pocket calendar, flipping through the diary-size notepad and her schedule. Madison smiled at the no-nonsense sand-colored leather. No flowery covers for Cora. "Ella mentioned she'd like to take a short trip somewhere, to get away for a few days to someplace cooler. Perhaps now is the time to go."

"That's an excellent idea! I just hope you can talk her into going."

CHAPTER EIGHT

Dexter presented his faxed request for gate clearance at San Quentin's gate and waited while the guard checked it on the computer.

The morning sun hit Dexter right in the eyes. Squinting, he tried to be patient as the moments dragged by. The year before, he'd been whisked right through, but that time he'd presented a mailed request enclosed in an official envelope. He checked the dash clock and saw that he had an hour before the hearing. He was okay—as long as there were no lengthy delays.

The guard made a phone call and Dexter ground his teeth. Was something wrong? As several more minutes passed, he feared the worst. If the fax hadn't arrived in time to generate a pass, he could miss the hearing.

He knew his testimony wouldn't prevent Bates' release if the board voted otherwise, but he had to try, had to make them understand the horror of the night that scarred Madison so terribly.

Finally, after an eternity of waiting, the pass was approved and Dexter was allowed through to the second guard station.

More than a hundred-fifty years old, the prison sprawled over four hundred acres about twenty miles north of San Francisco. It sat right on the bay, and with the palms, shrubbery, and outbuildings, including a post office, museum, and a gift shop, Dexter felt he could be in any government complex—except this one housed death row inmates and a gas chamber.

Once through the "sally port," a barred cage that's locked on both sides by floor-to-ceiling metal gates, a tall woman in her late thirties, her complexion reminding him of a rich café au lait, greeted him.

"Good morning, Detective Quinn. I'm Marsha Cummings," she offered her hand, "Victim Services Representative. I'll escort you through today's proceedings.

"I'm aware you've visited before and realize you must be familiar with the rules," she continued, "but I must reiterate Title 15, Section 3303 of the California Code of Regulations."

"The hostage rule."

Ms. Cummings smiled. "Just as law enforcement officials must quote the Miranda rule, we must make sure visitors know the Hostage Rule, which states, 'Employees must not permit inmates or others to use hostages to escape from custody or otherwise interfere with orderly institutional operations. Hostages will not be recognized for bargaining purposes. All inmates, visitors, and staff will be informed of this regulation.' In other words, Detective, if you're taken hostage, you're on your own."

Dexter nodded his acceptance. Nothing else he could do. He checked his watch; ten minutes until the hearing.

"We're fine, Detective," she assured him. "It's just around this corridor."

The hearing room, about fifteen-by-fifteen feet, was as tight as the one last year, but since only two other people besides Ms. Cummings and Dexter sat on the visitors' chairs lining the wall, he felt he could breathe. Recognizing the deputy district attorney from San Bernardino County as well as an assistant from the Major Crimes Unit, he nodded and took a seat. No one spoke.

A honeywood table about three-by-nine separated the visitors from the committee of two men and one woman. Files of loose papers covered the table, and steam rose from a carafe of coffee. Dexter would have liked a cup, but it wasn't offered.

Directly in front of Dexter, a lone straight chair, which he knew was for the inmate, faced the panel. Unfortunately, from his position, Dexter wouldn't be able to see Bates' face. He wanted to watch the dirtbag's expression when he told the panel about the savage slaughter that had left two dead and one woman afraid of the dark.

"Do you mind if I move to a different chair?" he asked Ms. Cummings. "I have a personal stake in the outcome, and I want to watch Bates when I testify."

After they took other seats, the door opened and two guards, one on each side of the prisoner, escorted Bates to the chair, matching the slow, shuffling steps that were all the shackles would allow. Once he was seated, the guards took standing positions directly behind him.

Dexter observed the relaxed figure, noting Bates' dark eyes scanning the parole board directly in front of him, then lowering his head in assumed repentance. But Dexter would stake his life that the dirtwad felt no such thing. Wearing jeans and a light-blue shirt with CDC PRISONER on the back, Bates appeared about the same as last year. Perhaps his mustache and beard were streaked with a little more gray, but Dexter still detected that belligerent demeanor. Bates was merely trying to hide it. At nearly six feet and dressed in black, he must have been a terrifying figure to a child.

As if feeling Dexter's stare, he raised his head and their eyes met for just an instant. He smiled slightly, an insolent smirk that Dexter wanted to wipe off his face with a fist.

"Good morning," the man in the brown suit began. With his high cheekbones and coal-black hair, Dexter thought he might be Native American. He identified Bates by ID and case number.

"This will be a subsequent parole consideration hearing for

Michael Bates," he said, then read the date Bates was received into San Quentin, "For Violation of Penal Code Section One-Eighty-Seven, causing the death of another person with malice aforethought." He gave the day's date, time, and location.

Dexter shifted in the tiny chair, impatient to get on with it.

"We'll start by establishing voice identification," the speaker continued. "I'm James Cordova, Commissioner, Board of Prison Terms." The woman and other man identified themselves as deputy commissioners, then the visitors, including Ms. Cummings, stated their names and occupations.

"The purpose today is to consider the suitability of parole for Michael Bates," Cordova said. "Mister Bates, you have the right to present relative documents to this hearing, the right to an impartial panel. We've reviewed your file, including psychiatric reports and psychological evaluations, your work in the library, participation in group therapy, and your educational achievements, which include obtaining your GED. Congratulations."

Bates preened.

What the hell is this? Oh, Christ, Dexter thought, they're going to let him go.

"A copy of today's transcripts will be sent to you," Cordova continued, "and you have the right to appeal within ninety days. We'll begin with the offense. You are not required to admit guilt. We'll accept the court documents as fact. Do you swear to tell the truth today?"

Bates nodded.

"Please state your answer aloud."

"Yes," Bates said.

The asshole wouldn't know the truth if it hit him in the ass, Dexter thought. Why the hell didn't the state fry him when they had the chance? A lethal injection like they did now was too painless for a cold-blooded monster like Bates.

Cordova read the court's account of the Youngs' murder,

reading all the known details. Bates listened with his head lowered.

"That's the statement of facts, Mr. Bates," Cordova said. "Is there anything you'd like to add?"

Bates said nothing for a long moment, then he raised his eyes. Holy shit, Dexter thought. The asshole had managed to work up tears.

"I'm so terribly sorry for what I did that night," Bates said. "I know nothing I could do will ever make it right, but all I can say is that I'm sorry. I've studied the Word of God since then, and I swear I'll never hurt another living soul as long as I live."

Dexter watched the woman's face. She's buying it, he thought incredulously. He couldn't believe it.

"Anything further?" Cordova asked Bates.

He shook his head and looked down as if humbled. "I'll just throw myself on your mercy."

"Now we'll hear from the deputy district attorney and the detective on the case."

Dexter listened as the DDA gave an account of the trial and told of Bates' hostile reactions at the defense table, which had included several outbursts of obscenities. One time he'd tackled the prosecutor and had been hustled out of the courtroom. Then it was Dexter's turn.

Inch by inch, he led the committee through the Youngs' home as if he were seeing it again.

"I'd only been on the job a year when my partner and I responded to the call. We entered the two-story house in Yucaipa and began our search. We found nothing amiss on the first floor, and cautiously, weapons drawn, we climbed the stairs. Four doors were closed upstairs and one was opened. A glow was observed under one of the closed doors, so I announced myself. There was no response.

"My partner entered the room with the open door and

discovered a child's empty room. He secured the rest of the rooms, then together, we entered the room with the light.

"We found Mr. and Mrs. Young's bodies in that bedroom. A small table lamp was lit on the floor next to the bed. We called for backup and emergency services, but my partner and I knew it was too late.

"Mrs. Young's nude body was on the bed, vicious stab wounds to her chest and abdomen. Blood covered the bed and the walls. In all the years since, I've never seen so much blood."

Dexter paused a moment. No one made a sound.

"She'd been raped, repeatedly, according to the medical examiner. I believe you have a copy?"

Cordova nodded, his face expressionless. "Please continue."

"On the floor next to the bed, Mr. Young had been propped against the wall, hands tied behind his back and a gag torn from Mrs. Young's nightgown around his mouth. His throat had been savagely slashed.

"More units responded to the call and a thorough search was made of the house. A child, Madison Young, six years old, was discovered crouched in the corner of her closet, wet from her own urine, so traumatized that she couldn't speak. Later, when Miss Young was able to communicate, she said Bates was coming after her when we arrived on the premises. He escaped out a lower window, but as you know, he was apprehended by officers surrounding the home.

"Mr. Cordova and members of the committee, I realize we're not here to retry Michael Bates, although I wish we could—"

"Detective Quinn," Cordova interrupted. "Please keep your narrative to what the law allows."

"When officers tried to remove Miss Young from her closet, she screamed and backed away. She's spent eighteen of the past twenty years in therapy," he went on, "and she still has nightmares.

"This *man,* if you will, should not be released into society. Before he murdered the Youngs, he was convicted of aggravated assault, for which he only served one year.

"He's violent and poses a threat to society. Studies on recidivism find that between two-thirds and three-quarters of offenders released from prison are arrested again within three years. Mr. Bates is a convicted murderer. We cannot, in all good conscience, release this man to kill again. Miss Young, her grandmother, Mrs. Ella Osborne—who assumed care of her when she was orphaned—and the community have the right to live without fear of their lives at the hands of convicted killers such as Michael Bates. Please protect our citizens by keeping him in custody."

Cordova finished his notes. When the court recessed, everyone stood. Just before the guards hustled Bates out of the room, he threw a backward glance at Dexter. For an instant, Dexter saw a chilling, shrewd smile, and he knew for certain that Maddy was still in danger.

CHAPTER NINE

Cramped in his tiny airline seat two hours after the parole board's decision, Dexter was still seething. Even after several shots of rye whiskey at the airport bar, he couldn't get Cordova's words out of his head.

"After careful deliberation and review of all the records, including psychological, educational, and work duty," Mr. Cordova said, "we, the members of the California Department of Corrections panel, have concluded that Michael Bates has demonstrated repentance and remorse for his crimes, as well as a commitment to decent behavior and a desire to contribute to society.

"While we recognize that his crimes were despicable, we believe he has successfully undergone rehabilitation while in custody.

"Therefore, parole is granted."

Parole granted. Parole granted. The words echoed in Dexter's head. How the hell was he going to tell Maddy and Ella something like that? No way could they ever feel safe with that shithole loose. The system was fucked. Citizens were fucked. Dexter wanted to hit something. Despite his size, he'd never been a man of violence, but now he wanted to feel that satisfying release when he sent something flying.

After landing at Ontario International, he snarled at the attendant, and when he pulled out of the airport in his Tahoe, he felt like ramming everyone out of the way. At the I-10 east on-ramp, he slowed, and cars behind him honked.

He lowered his window. "Fuck off, you assholes!"

This wasn't good. He was liable to kill someone in the mood he was in, so, instead of taking the freeway east to Yucaipa, he pulled into the nearest lot, a hamburger joint. He grabbed some coffee and sat down. In desperate need of a friend, he entered a special number on his cell.

As ring followed ring, disappointment washed the rage away. He sagged in his seat. It was if all the tension he'd carried in the past few days evaporated, and he felt drained.

Just as he touched the disconnect button, Pam answered.

"Well hey, stranger. What's up?"

"Oh, the same old, same old. You busy?"

"Not for you, big boy. Come on up."

Smiling for the first time in several days, he pulled back into traffic. Even driving like a sane man, it was only a few minutes until he pulled outside the gates of her Rolling Hills Drive complex.

Dexter's relationship with Pamela Evans spanned over thirty years. He and his Navy buddy had been standing in line for the roller coaster at the old Pike Amusement Park in Long Beach when Pam and a friend had come along. Soon after, they all double-dated, and he had continued to see her after his discharge and entry into the sheriff's department.

They'd discussed marriage, but he gave more to the job than to their relationship, and after breaking several dates in a row, they both knew it wouldn't work. Over the years, their relationship had evolved into one of complete compatibility. As long as neither was attached to someone else, they'd meet at her townhome, have a few drinks and dinner, perhaps take a swim, then make love until the wee hours. The next morning, each would return to their own world, Pam to the software corporate world, and Dexter to the business of chasing killers.

He had barely parked his Tahoe beside her Lexus when she flew out the door and flung her arms around him. In shorts and halter top, her auburn hair sleeked back with a bandana, she looked damned good. A sheen of sweat glistened on her tanned skin.

"Don't mind me," she said, still plastered against him. Almost as tall as Dexter, she was a perfect fit. "I've been doing some weeding in the back, and I'm all sweaty, but I'm glad to see you."

"Let's take a shower together," he suggested, heading for her back door. "After the day I've had, I could stand to feel clean." Arm in arm, they entered the house, the dark hardwood floors adding to the feeling of calm and comfort.

While Pam blended frozen lime daiquiris in the kitchen, Dexter shrugged out of his coat and unbuttoned his shirt. The family room opened from the kitchen, and Dexter took his drink and settled on an oversized easy chair he'd bought several years ago and stretched his long legs on the ottoman.

"Damn, this is heaven." He drained his drink in one gulp.

Pam, one eyebrow cocked, poured him another. "Okay, I know the pleasure of my company is to die for, but something else is going on. What's up?"

"Let me enjoy this drink and a shower first. Then we'll see what comes up." He waggled his eyebrows in a leer.

"Sounds like a plan." She grinned, and carrying her drink, reached for his hand. "Come on, let's take that shower."

After they took turns soaping each other, Dexter tenderly cupped her small breasts and bent to take a nipple in his mouth. She reached for him, and after a few more minutes of play, each so familiar with the other's body that the slightest touch was welcomed, they wound up on her bed.

Cora backed the family's Mercedes out of Ella's driveway and turned west to catch the southbound freeway. Madison waved one last time, relieved that Ella had not only consented to a short trip, but had mentioned the sea breezes in San Diego. The sisters thought it would be perfect, and Ella suggested leaving immediately so they could attend the evening's last performance of the new musical at the Old Globe Theater in Balboa Park.

They had certainly picked a perfect day to travel, Madison thought, lifting her face to the sky. The early afternoon sun was warm enough to leave jackets home, yet not hot enough to need air conditioning.

She locked the front door. Even though Ella never complained, Madison knew her grandmother had missed so much in life while taking care of her, and with Ella's health slipping lately, she'd been especially worried. San Diego was the perfect place to revitalize with its soft ocean breezes and plenty of shopping and sightseeing. And, since it was only about a two-hour drive, the ladies wouldn't arrive overtired from traveling.

Now that Ella was going to have some fun, maybe it was time she did as well. Maybe she'd call Greg and suggest dinner. She might even let him pay.

A while later, as the gray dusk was throwing the room in shadows, Dexter and Pam lay wrapped in each other's arms. Dexter felt drained, but he also felt as if a crushing weight had shifted. He might still carry the burden, but at least now he could breathe.

"You're so damn good for me," he said, giving Pam a peck on the tip of her nose. "Why didn't we ever get married?"

"Because I wouldn't have you." Lazily, she snuggled closer.

"Ah, well, there's that. I always knew you were smart."

She nuzzled his neck and reached down.

"Might as well forget that for now," he told her regretfully. "I'm an old man and I need rest."

She laughed and sat up. "Well, *old man,* you've taken advantage of my hospitality and my body, so what are you going to do for me?"

"How about I feed you?"

She jumped off the bed and headed for the bathroom. "Last one ready has to pay the tab!"

Seated later at their favorite seafood restaurant, they shared a platter of fresh oysters on the half-shell. By the time dinner arrived, a steam pot loaded with two kinds of crab, sausage, potatoes, and corn, Dexter felt ready to talk.

Attacking the shells with a vengeance, he told Pam about his trip to San Quentin.

"Why on earth would they release someone so dangerous?"

"Funding issues, overcrowding, and because the do-gooders of society think a murderer can be rehabilitated."

Cracking a long joint, he pulled it apart, and carefully peeled out a long string of crab. "Perfect," he said, dipping it in the drawn butter. He chewed slowly to savor the sweet flavor.

"You don't agree, I take it," Pam said.

He gave her a cynical look.

"But isn't it possible?"

"Anything's possible, but once someone has crossed that line of taking another life, something in their psyche is changed. I don't believe they can ever regain that certain respect for human life."

"I hope you're wrong."

"So do I, but I doubt it."

"What are you going to do now?"

"Watch him like a hawk," Dexter told her grimly, "and if he makes one move toward Maddy or her grandmother, I'll kill the son of a bitch."

"So, will you marry me?" Greg asked over his slice of pizza. A waiter passed their table with a tray of freshly baked Italian bread, and in the background, a ballad by The Three Tenors offered a touch of romance.

Madison choked and Greg handed her a glass of water to wash down her bite of pizza.

"Are you crazy? We haven't even discussed marriage."

"Just because we haven't discussed it doesn't mean I haven't thought about it," he told her calmly, his hazel eyes twinkling in the soft candlelight. "I knew I wanted you the first time I saw you. And take smaller bites."

"Oh for heaven's sake, I know how to eat. I've been doing it my entire life. And that's exactly why I won't get married again. I don't want you or anyone else telling me what to do."

"You need someone to look after you, and I'm the man to do it." Greg took another bite of pizza. "Delicious."

Taken aback, Madison stared at him. "Why you arrogant, uh . . ."

"Macho male? Stud?" he offered. "See? You need me. You don't even know what to call me."

"That's because my grandmother brought me up to be a lady."

"I like Ella. I thought I'd have to soften her up, but she surprised me. She's actually on my side. She also makes a mean peanut butter cookie, even better than mine, so I'll definitely hang around. If you won't marry me, maybe she will." He pulled another slice of pizza apart and put it on her plate. "Eat more. You've lost some weight."

After several months, Madison still didn't know what to think about Greg. Half the time he sounded serious, and the other half, she just didn't know. He had something, a certain old-time gentleman courtesy that she was drawn to, always walking on the outside, never forgetting to open doors for her. While several inches shorter than Dexter, he was tall enough to make her feel feminine. And, he always looked at her with a warmth that made her toes curl.

She did get lonely. But still, she wasn't ready to live with anyone and she didn't know that she ever would.

"Greg, I do like you—"

"*Like* me? Ouch, that hurts."

"I'm fond of you, more so than I've been about anyone, but I can't marry anyone right now. I have problems that are difficult to live with, to say the least."

"We all have problems. Look, I was married before too, but I learned from my mistakes. Now I put the seat down and pick up my socks. I even cook. What more could you want?"

He gave her such a charming grin that she couldn't help but smile.

"It's not that simple. I have control issues, serious ones. You'd rebel and walk out."

Greg put down his pizza. "Is that what your husband did?"

She nodded. "The thing is, I don't blame him."

"I know what happened to you when you were a child, Madison. Your grandmother told me. And I understand your fear of the dark. We can work around all your fears."

"This is all too soon. We've been out a few times but we don't even know each other."

"I know all I need to know."

"My husband thought he knew me, and I still managed to chase him away."

"I'm not your husband, Madison, but okay. We'll go one step at a time. I'll take you home tonight, then I'll call tomorrow and we'll arrange to go out again. And we'll keep going out until you feel as if you know me better. Do you like the mountains? How about a picnic at Big Bear Lake? I'll supply the food."

Later, when he walked her to her door, he took her key,

unlocked the door, and pushed it open to her well-lit living room.

"See?" he said. "Lights don't bother me. I want you enough to live with them. Hell, I'd even wear one of those frilly blindfold things to bed if I could have you."

"But why? How could you want me when you don't even know me?"

"I know you, Madison. I know how courageous you are, even if you don't. Your courage, for instance, when you covered the incident at Jimmy's even though it was painful."

"Some courage. I fell apart and Dexter had to rescue me."

"Doesn't matter. You were there, doing what you felt was right. I admire that. You have warmth, Madison," he told her, his voice husky. "You try to keep it hidden, but it's there. Your devotion to your grandmother, your love for Dexter. You have passion whether you know it or not." He ran his fingers through her hair. "I love the way your hair shines in the light. It reminds me of strands of liquid gold."

Madison met his gaze and the need she saw in his eyes made her knees go weak. She found herself leaning toward him, desperately needing someone to love, someone who loved her, but did she dare?

"I love your eyes," he continued in a whisper, "flashing fire at me one minute, melting me with softness the next. And your mouth . . ." he trailed off as he traced her cheekbone with his forefinger and thumb, then ran down her jaw line to her mouth.

Madison forgot to breathe.

Then he leaned down to kiss her, a light kiss that gently caressed her lips. "I love the taste of you," he murmured. "Makes me think of a perfect, ripe peach, ready to drown me in its sweet juices."

When he pulled her to him, Madison allowed him to hold her. To feel loved, wanted, and accepted was a powerful attraction. She wrapped her arms around him, drawing in his strength. It felt so wonderful to be held, and for one, tiny, nanosecond in time, the anxiety that she constantly lived with, eased.

"I love everything that makes you uniquely you." His voice was as soft as his lips. "Give me a chance, Madison. Give us a chance. Let me in, let me love you."

She wanted more of his kisses, wanted to touch him and wanted him to touch her, but the thought of allowing someone inside her home, of relaxing her guard even for a moment, was more than she could bear. She stiffened and pulled out of his arms.

"For God's sake, Madison. Don't do this. I love you."

"You don't understand, Greg. I'm not a complete woman, so I can't offer love. Not now, maybe not ever. If I were in any condition to love someone, it would be you. But I can't. I can't even love myself." She touched his face. "I don't think we should see each other any longer."

"But Madison—"

"I'm sorry, Greg." Without another word, she went inside and shut the door.

Once inside, she didn't try to stem the tears, weeping until she was exhausted. Would she ever be a normal person, capable of loving someone and allowing them to love her? Her first husband hadn't thought so. She still remembered how he'd recoiled in horror at her hysterical screams when he'd failed to lock one window.

She went on her nightly routine, making sure each window and door was locked. She pulled her revolver from the night-stand and touched each bullet in the cylinder just to be sure.

When she finally fell asleep, she dreamed of dark nights and heard again the terrifying sound of her mother's screams. She saw the killer's eyes, locked on her own as she stared at him through the louvered closet door.

Heart pounding, she jerked awake and lay sleepless until the alarm rang in the morning light.

Never had she felt so alone.

CHAPTER TEN

On his way to the bullpen, Dexter went over his list of names to contact about Bates. Ella and Maddy were first, of course, as he wanted the news to come from him. But after a sleepless night worrying about it, he still hadn't figured out the best way to break it to them.

One thing he was certain of. They should hear about the parole together so they could support each other. Or would it be better to talk to Ella first, so the two of them could prepare Maddy?

Just how the hell do you prepare someone to face the monster from her nightmares?

Dexter had always loved the justice system, believing in it so strongly that he'd spent his adult years putting his life in danger to defend and enforce its rules. Sure, it had faults, but it was a hell of a lot better than any alternative he could think of.

But now? He was taken aback that the system, for whatever reason, would allow a fiend like Bates back on the streets. Everyone knew it sometimes happened, but he couldn't let the injustice of that prevent him from continuing to track down the perps and see that they were put away. Now he was personally involved, and it was hell, and if *he* felt that way, he could imagine Ella's and Maddy's reactions.

He had to prepare them gently, carefully, praying that the news wouldn't send Maddy back into a mental and emotional relapse.

How the hell could he do that?

He should've been a shrink instead of—

A shrink! That was it. He'd call Maddy's therapist and ask her to accompany him.

Dr. King had given every sign of being committed to helping Maddy when she had been seeing her regularly, and he had no doubt she would be willing to pick up where she had left off. Especially under the current circumstances.

She had to.

So relieved at his brilliant idea that he could've broken out in song, he checked his Blackberry's address book and punched her office number. But when he asked to speak to her, the receptionist said she was on vacation.

A vacation? She couldn't be. Not now, not when Maddy's emotional health was at stake.

"When is she due to return?"

"She's due back in five days," the receptionist told him, "but she may extend her visit."

Five days? He didn't know if he could wait that long. With the overloads in the prison system, paperwork got behind and it often took a month for an inmate to walk through the gates. But Dexter had experience with those unexpected twists of fate, and Bates could be released at any time. Dexter didn't want to risk Maddy's state of mind.

"I need to speak with her on an urgent matter. I'd like her number, please."

"Are you a patient?"

Using all the authority he could muster, Dexter identified himself, adding that it was an urgent matter involving Ella Osborne and Madison Young.

She didn't give him the doctor's number, but in her cool efficient manner, she told him she'd relay the message—and she hung up.

Dexter stared at the phone. She hung up? He wasn't through speaking.

He resisted the urge to throw the phone on the floor and then head to the nearest bar, but he was afraid of how much booze it would take to calm the frustration and panic squeezing his guts. Instead, he called Senator Stone, the one man who could commiserate with him over Bates. However, after hearing the senator's voice, he kept the conversation brief. The older man hadn't sounded well at all, and Dexter hoped he'd take advantage of his downtime and get some rest.

The mayor and Marie were also on the list, but he could delay talking to them. Captain Silva needed to know.

Wanting to talk to Silva alone, he passed by Rico's desk, but to his consternation, Silva yelled for Rico.

"He's your partner, Dex. He needs to know what's going on."

Dexter ground his teeth.

Rico strolled into the office, nodded at the captain, and sat down. He avoided Dexter's eyes.

Christ, Dexter thought, he's still wearing that wounded expression. Too bad. He might actually like the guy if he'd act like a man instead of a pussy who didn't get picked for a sports team in gym class.

Dexter ignored him and brought the captain up to speed.

Silva's mouth tightened. He shuffled some papers on his desk, then dropped them.

"Yucaipa was Bates' last known residence," Dexter said, "so he'll be released back to his so-called community. Depending on their backload, it may take a few weeks for all the paperwork to get processed. That'll give us some breathing time."

Silva sat back and eyed Dexter. "I shouldn't have to say this, and I'm hoping it won't be needed, but Dexter, no matter what your rank is, you're first a law enforcement officer. Remember that. I know your history with Bates, and I can imagine how you must feel. But watch it. I don't need a half-crazed vigilante on my team."

"Yes sir, I understand."

"You hear me, Dex? I have enough problems."

"Yes sir."

Silva held Dexter's gaze for a moment. "Ah, get the hell out of here."

Dexter walked back to his desk. *Half-crazed vigilante?* Not him—not unless such action was needed.

"What's up with you and a parolee?" Rico asked, pulling out his own chair. "Sounds like something I should know."

"Maybe I'll tell you about it sometime."

Rico frowned.

"Over breakfast," Dexter added with a sigh. The things he had to do just to get a vacation.

When they were served, Rico's gaze went from his platter to the server, fixing her with a beady stare. His impression of authority, Dexter thought.

"One egg yolk is flat and hard," Rico complained, "and I asked for over-easy. Please take them back and have the cook prepare them the way they were ordered."

The server took his platter, but Dexter wasn't going to wait. He spread a generous layer of strawberry jam on his toast.

"Want a piece until they bring yours?" he asked, then ignoring Rico's scowl, he dug into his breakfast.

"The toast looks overdone," Rico told the server when she appeared with his breakfast, "but I don't want to wait again."

Just to keep from punching the guy, Dexter asked him about canvassing the area yesterday around the steakhouse. "Any luck?"

"The usual. No one saw or heard anything. If something doesn't break soon, we'll have an unsolved mystery right in town. Any ideas?"

"Maybe someone in one of those houses on the hill behind Jimmy's saw something. Worth a try, but with no leads, this case goes cold."

The words hung in the air as they finished their meals.

"What's the deal with this guy Bates?" Rico asked. "Why are you so attached? They warn us about getting too emotionally involved."

Over a refill of coffee, Dexter thought about his reply. If he were doomed to have that asshole as a partner, he should at least let him know why he felt so strongly about Bates.

"It's more than a case, Rico. Madison and her grandmother, Ella Osborne, are like family. Over the years, I've spent many evenings at Ella's kitchen table.

"At first my goal was to help them through," he went on, "but I discovered I needed them as much as they needed me. Ella comforted me through my marriage and divorce, plying me with cookies, pies, and my favorite, chicken and dumplings. I'd *help* Maddy make the dumplings, and I managed to get more flour on me than in the dough." He smiled. "And when she'd laugh, well, it was a delight. That child had been through hell, and for a while, none of us knew if she'd survive.

"And now, I'm going to have to tell them news that'll shatter the world they've managed to build."

"That's a tough break," Rico said. "I've seen her review columns, even tried a restaurant or two she recommended. That's rough, but neither woman is your responsibility."

Dexter put his fork down and let go. Otherwise, he was afraid he'd stab Rico with it.

"You have any kids, Rico?"

"A son, fourteen. Lives with his mother in San Jose."

"See him much?"

"I try to, but you know how it goes. He blames me for the divorce."

"Wouldn't you do anything and everything in your power to keep him from harm?"

"Of course."

"That's how I feel about Maddy."

"She's not a relative, though, right? I mean you're not legally responsible."

Dexter couldn't figure out the little prick. And he was supposed to trust him with his life? Soon as he could after vacation, he'd dump him, no matter how much the captain bitched.

Finishing his coffee, he picked up his cell. It had been a couple of hours since he'd left word for Dr. King and still no word.

"This is Detective Quinn again," he told the receptionist. "Dr. King has not returned my call."

"I left word, sir," she said, her voice just as detached as before. "Dr. Simmons is on call. Would you like to speak to him?"

"I'm sure he's a very capable man, but I want to speak to Dr. King. As soon as possible." Keeping his irritation in check, he left his name and number once more. Was the entire world fucked?

Next, he called Ella to see how she and Maddy were doing, to get a feel for their mood, and was switched to her voice mail. He tried her cell number. Same thing. She might be out shopping, but she usually answered her cell. He wondered if anything was wrong.

Just to make sure she was all right, he called Maddy, who assured him that her grandmother was fine and was just taking a short trip with Cora and her sister.

Although he didn't say it, he could only hope that she'd return rested enough to survive what he had to tell her.

"Willy Boy" Martin stood in the Arizona sun, waiting in line with a handful of other people near the food bank semi parked at a local church. By the time they opened the doors in an hour, the line would be three times longer, and there never was enough food for everyone. Willy wanted to make sure he got his share.

He took a deep drag of his cigarette and blew a heavy plume of smoke, ignoring the irritated glances of the other people in line. They didn't like it, piss on 'em. They could leave.

The fat broad in front of him turned around, but before he could tell her to go fuck herself, she smiled.

"Wonder what we'll get this time," she said, eyeing him as if he were a choice cut of steak. About as wide as she was tall, she was in her thirties and wore one of those skimpy little tops that barely covered her floppy boobs. Dimpled flesh hung over her short jean cutoffs and rippled down her heavy thighs. But hey, he never turned down a piece of ass, no matter how big, so he poured it on, paying attention and laughing inside when she smiled at him. After making a date, he lost interest in her silly chatter and she finally gave up and turned around.

The sun burned hotter and he brushed sweat from his forehead with his arm. His dingy T-shirt was soaked. Tired of standing, he plopped down on the pavement. Waiting for food was woman's work, but Shantel got called in at the diner, and if he wanted a meal and a fuck later, he had to pick up the box of food.

Man, he had a good thing going; he'd sell what he didn't eat right out of the box. In his neighborhood, buyers didn't always have money, but they traded services, especially that little Asian broad. She really knew how to use her tongue, and it only took a few moments after stepping into the alley. He got a hard-on just thinking about it.

"Waiting's hell in this heat," a voice said.

Willy looked up and could just make out an outline of someone wearing jeans silhouetted against the afternoon sun. He shaded his eyes with his hand and couldn't tell if it was a man or woman.

"Hey man, you a him or her? Not that I usually have a problem telling," he added with a snicker.

"You can't tell?"

Willy patted the pavement beside him. "Tell you what. Sit here and I'll feel your tits. Then I'll know." He threw out his chest. "I'm an expert on tits."

"I'll sit, but keep your hands off my boobs. Just think of me as an *it*, like in Cousin Itt from the Addams Family. You ever watch it?"

"Yeah. *Thing* was cool."

Itt sat heavily beside him and stared at him from behind huge sunglasses. Instead of something light, Itt wore one of those long-sleeved sweatshirts with the hood pulled halfway over gray hair.

"Man, you crazy? Wearing that thing in this heat?"

"Keeps the sun off me."

Willy shrugged. He didn't give a rat's ass what Itt wore.

"You have a family?" Itt asked.

"Nah. Got me a woman, though. Her bratty kid lives with us."

Itt nodded and kept looking at him. Even though Willy couldn't see Itt's eyes, he felt the stare. Shit, man, as horny as he was, he wasn't hard up enough to go for an old woman—or man.

"Let me tell you a secret," Itt said, leaning toward him. Willy wasn't sure he wanted that close, but he was willing to listen. Hell, listening never hurt nobody. When Itt cupped his ear with its hand, he waited.

"What's the secret?" he asked, getting impatient. He didn't want no one seeing him too friendly with this thing.

Itt pulled an envelope from a front pocket and showed it to him. Printed on a sheet of paper was something about some society and a time and date.

"That's today," Willy said. "That supposed to mean something to me?"

"That tells when you're going to die," Itt whispered.

Willy jerked back. Just then, he felt a sharp prick in his right side and looked down to see Itt's hand push the plunger on one of those syringes.

"What the fuck?" He swatted it away, but not before he felt liquid fire spreading through his body.

"Oh, Jesus," he moaned and tried to stand. He got to his knees but a wave of contractions doubled him over and took his breath. He tried to call for help, but he had no air left. Suddenly, his arms and legs wouldn't work. He couldn't speak. His eyes watered, and his jaw froze in a silent scream.

The thing beside him stood and dropped the syringe into its shirt pocket and hurried away. Someone screamed and the broad in front of him bent down.

Her round face was the last thing Willy Boy ever saw.

CHAPTER ELEVEN

Mornings in Marie's office were occasions Madison tried to avoid. The ringing phones, the constant ping of new emails from her two computers, reporters barging in with the latest emergencies, all were maddening to a quiet person with too little sleep. But Marie needed information about the vice-president's trip to the Near East, and Madison was recruited to search the newswire service.

"You may have to check back a few days," the editor told her, punching numbers on her fax machine. "They've kept details under wraps."

When Marie turned away to answer her phone, Madison was ready to scream. She tried to think of reasons to escape, desperate enough to wish for a sudden appendix attack. Instead, she swallowed a couple of aspirins and tried tuning out the noise.

Inching Marie's little green stuffed frog away from the keyboard, she scanned the front page of the service before scrolling through the new releases covering everything from entertainment news to the latest hot software. She clicked on the unfiltered political news and printed all the information she could find on the vice-president's upcoming trip.

Just as she was ready to log out, something she'd bypassed on another page nagged her, so she clicked back and browsed the stories until she found it:

Yuma, AZ—William "Willy Boy" Martin, 27, died today of undetermined causes while waiting in line at the food shelf on Impala

Drive. A witness in line with Mr. Martin stated he was seen talking to a senior individual also in line. That person fled the scene. The coroner's investigation into the exact cause of death is ongoing.

Madison read the story a couple of times and couldn't determine what there was about it that bothered her. She would have liked to send the item to her own computer, but Marie's was the only one with a subscription to the newswire service. Instead, she hit the print button.

"I'll find out," Marie was saying into her headset. "Madison, Tom thinks there's five dialects for the Arabic language. Check on that, will you?"

Back at her desk an hour later, her headache still a dull throb, Madison scanned the story from Yuma onto her office computer and emailed it to her laptop. Something about it still nagged at her, but she didn't have time to think about it now. She was behind on her reviews, so she considered revisiting one of her favorite Thai restaurants in the area, but she was scheduled for the Japanese place in Colton the next evening and didn't want to sample two Asian meals in a row. What other restaurant could she review on short notice?

Then she remembered a neighbor asking her about a new deli that had opened a couple of days before the shooting. Perfect, she thought. She could do a fast review, write it up, and get it to Marie before the deadline.

Just as she was calling the deli manager for permission to take photographs inside the restaurant and of the food, her cell phone rang. She almost let it go to voice mail, but the ID told her it was Cora. That was odd. Why would Cora be calling her? She put the deli owner on hold, something she hated to do, and clicked to accept Cora's call.

"Is anything wrong, Cora? Is Gran all right?"

"Now don't get overly concerned, Madison, but Ella hasn't been feeling well and we're on our way home."

"I'll meet you at her doctor's."

"She refuses to seek medical help. I'd object, but I don't think it's that serious. She's weak and nauseous, but I'm sure it's one of those bugs or something she ate. She rested all day yesterday and may need to stay in a few more days. She'll feel better in her own bed. We're taking our time, so barring heavy traffic, we should be home in a couple of hours."

Madison wanted to get her grandmother's house ready, but she didn't dare postpone another review. Marie had been a tolerant editor, but Madison didn't want to push her luck. No matter what happened in a reporter's personal life, the newspaper still had to go to print each day.

At the deli twenty minutes later, Madison chatted with the owner about the quality of the cold cuts he used and dutifully made notes about his wife staying after hours to make fresh potato and macaroni salad. She complimented them on one of their specials, a soup and half sandwich meal, which came with a miniature black and chrome kettle that sat on the table and held two cups of homemade soup.

Madison tasted a spoonful of soup, her mind on her grandmother. How much longer until Cora made it home? If Ella was nauseous, she'd need nourishing, easily digested food, so Madison decided to buy as much soup as the deli could spare.

She snapped photos of the inside of the restaurant, the plates and salads, and also of the owners, then she thanked them and took her leave.

Once at her grandmother's house, she put the soup in the fridge and checked for juices, oatmeal, and other staples she thought would be needed over the next few days. After opening windows and turning down the bed, she walked to the front porch to check for Cora's red Mercedes, and finding it nowhere in sight, took her computer from her briefcase to do some work.

She entered the title of her review and downloaded the photos from her camera, but instead of picturing the restaurant and describing the food for her readers, she found herself listening for the car. Twenty minutes later, still no further along in her article, she heard the engine and ran to the porch and down the steps.

Cora had opened the back door to help Ella out, and when Madison saw her grandmother's face, she was so shocked that she came to an abrupt halt.

Although Jimmy's Steakhouse was still closed, Dexter and Rico tracked down the personnel who'd been on duty the night of the shooting and questioned them about the woman in the straw hat. The results were the same as they'd been the first night: no one knew her, no one remembered seeing her in the restaurant. Some had heard the shots but thought they were backfires from the busy boulevard.

On their way back to the bullpen, Dexter tuned out Rico's prattle and checked his phone again. Dr. King hadn't returned his call yesterday, and now it was the afternoon of the second day and he still hadn't heard from her.

He called the office. Again.

"I'm sorry, but Dr. King can't be disturbed," the receptionist said in a brisk voice. "I'll be happy to connect you to her associate."

Until then he'd been polite. Now he switched to his professional voice, the low menacing growl that intimidated the toughest gangbanger.

"What's your name, young lady?" he demanded, and then, when she told him, "Rebecca, please tell the doctor that if I don't hear from her in the next half-hour, I'll show up at the office with a subpoena."

"A subpoena?"

"Tell me, Rebecca. Is your waiting room full of patients right now?"

"Of course. She and her associate are highly respected doctors."

"I'm glad to hear that, but I have to wonder how all those patients would react to several cops bursting into the office demanding access to the records."

Rico stared at him, clearly startled, but Dexter ignored him.

"Think it would shake their faith in their doctors just a bit?" Dexter asked smoothly. "Do you, Rebecca? Then why don't you save us that trouble and get Dr. King on the line. Now." Dexter hoped she wasn't versed on legalities and able to recognize bullshit when she heard it.

"I'll see if I can reach the doctor immediately," she told him stiffly.

"Young lady, I've heard that before. A half-hour, then I'll be at your door."

When Madison saw her grandmother leaning on Cora beside the car, she couldn't believe what she was seeing. Ella's entire body sagged as if she'd aged twenty years, and her face was as white as Madison's typing paper and so translucent that Madison could see the blue veins in her cheeks and forehead. Her eyes were sunken and rimmed in red.

"Gran," Madison breathed. What in God's name had happened in just a couple of days to cause such a change?

She'd always known that in the natural order of things, Ella would pass on before her, but that was an abstract knowledge, not something she'd had to think about or face. But seeing her condition now, observing how she could barely stand on her own, forced Madison to realize that one day she'd lose the person who meant more to her than anyone else on earth. And that realization terrified her.

"I'll take care of the luggage, Cora." She put her arms around her grandmother. "You and Clara go on in and have something to drink. I'm going to take Gran to her doctor's."

"No you're not, Maddy," Ella said. "I'm home and this is where I'm going to stay."

"Now Gran—"

"Madison, I don't feel strong enough to argue, so I want you to listen. I'm not dying. I just need some rest in my own bed. If you insist on fussing, I'll go to Cora's."

Madison glanced helplessly at Cora, who simply shrugged.

"What can I say? The woman is so obstinate that you can't reason with her."

Clara looked sharply at her sister, and Ella managed a chuckle.

"Who's calling whom obstinate?" Clara asked.

Cora ignored them all and marched up the steps to the house.

After Madison settled her grandmother in bed and brought some soup, she sat on the edge of the mattress and tried to help.

"I can feed myself, Maddy. Now don't hover."

"I'm sorry, Gran. It's just that you took care of me all those years, and now I want to care for you. I love you, you know," Madison added, her eyes filling, "and I don't know what I'd do if I lost you."

"Well, you're not going to lose me, honey, at least not today. So don't fret. I just caught something, or perhaps the shellfish we had before going to the theater didn't agree with me. But whatever it was, it'll pass. I'm already feeling better."

Her face was regaining some of its rosy color, Madison observed with relief. She'd been so terrified that she could barely breathe and only realized it when she took a good, deep breath.

She leaned down and touched her grandmother's soft cheek

with her own, a gesture Ella had done many times that first year after Maddy came to live with her. How wonderfully comforting it had felt to the six-year-old who'd just lost her parents. Now the touch was more for her than for her grandmother.

"I'll let you rest now," she said, gathering the dishes. "I'll be staying here the next few days to take care of you, and if you protest, I'll hover."

"Thanks, honey. That'll be nice. Now go away so I can sleep."

Back in the kitchen, Madison fixed egg salad sandwiches while Cora made a pitcher of iced tea.

"Now tell me," she asked her grandmother's friend. "What happened?"

Just as Dexter had decided to head for Dr. King's office, sans a subpoena of course, his phone rang. It was the elusive Felicia King.

"What the hell do you mean threatening my receptionist?"

"I didn't hear back from you, so I had to do something to get your attention."

"I should file charges against you, Dexter. I don't like threats, and I certainly don't like bullies."

"Who, me?"

"Don't sound so innocent. You pulled similar stunts in the past when you tried to pry information out of me about Madison. It didn't work then and it's not going to work now. I don't have much time, so what do you want?"

"Actually, Felicia, I need your help." He brought her up to date about Bates' release. "Ella and Maddy have to be told, and I'm not sure how they're going to handle it. Ella is more grounded, but Maddy still leaves all of her lights on. I'm afraid the news will send her into a relapse."

"Oh, no, Dexter," King said. "I'm so sorry this has happened. Call my associate. He's good. I picked him myself."

"I don't want your associate. Maddy's used to talking to you. Besides, you know all of her history, and an associate couldn't pick it all up from a file."

"I wish I could help, but I can't get away."

"Look. If it's the fee, I'll pay. I'll even spring for your airfare home and back again."

"I'm sorry, Dexter. I can't."

"What's so damned important that you can't leave?"

"My father is dying. He's on life support and I have to be here."

Cora and Clara told Madison about the enjoyable time they'd had on the way to San Diego, how they'd stopped for lunch at a delightful restaurant south of Temecula. Other than being quiet and eating very little, Ella had seemed okay.

After checking into the hotel, they'd had dinner at an oceanfront restaurant, then gone to the musical. When they took a taxi back to the hotel, Ella had told them she was feeling tired and retreated to her room. The sisters had tea and dessert in the hotel coffee shop, and when they retired to the room they shared, they found a message from Ella saying she'd been throwing up and wanted to stay in bed the next day to rest, that they should go ahead with their own plans.

The next day, Ella had the Do Not Disturb sign on her door, and not wanting to wake her if she were sleeping, the sisters had gone about their plans. The morning after that, which was today, Cora called Ella's room, and after speaking to her, decided to take her home.

"I tried to get her to the doctor's," Cora told Madison, "but you know your grandmother. And actually, she seemed to perk up a bit on our way back home. I'm sure she'll be all right now."

After the sisters left, Madison tiptoed to Ella's room and

stood outside the partially opened bedroom door. When she heard her grandmother's soft snore, she gave a silent thanks and crept back to the kitchen to do some work.

In front of her laptop, her notes neatly stacked on the kitchen table, she wrote the deli review and sent it to Marie. Then she clicked on the Yuma story and read it several times. What was it that bothered her? What kept her going back to read it again and again? It was only an unexplained death, and God knows there were plenty of those in the news. So what nagged at her?

When her cell rang, she ran to the table to grab it.

"Hi, honey," Dexter said. "Any word on when Ella will be home? I'd like to stop by when she gets back."

"Actually, Dex, she's home now, but she's resting." She explained what happened. "I'll be staying with her for a few days, so why don't you tell me and then I can let her know?"

"That's okay, Maddy," he said, and for a second, she was aware of a change in his voice. "I'd rather speak to both of you at the same time. Just let me know as soon as you feel Ella is strong enough for a visitor."

"Since when are you a visitor? You know you're welcome any time."

"I know, but I'll let her rest today and check tomorrow. In the meantime, is there anything I can do?"

After hanging up, Madison wondered what Dexter thought important enough to want an appointment to talk to them. For as long as she could remember, he'd dropped by the hillside house for coffee and cookies in the kitchen whenever he had some spare time, sometimes bringing a pizza for the three of them to share, or simply to relax in Ella's homey kitchen.

He never talked about his job or the atrocities he'd faced over the years, and while Madison had been curious at times, she learned to recognize the tight lines around his eyes and mouth and could hear the edge in his voice. During those times, she knew that whatever he'd faced had been bad, and she'd wanted to help her grandmother soothe away the demons just as he'd helped her.

Now, no matter how he'd tried to mask it over the phone, she'd heard that edge. Taking a sip of iced tea, she wondered why he felt it was important to talk to Ella and her.

Damn. It was bad enough to have to tell them about Bates, but to have to do so when Ella felt unwell made it worse. Dexter wondered how long he could safely postpone talking to them.

"Wait up!" Rico yelled from across Impala Drive.

He and Rico had been knocking on doors of houses behind the steakhouse in the hope someone knew something or had seen something they didn't realize was significant. So far, they had picked up nothing. Zilch.

He checked his watch. Six-thirty. Josh Gidding had probably left for the day, but Dexter hoped he'd still be in. Like others in public service jobs, parole officials put in hours of overtime. He punched Gidding's number.

With his phone to his ear, he loosened his tie and made his way to his car. Rico trailed behind. The mercury had soared to the high nineties, and although it was starting to cool down, it was still hot enough to make an iguana happy. Good ol' Inland Empire, he thought. Winter one day and full summer the next.

Gidding's number rang and rang, and with each ring, Dexter's guts squeezed a little tighter. He finally left an urgent message on voice mail. Once inside his Tahoe, he turned on the air and aimed the vents for his face. He was getting too old for this shit.

Christ! Couldn't one damned thing go right? He yanked off his tie and unbuttoned the top two buttons of his shirt.

He glanced at the sandy-brown hills surrounding Yucaipa and longed to escape to a campfire near a river. Maybe it was age, perhaps it was burn-out after a lifetime of dead bodies, grieving families, and the fucked-up justice system, but with each day, the longing grew to hear the sound of water rushing over rocks or down a waterfall. Instead of sirens, he wanted to listen to the wind rustling through leaves on a shade tree and feel a cooling rain on his face.

Why the hell didn't he retire to a nice, rural state where everything was green, a place where he could sit under trees and throw a casting line into a river?

Hell. It had been years since he'd even seen a river, much less camp near one, but that was going to change. Less than two weeks and he was out of here. Only one thing could stop him, and that was Bates in his town, walking the same streets as Maddy and Ella.

Rico opened the passenger door and slid in.

"*¡Válgame Dios!*" He wiped sweat from his face. "This is brutal. How about we knock off for something cold to drink?"

"Best suggestion you've made all day."

When Rico headed for the men's room at Denny's, Dexter made an appointment with the mayor for the next morning. They'd need to call a special city council meeting to alert the city that a parolee with a violent history was about to be released into its midst. Since there was no official word on the exact date Bates would be released, Dexter didn't want to delay too long.

He'd also talk to Marie, let her know what he was planning. As editor of the local newspaper, and especially considering her involvement in the community, she deserved to know.

He knew he should clear all of this with the captain, but he didn't want to risk Silva nixing the idea. Bates might not be released for another few weeks, but he didn't want to risk waiting. Fate had already thrown one of those fancy twists that put the screws to everyone's lives, and if another happened, he was damned well going to be prepared.

When he called Marie, the only off-time she had available was that evening, so, trusting that she had enough decency to hold the story until he'd had the chance to talk to Maddy and Ella, he decided to go ahead and meet her.

He just hoped Ella would be strong enough the next day to hear the news.

CHAPTER TWELVE

Jericho One stood at the carved wooden door, ready to welcome each Society member with a handshake before leading them to the table and encouraging them to help themselves.

Instead of the usual tray of fruits, pastries, and finger foods, the sideboard held iced platters of crab legs, shrimp, and oysters on the half-shell. Delicate glass side dishes held lemon quarters and seafood sauce. For the two members who didn't care for seafood, a platter held halved sourdough loaves topped with reddish-rare prime rib slices. Cantaloupe quarters held chunks of mango, papaya, and kiwi, and two carafes, one for water and the other for wine, stood in the center of the table between the two lamps. A coffee carafe stood by Number Three's place.

When all six had arrived, Jericho selected a few food items from the buffet, took the chair at the head of the table, and chatted amicably with the members.

After the table had been cleared, Jericho began the meeting.

"Thank you all for attending this emergency session. I know some of you have traveled a great distance, especially you, Number Five, but I'm sure you're aware that I wouldn't have called this meeting if it were not urgent." After a pause, the chairperson continued.

"A situation has arisen and intervention is immediately needed." Jericho handed two sheets of paper clipped together to each member.

"Michael Bates, forty-seven, Caucasian, from Yucaipa,

California, was convicted twenty years ago for the torture and murder of Mr. and Mrs. Daniel Young, also of Yucaipa. A daughter, Madison, age six, was in the home, and after Bates brutally murdered her parents, he entered her room as well. He testified at trial that he'd intended on 'getting her too,' but fled when he heard police sirens."

Jericho recounted in detail the acts Bates had committed on the Youngs, then passed glossy photos of the two victims, of the six-year-old child, and of Michael Bates at the time of conviction and also one taken at his last parole hearing.

"He was sentenced to execution at San Quentin, but Bates got lucky. The courts were arguing that execution was unconstitutional, and a temporary moratorium on capital punishment was enforced. Bates' execution was converted to a life sentence. And because of that life sentence, he's been eligible for parole and has, indeed, been before the board several times. Fortunately, the request has been denied—until the last hearing. Mr. Bates will be released as soon as the paperwork can be completed." Jericho paused to take a sip of water.

"I think you'll agree, after reading his history," the chairperson continued, "not only would his execution have saved the taxpaying citizens the expense of his care, but it would have eliminated the threat to those still living. He's an imminent danger not only to the community to which he'll return, but to the lives of the remaining family he brutally slaughtered.

"Mrs. Young's mother, Mrs. Ella Osborne, still resides in California as does Miss Young, who was severely traumatized and, judging from psychiatric records, still carries emotional scars," Jericho explained. "But the reason for this intervention is that during his trial, Bates vowed to return for the daughter. It may have been a blusterous threat, but the petitioning member does not want to take that risk."

Several members studied the photos as if to reinforce the

necessity of their proposed actions.

"The requirements for the execution have been met," Jericho went on. "All that's needed is your approval."

As was the custom, the ruby bowl was passed somberly around the room for each member's vote. After they were counted, Jericho announced the decision.

"So what's up?" Marie asked, scooping salsa onto a tortilla chip. She'd changed from her usual pantsuit into a sleeveless blouse over linen trousers and her hair was swept back into a French braid.

Dexter sat across from her in a Mexican place in Mentone, a small hillside community near Yucaipa. He swirled the crushed ice in his margarita glass, trying to decide how much to tell her. While he knew of her impeccable character, he also knew she was a devoted newspaper editor.

"Can I trust you not to print the information I'm about to give you? At least not yet?"

"Sounds ominous."

"You haven't answered my question."

"How can you ask me something like that? The people are entitled—"

"Don't hand me that shit. I want an answer. Not from the newspaper, but from you. Otherwise, this meeting is over."

"Why such hardball?" Then, when stony silence was his response, "At least tell me why I can't print it, then I'll give you my answer." Marie took another handful of chips and washed them down with a swallow of her drink.

"I don't want the two people personally affected to read about it before I have a chance to talk to them. And I can't talk to them until tomorrow, or possibly the day after."

"You must think a lot of them to feel so strongly."

"I do." Such a simple answer, Dexter thought, to express

twenty years of feelings for the Young family. "Look. All I'm asking for is a couple of days. And I don't have to tell you anything. You can find out at the special city council meeting just like everyone else."

"I'm not aware that a council meeting's been scheduled."

"It will be."

Marie eyed him for a long moment. "So why tell me now?" she asked.

"Because of our long association."

A skeptical look crossed Maric's face.

"And there's always the risk you'll find out and print it before I'm ready," he added.

"I've worked with you on committees and other volunteer projects over a lot of years," Marie said, "and it doesn't take much deduction to know how important Ella and Madison are to you. And something this serious must mean news about Bates."

Dexter was taken aback. He'd almost forgotten how good she was at her job, how she made it her business to know the important things about the community and her employees.

"Close your mouth, Dexter. You don't want to catch flies."

He grinned. "You never cease to amaze me." He told her about the trip to San Quentin and the board's decision. "Ella's been ill, so I haven't been able to break the news to them yet."

"Nothing serious, I hope."

"I don't think so or Maddy would have her at the hospital."

When their food came, they dug into fish tacos with cabbage and fresh cilantro, and chiles rellenos with beans and Spanish rice as accompaniments. One thing about it, Dexter thought. He might hate the heat in the Yucaipa Valley, but the area had damned good food.

Marie stirred her drink. "I can't believe they'd free Bates, not after what he did. I'd hoped they would've fried his ass."

Dexter's eyebrows climbed. "Such language. I'm surprised."

"Can it, Dexter. We have to do something. That piece of shit shouldn't be allowed in our community."

"We can't stop it, Marie. You know that."

"We'll see."

After dinner, Madison settled her grandmother on the sofa with the TV remote in her hand, then she set her laptop on the coffee table.

Although Ella claimed she felt stronger, watching her declining health caused Madison to realize what had caught her eye about the Yuma and Yucaipa articles.

She read the article once more, then pulled up her notes on the Yucaipa shooting. Middleton, the man she'd interviewed, had mentioned an older woman with Hawley.

In the Yuma story, she highlighted the word "senior" and sat back and compared the two stories. There it was. Two sudden deaths with references to senior citizens.

Could there be a connection? A sudden image of a gun-toting old lady going around shooting people popped into her head, and she dismissed it as absurd. Besides, the first shooting had been in Yucaipa, California, and the other death, which the police hadn't even called a murder, had been in Arizona.

She ran several searches on her computer, looking for unexplained deaths or murders with the word "senior" or "senior citizen" included. What came up was disappointing. Page after page of articles including items about senior officers, senior relatives, senior advisors, and even one about a short story as a senior thesis. Not at all what she wanted.

As much as she dreaded entering the den of fire, she'd ask Marie's permission to run the newswire service. She didn't know why this nagged at her, and normally she'd avoid anything with violence. Perhaps working in a newspaper office had taught her to instinctively know when something felt amiss.

Two hours later, after settling Ella in bed and checking each door and window, she found a comfortable spot on the pillow and closed her eyes—but only for a moment. Her gaze swept her old room, the light from her bedside lamp brightly illuminating every corner, and she could see the light from the hallway, also on as well. Maybe it was time she grew up and started living like a normal person.

Determined to give it a try, she reached for the knob on her pink hurricane lamp, the same one she'd had as a child, and switched it off.

There. She'd done it. It wasn't so bad.

Instead of inspecting the dark room again, she firmly closed her eyes.

From outside her darkened window, behind the ruffled curtains and closed shutters, she heard a slight rustling sound. She tensed, but told herself that everything was okay, that she was safe in her grandmother's home.

She closed her eyes again, but instead of relaxing, she listened for the next sound, hoping, praying she wouldn't hear it.

Just as she began to relax, she heard it again, that same sound, only slighter louder.

She sat up. Was there a breeze tonight? She didn't remember noticing one before. Please God, let there be a breeze. She crept to her door to listen, and heard something that sounded like shingles rattling on the roof.

Except that shingles didn't rattle, even in a strong breeze. Or did they?

She didn't know how long she stood, alert to any noise she couldn't immediately identify, but after hearing nothing more, she crept back to bed. The wall sconce in the hallway was still lit, a habit her grandmother had begun when Madison first came to live with her. The yellow light spilled into her room and illuminated her doorway, so if she kept her eyes on it, she would see a shadow if someone were moving toward her room.

Her eyelids felt heavy. She needed rest, needed to wake in the morning strong enough to care for her grandmother. Watching her doorway all night wouldn't help either of them, but how could she relax enough to fall asleep?

Then she remembered how she'd loved to draw, the one way she could relax and forget everything. Digging in her closet, she pulled out the box holding her artist supplies, items she hadn't used in years.

In bed moments later, surrounded by her sketch pads, spiral notebooks, crayons, and charcoal sticks, she began her charcoal strokes, thinking about Greg, wondering if she could replicate the way his eyes softened when he looked at her.

A half-hour later, she stared at the sketch she'd drawn, so horrified that she shoved all the supplies onto the floor.

Before her was Michael Bates, his piercing eyes staring at her from the sketchpad.

CHAPTER THIRTEEN

A little bribery never hurt, Madison thought, entering the office carrying Marie's favorite breakfast, a dish of hot cinnamon rolls smothered with cream cheese frosting. All heads turned as the spicy, sweet aroma wafted through the office. Luckily, she'd brought enough for everyone or she'd be tarred, feathered, and run out of town.

"Marie in?"

"Give me one first, then I'll spill," Sue said.

Madison laughed. "I promise I'll save you one, but Marie gets first pick."

She'd set the alarm an hour early and had popped the rolls into the oven while fixing breakfast for her grandmother.

Thank goodness Ella was looking more like herself. A sure sign that she was feeling better was bossing Madison in the kitchen and refusing to be pampered. Madison was so relieved by her grandmother's recovery that she felt more lighthearted than she had in years.

Marie was bent over her PC. Good, Madison thought, the Mac was free.

As soon as Madison entered the room, Marie sniffed the air. "Cinnamon rolls. Okay, what do you want? My prized pooch? My five-year-old car? Whatever it is, you got it." She jumped up, took a couple of paper plates and plastic cutlery from a file drawer, and helped herself to a roll.

"What else do you have in those drawers?" Madison asked.

"Top secret stuff that I'll never tell. So what's up? You didn't go to all that trouble just to see me smile." She licked a dab of frosting from her finger and sighed in ecstasy.

"I'd like to use the wire service and do a search for any stories that might tie in with these," Madison said, handing the articles and notes from her briefcase.

Marie glanced at the notes and helped herself to another roll.

"These what, Madison? I don't see anything relevant."

"It may not be much, but I'd like to check them out. Look. Both stories are about someone dying, and in each, there's mention of a senior near them before they died."

"So? According to statistics, there are over thirty-six million seniors in the country."

"But read the articles. One's a murder and the other is an unexplained death of a man in his twenties. Don't you find that strange? Let me do some research, see if I can find any other stories like that. You're always talking about training me to be a news reporter, so now I'm interested."

Marie put down her plate and slowly, carefully, wiped her hands on a paper towel.

Madison knew her editor well enough to recognize the signs of disinterest. Only then did she realize how important it was for her to investigate.

"I don't have the time to train you right now and frankly," Marie said, not meeting her eyes, "I don't see a story here. You're wasting your time. Besides, I'm using the computer."

"What if I do it on my own time? I plan on checking on Gran at lunch, and I have the review at the Japanese place this afternoon, but I could work it in. I could come in after hours, do some checking on my own."

"You know the publisher doesn't approve overtime."

"Marie, this would be on my own time. What's the problem?"

"Our insurance doesn't cover anyone after office hours."

That didn't sound right to Madison. She'd heard Marie talk several times about the late evenings she'd spent putting the paper "to bed," but since she wasn't familiar with business insurances, she didn't argue. Besides, she could see her editor's lips tighten and knew it was time to drop the subject.

"I hope Ella's feeling better." Marie handed the dish of rolls to Madison. "Thanks for bringing them in. Just pass the rest around the office," she added, dismissing Madison by turning to her PC.

Madison stood like a statue holding the dumb rolls, watching Marie ignore her, trying to understand what had just happened.

"Marie—"

The ringing phone interrupted, and Marie's relief was obvious. She grabbed it and again turned her back to Madison.

Madison waited a few moments, hoping Marie would finish her conversation and get back to her so they could talk, but as soon as Marie hung up, she rushed out of her office to talk to Sue. She said nothing more to Madison, didn't even glance her way when Madison walked back to her desk.

It didn't make sense. Madison had never known Marie to discourage any of her staff from investigative reporting. On the contrary, she'd always welcomed it. And, she hadn't been using the Mac; she'd been at her PC instead.

Madison left Marie's office feeling as if she'd been rudely dismissed, and she had no idea why.

The conference room in Yucaipa's city hall was as familiar to Dexter as his own squad room. The Honorable Walt Goodman had always been active in city affairs, attending as many Yucaipa functions as he could, believing city government should personally be involved in its community. He'd attended Little League games as well as the opening of new businesses, and he, Marie, and Dexter had spent many evenings drafting new incentives and scholarships for the city's youths.

Today, Dexter had the unpleasant duty of having to tell the mayor about the threat to his city.

"Thanks for seeing me on short notice." He shook hands with his friend. At nearly seventy, Goodman stood as tall as he had in his younger days. His military posture was softened slightly by his thick white hair.

"It sounded urgent, Dexter. Come, sit down, have a cup of coffee." The mayor led the way to a highly polished conference table. But the true focal point of the room was the view through the wide bay windows of the city. As before, Dexter took a moment to gaze at the city from the bluff on which the city hall had been built.

His community, his adopted home.

He'd watched Yucaipa grow from a quiet little town full of orange groves to a thriving community with a population of over fifty thousand. Nestled in the foothills of the San Bernardino National Forest about seventy-five miles east of Los Angeles, the city maintained its home-town atmosphere. Citizens were involved in city government as well as with community events. Each Fourth of July, the city celebrated at the high school stadium with bands, games, fireworks, and flyovers from March Air Reserve Base. The Elks, the Moose, and the American Legion held lunches, dinners, and other events open to the public. Even in the near-desert heat, the recreational areas flourished, and people flocked to the regional park or to one of the several golf courses. A top-ranking community college overlooked the city from the top of a foothill. Gang activity was almost nonexistent and the overall crime rate was low. The shooting at Jimmy's was an anomaly. Citizens felt safe, which was the way Dexter wanted to keep it.

Goodman poured coffee into two mugs and took them to stand next to Dexter. They sipped in companionable silence and gazed over the city they each loved.

"We have a problem," Dexter said.

Madison spent the rest of the morning working on her outline for the review scheduled that afternoon, making notes on the items she wanted to cover, but she had trouble concentrating. Several times Marie had walked past her without speaking or even glancing her way. Madison replayed the morning several times, but she still had no idea what had happened. Or why.

The morning's bright spot had been her call to her grandmother. She'd planned to stop by the drugstore for camera batteries, then pick up sandwiches for the both of them. But when she called, she was astonished to learn Ella had lunch waiting for the two of them.

Madison's favorite tuna salad recipe with chopped apples spread between Ella's homemade bread and green salad was an unexpected treat. The table was set, and Madison poured iced tea.

"I thought about setting up the patio table on the porch," Ella told her, "but it got too hot even for me."

"This is wonderful, Gran, but you shouldn't do too much. You need rest to get your strength back."

"I know my limits, so don't think you can mother me. I'm too old for that. Besides, I need to keep busy and you know cooking is my pleasure. Now eat your lunch like a good girl and let me enjoy myself."

Madison grinned and gave Ella a kiss on the cheek. Now that she knew her grandmother was okay, relief fueled her appetite and she realized she hadn't eaten more than a nibble for several days.

However, Ella only picked at her food.

"I don't want anything heavy in my stomach," she said. "Don't worry, I'll be just fine."

But she didn't seem fine. Now that Madison had finished her lunch, she noticed that Ella was continually checking the wall clock over the door and rearranging the silverware. If Madison hadn't known better, she'd say her grandmother was fidgeting, something she never did. Perhaps she was on new medication, but Madison didn't remember a recent trip to the doctor. Ella didn't tell her everything, she knew, and now that she was getting older, and especially after how she'd looked yesterday, Madison vowed to keep better watch over her.

She'd planned to discuss what had happened with Marie, but now she hesitated. Not only did her grandmother seem a little unsettled, but she'd worked with Marie on community projects for years, and Madison didn't want to put her editor in an unfavorable light. She knew how loyal Ella was, and even though she considered Marie a friend, Madison came first. Always.

"Cora's coming over this afternoon," Ella said. "She's taking me to the cemetery. Would you like to go?"

"You know I have that review this afternoon."

Ella said nothing for a few moments, then took Maddy's hand.

"Honey, your parents' death wasn't your fault. I hope one day you realize that."

"I know." Maddy automatically patted Ella's hand, then grew quiet.

"What is it?"

"I don't remember her, Gran. Even though I was only six, I should remember something. I can see my dad's face, I remember him throwing me in the air and catching me, but I don't remember my mother."

Ella rose and gave Madison a hug.

"You will, honey, when you can forgive yourself."

Madison blinked back tears. "Now, about you," she briskly said, determined to shove her guilt to the side. "Do you really think you should go out today?"

After a long look at Madison, Ella took her seat. "I'll enjoy the outing. Besides, Cora's almost as bad as you. She won't be satisfied until she sees that I'm not on my deathbed." She opened her half-sandwich, took a small bite of the tuna, then put her fork down.

"Gran," Madison, said, wanting to phrase it delicately, "are you, by any chance, taking any new medications?"

"Of course not. Why would you ask?"

"Just wondering. You seem a bit . . . anxious."

"Maybe I'm feeling cooped up. You know I like to get out and walk, and with the trip and all, I haven't had any exercise for a week."

Madison hoped that was all it was. "Would you like something from the sushi restaurant?"

"Are you kidding? I might be willing to try new things, but raw fish isn't one of them. Back when your grandfather was alive and we all went fishing, we used that stuff for bait."

Madison laughed. What great times they'd had, going up the mountain to Big Bear. She missed them and decided, just as soon as Ella felt a little stronger, to take her up to the lake for a picnic. It would be good for both of them.

When the wall phone rang, Madison wondered if it were Dexter. As highly as she thought of him, she hoped he'd wait another day or two to talk to them. He hadn't sounded as if he had good news and she wanted Ella to have another day's rest.

The conversation only took a few minutes.

"That was the senator checking up on me," Ella told her. "He wanted to let us know about a garden party he's hosting in a couple of weeks. How very fortunate I am to have him as a friend."

But the look in her eyes told Madison that she was thinking

of something else entirely.

Afternoon traffic on I-10 west was so light that Madison made excellent time covering the eighteen miles to Colton, a neighboring city rich in Old West history.

Originally a railroad town laid out in the late eighteenhundreds when the Southern Pacific Railway moved eastward from Los Angeles, it had been home to the Earp family. Nicholas P. Earp, father of the Earp brothers, had owned a saloon, and Virgil Earp had been the town's first marshal. It also had a large slice of the region's citrus industry, which, by the late eighteen-hundreds, could boast half a million citrus trees, most of which, today, had been replaced by light industry and single-family homes. Colton was one of the fastest growing regions in the Inland Empire.

It also housed one of Madison's favorite Japanese restaurants. Today, though, she was going to bypass the grill tables in favor of sushi for her readers.

She made her way past the outside gardens, and once inside, instead of taking the walkway to the teppan-yaki tables—teppan was Japanese for iron plate, she'd learned, and yaki meant grilled—she took a seat at the S-curved sushi bar in the back. Then, while three chefs performed their magic for appreciative customers, Madison took photos and notes.

The manager suggested a spicy tuna roll topped with avocado and a spicy sauce, which turned out to be her favorite, and she also ordered a dish of sushi, rice in finger shapes topped with filets of raw fish—red tuna, salmon, which was orange with white marbling, and pink yellowtail. Madison thought she'd try chopsticks, but she dropped everything and soon went back to her fork. No wonder the Japanese were slim people.

One of the ladies in a group of three seniors kept watching Madison take photographs and make notes, and after about a half-hour, the woman finally came over and introduced herself.

"My family and I enjoy your columns, Miss Young," she said, "and we always look forward to your next one. I was just telling my friend, Grace, that I've run into newspaper people several times the past couple of weeks."

"Oh?" Madison said politely. Ready to leave, she was packing her equipment and only half-listening.

"I stopped by that little lounge on Kipling Avenue the night of that terrible murder," the woman prattled on, "not that I frequent bars, you understand, but—"

Madison tuned out the rest of the woman's chatter. Maybe she'd stop at the market and pick up some of Ella's favorite ice cream.

"—saw your editor there."

"What? You saw my editor the night of the murder? I think you're mistaken. She was working on a story out of town."

"It was your editor, all right," the woman assured her. "I've seen her often enough at town meetings to know her anywhere. It must've been right after the shooting, because we could hear the sirens from inside. She was washing her face in the bathroom and fixing her hair. I even spoke to her, but I didn't let on that I recognized her. You know how some people are, they don't want to be seen in bars."

CHAPTER FOURTEEN

Captain Silva sifted through a stacked pile of manila envelopes on his desk. "Time to move on. Too many other cases stacking up."

"I'd agree, but something doesn't add up." Dexter sat in the cramped chair, his long legs sprawled in front of him. "I haven't located the woman in the straw hat, and she's important to the case."

"You've canvassed the area, checked leads, and you still have nothing. Hell, the woman could've been a passerby."

"He's right," Rico piped up. He sat so stiffly in the other chair that Dexter thought he could've had a rod stuck up his ass.

"Shut up, Rico."

"Tish and Chris have their hands full," Silva went on, ignoring the exchange between the two detectives. "Frank's appendix finally landed him in the hospital, Bob's still on vacation, and I need the manpower."

Although the number of homicides in San Bernardino County had been falling for the past couple of years, some asshole, rage fueled by the summer heat, always shot, stabbed, or beat someone else to death. A large percentage of the murders were gang-related, but with a population of over two-million people, there were other cases just as senseless. Robberies gone wrong and domestic violence were year-round events.

"Mayor Goodman just alerted me about the special city

council meeting he's calling." Silva said. "You'll be there?"

"If he gets it done before I leave," Dexter told him. "Eight days and counting."

"Your project, you be there."

"What project?" Rico asked.

Silva eyed Dexter wearily. "You didn't mention it to him?"

Dexter shrugged.

"What's going on?" Clearly puzzled, Rico looked back and forth between them.

"Better explain it to your partner."

Dexter skimmed through an explanation.

"All this is going down and you didn't bother to tell me?" Splotches of red dotted Rico's face. "We're supposed to be partners."

"We are partners, but we're not joined at the hip. Besides, it's old business."

"If it's going on now," Rico told him, "it's new business. And if it involves you, I need to know."

Christ. As much as he hated to, Dexter had to hand it to Rico on that one.

Madison felt shaken. Marie at a bar in Yucaipa rather than in Long Beach? It didn't make sense. All the way back to the office, Madison kept hearing the woman's words. Surely she was mistaken.

But she'd sounded so positive that Madison had no choice but to believe her.

Rush hour on I-10 was slowing everyone to a crawl, so she was glad she was close to the Yucaipa exit. She took the off-ramp and glanced at the gas station, but the islands were crowded and it was still too hot to wait in the sun. She headed up the boulevard toward the office.

Why would Marie lie? And especially that night. The woman

said Marie had been washing her face and fixing her hair. Fixing her hair could be explained; many women touched up their makeup and hair while in the ladies' room. But washing her face?

Then a horrible thought slammed her. Could Marie have been the mysterious woman with Hawley the night he'd died?

But no, she couldn't be the one. Middleton had said that it had been an older woman. Even though in her late forties, Marie would never be classified as an older woman.

Or would she?

Madison had heard Dexter voice his frustrations about the justice system enough to know that, contrary to popular belief, witness testimony was often far from accurate. Perception, memory, and the witness's own bias always came into play. And Middleton had admitted he hadn't seen the woman; he'd just heard Mr. Searl mention her to the deputy.

So it was possible that Marie had been that woman. But if she had been, why had she been with Hawley? They certainly weren't friends going to dinner together.

Madison needed some time to gather her composure, so she pulled into Jimmy's parking lot. The yellow tape was still there, the only sign that an investigation was in progress.

She walked to the area where she'd been standing the night of the murder, hoping that by some miracle, she'd realize that her suspicions of Marie's involvement were ridiculous. However, after a few moments of feeling nothing but the ninety-degree heat, Madison got back into her car, no closer to answers than she'd been before.

A few irritated honks from behind alerted her to her absent-minded crawl on Yucaipa Boulevard, no doubt due to her reluctance to go back to the office.

What should she do with this new information? Should she mention it to Marie? Even if she tried to sound casual, Marie would surely take offense. If things were awkward now, that would wipe out any chance of restoring their friendship—and, Madison realized, perhaps her job as well. How could she work in an environment where she'd accused her boss of lying?

She could tell Dexter, of course. He'd laugh at her wild imagination and convince her she was way off-base.

At least she hoped that was what he'd do.

She picked up her cell phone, deciding there was only one way to find out.

"How about if I stop by Ella's this evening?" Dexter suggested, his long legs spread in front of his desk chair. "I still want to talk to the both of you, so it'll be a good opportunity to discuss your concerns as well as mine."

"No!" Maddy almost shouted over the phone. "I don't want Gran to hear this."

"Is it her health?"

"It's nothing to do with her. Please, Dex, I need to talk to you now, or as soon as possible."

Dexter had never heard that sense of urgency in Maddy's voice. Had she found out about Bates from someone? But no, she'd said it had nothing to do with Ella. And no one else, at least anyone who knew the family, had information about his release.

So what else could it be?

He rose, took his jacket from the back of his desk chair, and slipped it on. Rico looked up.

"What's up?"

"Gotta see a man about a horse." Christ, Dexter thought immediately afterward. He swore he'd never use that phrase, the one his father had always used when he'd wanted to give his son the slip. He'd leave the house and disappear for days before finally disappearing for good. Dexter had been nine and he hadn't seen him since.

Rico sprang from his chair. "Saddle it up for two, because you're not leaving without me."

Dexter grinned. Strike another one for the little prig. It might be interesting to see how enthusiastic he was when he found out what he was getting himself into.

The coffee shop east of Calimesa off I-10 was known for its fast and cheap family meals. Easy to clean orange vinyl booths lined the walls and small tables stood in the center. Plastic potted plants in plastic tubs were scattered about and Country and Western music played softly in the background. Dexter spotted Maddy in a back booth behind one of the potted plants.

"Kind of 'cloak and dagger' stuff, isn't it?" He teased.

She smiled briefly, but seemed taken aback at Rico's presence. After introductions were made and they took a seat opposite of her, she went quiet.

"My," Rico said, leaning toward Madison, "you're even prettier than the photo with your column, which, by the way, I always enjoy reading."

Madison actually blushed, and Dexter felt as proud as if he were directly responsible.

"Thank you." She kept her gaze down and said nothing more.

A teenage boy bussed the table next to them. Dishes and utensils clattered. Even the cleaning fluid spray sounded loud.

"How's your grandmother?" Dexter asked to get her talking. He doubted she'd asked to meet him to discuss the weather.

"She's much better. She rested most of yesterday and it seemed to do her good. She was even going to do a little shopping with Cora today." Her gaze went to Rico and she grew quiet again.

"How about giving us some time alone?" Dexter told him. He jerked his head toward an empty booth across the room.

"Dex—"

"It's personal, Rico."

But even after Rico stomped to another booth, Madison still couldn't get the words out.

"What is it, Maddy? What's so difficult for you to talk about?"

"It's Marie, Dex. Now that you're here, I don't know how to begin. I feel as if I'm betraying someone who has done nothing but help me, and I'm not even sure there's cause. You'll probably think I'm being silly."

"Why don't you let me decide? Start at the beginning and tell me what happened."

She started talking, hesitantly at first, telling him how something she'd read in the newswire stories had bothered her and how, at her grandmother's, she'd realized what it was. She related asking Marie permission to use the newswire service and her editor's strange reaction.

Dexter listened patiently, relieved to hear it was nothing serious. He was sure Marie had simply doubted the wisdom of letting Maddy get involved in a story when Bates was due to be released.

But since he hadn't told Maddy about Bates, he couldn't tell her why Marie behaved as she had.

So he simply listened.

"Then that woman said she saw Marie the night of the murders. Here in Yucaipa, Dex. Can you imagine? Marie told me she was in Long Beach, so why would she lie? And why would she have been washing her face? Women don't usually do that in a public restroom."

"Wait a minute," Dexter said, leaning toward Maddy. "This woman said she saw Marie in Yucaipa? Was she sure it was Marie? She could've been wrong. Happens all the time."

"That's what I thought, but I questioned her. Discreetly, of course, and she recognized her from town meetings. There's no question, Dex. It was Marie."

Dexter sat back. That threw him. He could explain Marie's reaction to Maddy getting involved in a story, but not why she lied about being in Yucaipa the night of the murder. If it had been any other reporter assigned to the story, Dexter wouldn't have thought anything of it, but Marie knew about Maddy's aversion to violence, knew the trauma she still experienced as a result from what happened that night years ago. Marie was too good a person to put Madison on the scene unless something else was going on.

Just what could've been so important that she'd risk Madison's emotional health?

CHAPTER FIFTEEN

Except for an occasional surly look at Dexter, Rico stared silently out the passenger window all the way back to the bullpen. Dexter managed to ignore him until he sighed, a loud, contrived sound that conjured up images of Dexter's ex-wife when he'd missed dinner, a party, or had worked until the wee hours of the morning. Sometimes it had seemed that he never stopped cajoling her out of her exasperation or apologizing for doing what was, after all, his job. Now, by God, he didn't have to apologize to anyone. Certainly not to the prick next to him.

"All right," he said, pulling into the parking lot. He shut off the engine. "Spill it."

Rico's mouth set into a rigid, thin line.

Dexter waited, but the late afternoon sun beat through the windshield and it was too damned hot to sit long. Finally, just as he grabbed the handle to open the door, Rico spoke.

"Just what is it going to take for you to accept me as your partner?"

Ah, Christ-all-Friday. On the rare occasions when Dexter felt lonely enough to consider marrying again, all he had to do was think of that tone in his wife's voice. He didn't blame her for wanting a husband home each night, but he was a cop who loved his job, and as long as he continued his career, nothing, certainly not her disapproval, could interfere with his dedication.

And now, instead of a wife, he had a partner. While he

125

resented Rico's intrusion, he could understand his reaction.

A partnership in law enforcement was like a marriage. Two people spent the major part of each day working and eating together, making life decisions together—only instead of taking the hours, days, or months to come to a decision that a normal couple contemplating a future might make, life decisions on the job were often instantaneous, made with the knowledge that the decision could eliminate your future.

Do you follow your instincts, and, weapons drawn, rush the perp, or do you first consider the danger to each and every face in the crowd? Do you take aim when a perp points a gun at a bystander's head and uses him as a shield, or do you try to talk him down? Which partner kicks down the door during a nanosecond's lull in gunfire and enters the perp's residence? Life decisions, decisions that have to be made in an instant. And during that instant, you'd better know your partner will cover your back.

Was he sure Rico would cover his?

What was it about Rico, he wondered, that irritated the hell out of him? He was a self-righteous asshole, but what the hell, everyone had their faults, and Dexter had adjusted to several partners during his long career.

Was it the way Rico dressed? Instead of yanking something off the rack like the other detectives, Rico wore finely tailored pin-striped suits in dark colors with shirts a shade or two lighter. Today he wore a charcoal suit with a dark gray shirt and an iron-gray tie, an outfit that made him look like a pit boss for the syndicate.

"Why do you wear clothes like that?"

"What the fuck do my clothes have to do with anything?"

"I'd just like to know why you don't dress like everyone else."

Rico expelled another drawn-out sigh. "Honestly?"

"No, Rico. I want you to lie."

"God, you're an asshole."

"Then why don't you make us both happy and partner with someone else?"

"You think I haven't tried? Silva refused my request, so like it or not, I'm stuck with you."

Stuck with him? Dexter hadn't considered that possibility. Just like a thick-headed husband, he'd never considered that Rico's dislike for him was just as strong. He'd only considered his own feelings. If that was an inkling into his married life, no wonder his wife skipped.

"My clothes are camouflage, Dexter, to answer your question. It's something I learned in the military." He talked about the importance of commanding attention, having a sense of what he called "presence."

"I'm a short man," he said, as though Dexter hadn't noticed. "And I work in a world where height is important. So I wear power suits. I'll use any trick in the book to command just an ounce of the respect men like you take for granted."

For once in his life, Dexter was speechless.

"While we're both stuck in this arrangement," Rico continued, "I suggest we make the best of it, and that means I'm included in everything you do, think, or feel while we're on the job. I may not like you and you've certainly made it clear you don't like me, and while I wish it were different, it's not. So let's accept it and figure out how we can work together."

Good God. Was the little shit actually making sense? And was that a smidgeon of respect he was feeling?

"What was the meeting with Madison about?" Rico asked. "I should've been included, not dismissed like an errant child."

He had seemed genuinely glad to meet her, Dexter admitted. So maybe he did have a human side.

"Not everything during the day is job-related, Rico. Like I told you, it was personal."

"Nothing job related?"

Dexter wasn't sure he could answer that. He thought of Marie, washing her face at a joint in town the night Hawley was shot. If she had been in Yucaipa, why lie about it? Could she have been the woman with Hawley? If so, why would she spend time with a convicted pedophile? To get a story? If that were true, why would she have run from the crime scene, leaving Madison, who was a novice? Questions Dexter knew he'd have to answer. As highly as he thought of her, he was first a cop, and he needed some answers.

Making one of those life decisions, Dexter opened the car door.

"Come on," he said. "We've got work to do."

Inside the squad room, Dexter told Rico about Maddy's conversation.

"I want Searl to see a photo of Marie, but I don't have one and I can't ask her."

"How about the newspaper? Isn't her picture there? You can have it blown up at Kinko's."

"By God, Rico, there might be a brain under that dandy suit after all."

Rico smirked in a satisfied way, but for once, Dexter didn't mind. At last they had a lead.

Madison knew she wouldn't be able to face Marie in the morning, so knowing it was the coward's way out, she sent the review by email and enclosed a note saying she'd caught her grandmother's bug. That would give her a couple of days to decide what to do.

She glanced at the clock and realized Gran and Cora would be home soon. She'd fix a light supper for the three of them, and borrowing a phrase from Scarlett O'Hara, she'd worry about Marie tomorrow.

While preparing a pasta salad with shrimp and crusty French bread, she listened for the door. Gran and Cora were late, and Madison was beginning to worry. Where were they? Was her grandmother all right? She hoped the day's outing didn't exhaust her.

When they finally arrived, Cora led Ella to a kitchen chair and shot Madison a silent look.

What did that mean? Had Gran become ill while they were out? Madison would ask as soon as she could get Cora alone.

"Don't fuss," Ella said with a scowl. "I'm all right."

During dinner, Ella only pretended to eat and Madison thought her edginess seemed more apparent than the day before. Her grandmother picked up her knife to butter a slice of bread only to put it back down with a clatter. And once she jabbed her fork into the salad so hard that a stray piece of celery went flying onto the table.

Cora's brows lifted. "You don't have to kill the shrimp, Ella, they're already dead."

"Very funny. You should be on late-night TV."

"If you don't start eating better, you'll be as thin as me," Cora answered. " 'Skinny as a rail,' my father always said."

"You do all right."

"Maybe so, but you're built differently. Listen to Madison for once and build yourself up."

Madison listened absently to the two friends' banter, something they'd done for as long as Madison could remember. But now, fork poised close to her mouth, she stared at Cora. Had she really suggested that Ella listen to her? That was a first.

Madison walked Cora down the steps to her car. The evening air felt soft after the day's harsh sun, and the lights in the valley gently spread before them.

"What was that look at dinner about?" She held the door, but instead of sliding behind the wheel, Cora raised her face to the night sky.

"How beautiful the stars are, Madison, and what tiny creatures we are under them. I sometimes wonder at our place in the universe."

Madison waited silently. Whatever it was, Cora was having a difficult time talking about it. That in itself was alarming. She'd never known Cora to be anything but painfully blunt.

"I've known that woman most of my life," Cora finally said, "and we've been best friends for at least thirty of those years. But she's changed. She looks the same, thinner of course, but inside, where it counts, she's different."

Oh God, Madison thought. Cora had noticed the change in Ella as well. Now she was truly alarmed.

"No matter what life brings," Cora said, "my best friend was always gentle and kind, the Yin to my Yang. I don't know this woman. She's edgy. Sharp, almost. And she can't make up her mind. One minute she says one thing and the next, another. She's had a personality change."

Cora took Madison by the shoulders. "I hate to even suggest it, but ever since we got back from San Diego, I've been reading up on Alzheimer's, and I think you should ask Ella's doctor about it."

Alzheimer's! Please God, not that. Please don't let it be that serious.

It wasn't fair, she thought while loading the dishwasher. Not now, not when the work of raising her granddaughter was finally over, not when Madison wanted to spend more time with her doing some fun things together, like traveling to places Ella never had the opportunity to see.

Tomorrow Madison would make an appointment with her grandmother's doctor and take her there, no matter how much she protested.

She prepared two cups of soothing herbal tea and took them to her grandmother in the living room.

"Want some ice cream?"

"I couldn't swallow another bite," Ella told her. "The salad was perfect."

"How could you tell? You didn't eat but two bites."

"Don't give me any sass, Maddy. I'm still strong enough to turn you across my knees."

Madison smiled. "You've never spanked me in your life and you never will."

"And that's your trouble, young lady."

"Drink your tea before it gets cold," Madison said, kissing her grandmother on the cheek.

Ella took a sip, then put the cup on the coffee table.

"I've loved your help, Maddy, but don't you think you should get back to your own life?"

"I will, Gran, just as soon as I feel you're strong enough. Not that there's anything exciting to get back to."

"That's the point. I'm concerned about your life, Maddy. You need to do something, make a life for yourself, not waste it taking care of me."

"A waste? How could anything I do for you be a waste? I love you, Gran, and I consider it a privilege to be with you. But I'm worried about you."

"I'm perfectly fine." Ella picked up the TV remote and scrolled through the channels before putting it down again.

"What is it, Gran? Is something bothering you?"

Ella rested her head on the back of the sofa and closed her eyes. For the long moment before she spoke, Madison studied her pale skin, taking note of the blue veins in her cheeks, the dark circles under her eyes. She was losing weight at an alarming rate. And was that a tear escaping from behind her closed eyes?

What in God's name was wrong?

"I just feel so helpless," Ella whispered, her voice so low Madison had to lean in close to hear, "as if life has spiraled out of control."

"What do you mean, Gran? What's out of control?"

Even though Ella swiped the tear and sat up, her once-proud shoulders curled and her entire body sagged as if the weight she carried was too much to bear.

Madison gently took her grandmother into her arms, holding her in a warm embrace, hoping she could feel the love and support Madison offered.

"What's wrong, Gran? Won't you tell me?"

"We try to do our best, going along in our own little worlds living moral and ethical lives, raising our children to do the same."

"What are you talking about? I don't understand."

"We know evil is out there, but unless or until it touches us, we're not personally involved. And when it does, we're changed. We find ourselves considering things that would have mortified us only a short time before."

"What things, Gran?" Madison took her hand. "You're scaring me."

For the first time, Ella took a long look at her granddaughter, and, during that time, Madison could see the gradual change in her eyes. It was as if she were back from wherever she'd drifted, facing her granddaughter, allaying fears as she'd done since Madison was six. She straightened and her entire demeanor changed.

"Nothing, dear," she said, patting Madison's hand. "I'm just an old woman who sees shadows when I should be counting my blessings."

"I'm going to make an appointment with your doctor."

"You'll do no such thing. There's nothing wrong with me

that a little rest won't cure, and I'm not going to pay that quack good money just to tell me so. Now I don't want to hear another word about it." She rose from the sofa. "I'm going to bed."

Madison knew whatever was bothering her grandmother would remain a mystery until Ella was ready to talk about it, and nothing Madison could say or do would convince her to say anything more.

She'd keep a close watch on her, and if the problem got worse, she'd get her to a doctor no matter what it took.

Brandon Searl, wearing jean shorts and flip-flops, led Dexter and Rico into the living room of the mobile home near the shopping center.

Geared toward families, the community court had a swimming pool and basketball hoops at the recreation center. Palm trees dotted the paved streets and couples were walking, enjoying the cooler night air.

Once seated, Mrs. Searl offered lemonade, explaining that it was from the lemon tree in the back yard.

"I don't know what I can tell you that I haven't said before," Searl said.

Dexter handed him an eight-by-ten photograph of Marie.

"I'd appreciate if you'd take a look at this and see if you can identify this woman."

Searl studied the photograph. "She looks familiar, but I can't place her." He passed it to his wife beside him on the over-stuffed sofa.

"Could she have been the woman with Hawley?" Dexter asked.

"Possibly. I don't know. I just saw her for a few moments."

"Honey," his wife said. "Isn't she with the newspaper? I think I've seen her photo with her column."

"Of course! That's why she looks familiar."

Dexter took back the photo and handed it to Rico, who retrieved a small box of colored pencils from his coat pocket.

"What did the straw hat look like? What color was it?"

Searl shrugged. "What color's straw? Brown? No, tan. Sorta light tan."

"How big was it?"

Searl frowned, then drew a wide circle in the air around his head.

"I don't know. Big. Covered her head and most of her face. At least the top part."

Rico drew a hat, colored it, and showed it to Searl. "Like this?"

"I suppose. But I still can't say this woman is the one."

"What kind of blouse did she have on?" Dexter asked.

"How am I supposed to remember something like that?"

"Try."

"Now that I think about it, it was . . . different. Roomy, like a big man's shirt. A bluish-plaid, I think. And it was loose, sorta draped over her clothes."

"Draped over her clothes?" Dexter repeated, exchanging a glance with Rico. That opened all sorts of possibilities.

People usually draped something over their clothes to protect them. What would the woman with Hawley want to protect her clothes from? Blood? If so, that would mean she knew he was going to be shot. Had she been the one to pull the trigger or had she had an accomplice? After all, older women were not usually killers.

So who else had been involved?

"Try a blue-plaid shirt over Marie's blouse," Dexter said. Rico drew the shirt, then handed it back to Searl, only to have him shrug.

A few moments later, Dexter and Rico returned to the Tahoe.

"One good thing came out of tonight, even if Searl couldn't

identify Marie." Dexter eased onto Valley Road. "It's looking more and more like the mystery woman was the shooter. Or at least knows who was."

"Now if we can only find her."

CHAPTER SIXTEEN

When Dexter's cell phone rang on the way to work the next morning, he hoped it was Josh. He was surprised to see Marie's name.

"Hey, friend," she said, "I still haven't heard about a special council meeting, so what's up? Do you know when Bates will be sprung?"

"I'll have to get back to you on that. Have to make a couple of calls." Dexter waited for Marie's response, but for once, she went silent. The pause stretched so long that Dexter wondered if the call had been dropped. "Marie? You there?"

"I'm running the story tomorrow," she quickly said, running the words together so it sounded like one long word. Dexter had to say it himself before he got what she was saying.

"What? You can't! Ella's been ill and I haven't had a chance to talk to them."

"I've honored your request to wait up to now, but this is news, Dex, news the community has the right to—"

"Cut the crap, Marie. Are you at the office?"

"Where else?"

"I'm coming by. I need to talk to you."

"Sorry, Dex. I think the world of Madison and Ella, but it's set. I have to release the story. The entire community is affected by—"

"See you in fifteen minutes."

He clicked off and punched Josh's number. Even though it

was before eight, Dexter knew his friend was an early riser. He heard a click, then finally, it rang. And rang.

Come on, Josh! After several rings, the voice mail clicked on. Damn. Where the hell was he, and why hadn't he returned Dexter's calls?

The newspaper parking lot was vacant except for Marie's 4Runner and one other car.

She poured coffee for both of them.

"Got any of the doughnuts you cops are famous for?"

"I didn't take the time," he told her, dropping onto the other office chair. It whooshed in protest. "Listen, Marie. I'm officially asking you to hold the story a couple more days."

"Sorry, Dexter, can't do it. The owner got word about Bates and demanded that I run it."

"Christ-all-Friday! How the hell did that happen? Did you tell him?"

"Of course not. I don't know how he found out, but he did, and he says to run it. I have no choice."

"You must make some excuse and hold the story, at least a couple more days. I'll stop by Ella's today, but they should have more time to adjust before a big fat article in the paper slaps them in the face."

"I've always juggled stories when you've needed confidentiality, Dexter, out of respect for procedure, and because you've asked. But I can't hold this any longer. You'll just have to talk to Madison and Ella today."

Dexter had never abused a woman before and detested men who did, but the urge to shake Marie was so strong that he made for the door to put distance between them.

"I'm not surprised you have no regard for Maddy's reaction, Marie. After all, you didn't think about her the night of the shooting."

"What are you talking about?"

"I'm talking about Jimmy's Steakhouse. I know you were here, in town, instead of on the coast. I have a witness."

She blanched white, but said nothing.

"Just what was so important that you'd place Maddy at a violent crime scene?"

"That was unfortunate, but I don't owe you an explanation."

"Do you have a straw hat, Marie?"

"A straw—oh, my God. You think I was the woman with Hawley that night? You know me, Dex. You know I couldn't do something like that."

"I've begun to wonder if I know you at all. Do you want to tell me about that night here or in the squad room?"

"You wouldn't!"

"This is a murder investigation, and I'll do what's necessary."

"After all the years we've worked together, you have the audacity to ask me something like that? Go to hell. I'm not telling you a damned thing."

Dexter said nothing, but his lips thinned. Keeping eye contact with her, he punched Rico's number on his phone.

"I'm at the newspaper office," Dexter told Rico, "and I want you to question Marie Campbell. I have to leave on an urgent matter, but I'll wait until you arrive."

"You son of a bitch," Marie said after he slipped his phone back into his pocket. "You're actually going to question me about that pervert's murder?"

"Where were you, Marie, and what was so important that you'd risk sending Maddy over the emotional edge?"

"Unless you arrest me," she said, her voice cold, "I don't have to answer any questions. And by the way, aren't you forgetting to read me my rights?"

"You're not in a custodial situation. That means you're free to leave at any time."

"May I remind you that you're in my office? If anyone leaves, it'll be you." When Dexter said nothing, she added, "Why don't you arrest Mayor Goodman? He hasn't said where he was that night. For that matter, pick any female off the streets and ask her. You'll get just as far."

"Right now I'm not interested in the mayor's whereabouts that night. I'm interested in yours. Why were you at a bar in town? And why were you washing your face? Was it to wash off splattered blood? Do you have a blue-plaid man's shirt?"

With a look of disgust, Marie turned her back to him and punched keys on her computer. That suited Dexter just fine. Two could play at that game.

When Rico arrived, Dexter apprised him of the situation.

"Shall I take her in for questioning?" Rico asked.

Marie spun her chair around.

"You've got to be kidding. This has gone far enough, Dexter."

"Just talk to her," Dexter told him, not bothering to lower his voice. "See if she'll tell you anything about that night. I have to leave."

"I'm still running the story tomorrow," Marie said, turning her back to them again.

Now, sitting in his Tahoe, Dexter wanted to hit something. In all of his years on the job, he'd never felt this frustrated. Always before, there had been something he could do to maintain the illusion he was in control. But now, for the first time in his life, he truly felt helpless. He'd received zilch cooperation from Marie, and as a result, he had to do the one thing he'd prayed he would never have to do—tell Maddy that her nightmare was about to come true.

He'd rather face a Mafioso hit man.

Maybe it was a good thing he'd never had children. He had just seen what concern over Maddy's well-being could do to him, what it could drive him to say. In normal circumstances, he would never have mentioned his suspicions about the straw-hat lady to Marie, but his emotions overrode his judgment.

Emotional detachment was the mantra every law enforcement officer learned, and for good reason. Once an officer becomes emotionally involved, good judgment flies out the window. Mishaps occur, and in their line of work, one mishap could cost lives. His run-in with Marie showed that his judgment had slipped.

Slipped? Hell, it had taken a nosedive.

Maybe it was time to cash it in. That campsite next to a river had never looked so good.

His phone rang. Josh, thank God. He'd been down with a virus, but he estimated the paperwork on Bates would be completed in two weeks or less.

Two weeks! Dexter could kiss his vacation goodbye. No way in hell could he be out of the state when that asshole showed up.

He wished he had two weeks to prepare Maddy and Ella, but time had run out.

If only Felicia could join him today, even for just an hour or two. He decided to call again to make one last plea.

"It's down to the wire, Felicia," he told her. "I have to tell Maddy and Ella now. Today. I know your circumstance, but could you possibly come for a couple of hours, just to stand by in case Maddy needs you? I'll pay for your tickets, pick you up at the airport, and take you back. You'd only be gone a few hours."

"Dexter, I told you. I can't possibly leave right now, and that's the end of it. I've called my associate and he'll work Madison in tomorrow."

"That's not good enough," Dexter said. "I need help today."

"I'm sorry. That's the best I can do."

"Christ. What do your other patients do in a crisis, Doctor? Slit their wrists?"

"That's not fair."

"Few things in life are."

He clicked off and held his phone, staring at it as if it were his enemy, dreading the call he had to make.

He had never been a man to postpone the inevitable, but now he wished he were anywhere on earth other than right here, right now, forced into an action he'd prayed he would never have to perform.

He punched the speed-dial.

"Hey, sweetheart. Is Ella awake? How's she doing? I need to stop by."

Madison hung up and wiped her hands on the dishtowel slung over her shoulder. Something major was wrong. No matter how hard Dexter had tried to act as if nothing were the matter, he'd had *that* sound to his voice, that strained, forced tone he used when he was trying to keep her from hearing something really horrible.

He'd used it when she was growing up and asked about a murder she had heard on the TV or radio. Dexter believed in honesty, so he'd always answered her questions, but she knew he glossed over the details and made a point of sounding as detached as possible.

She stacked the breakfast dishes, carried them to the sink, and wiped the table. She'd let her grandmother know he was coming, and concentrate on staying calm and strong for her.

She heated the cinnamon rolls she'd made to tempt Ella's appetite, then put on a pot of coffee. It was only when she dropped the carafe, spilling water all over the counter and her shoes, that she realized her hands were trembling.

CHAPTER SEVENTEEN

Dexter tried to relax in the house that was as familiar as his own, but he couldn't get comfortable. He sat on the edge of Ella's overstuffed wing chair, his favorite, but even after stretching out his legs, he still felt too large and awkward.

He moved to the loveseat and then back to the wing chair, aware that Ella and Maddy were watching him closely, glancing back and forth at one another, Ella's face growing more pinched by the minute.

"Are we playing musical chairs?" Maddy's voice was pitched higher than normal.

"Whatever it is, Dexter," Ella said with a surprisingly firm voice, slipping one arm around Maddy protectively, "you might as well get it over with."

Dexter nodded, took a swallow of his too-hot coffee, and burned his tongue. He set down the cup.

"Honey, I have some bad news. About Michael Bates."

Madison wrapped her arms around herself. "I don't want to hear this."

Ella held her tighter, and Dexter moved out of his chair to kneel in front of her. He took her cold hands in his.

"Don't be afraid, honey. I'm right here with you. But you have to know what's happening. You have to be prepared. I've done everything I could to avoid this, and so has the senator, but Bates had another parole hearing—"

Madison rocked back and forth, clutching herself, repeating,

142

"I don't want to hear this," over and over.

"Look at me, Maddy. You have to know. This time he was granted parole."

"No, no, no," Madison chanted.

"He'll be released in about two weeks, maybe less. You have to be prepared."

Madison stiffened and stopped rocking. Her eyes went wide.

"Oh, honey," Ella said and tried to hold her granddaughter. "I'm so sorry . . ."

Dexter gripped her hands harder. "Honey, listen to me. You have to know this. I, and all the other law enforcement officers in the area, will keep him under surveillance at all times. But he will be coming here, to Yucaipa."

"Here?" Madison moaned, then began a low keen, sounding like a wounded animal in too much pain to do anything except cry a mindless sound of agony. Her breathing became rapid and shallow. Her eyes lost focus.

"Maddy!" Dexter said, rubbing her hands, her arms. "Madison, look at me! Can you hear me?"

He checked her pulse. "It's too rapid," he told Ella. "She's going into shock. Call nine-one-one and bring me a blanket." He briskly rubbed her shoulders, her arms.

Ella made the call and hurried from the room.

When Ella returned with blankets, he wrapped them around Madison. She'd begun rocking again and making that terrible sound.

"Are you all right, Ella?"

"Call her doctor, Dexter," she said, holding Madison tightly. "He'll know what to do." She recited the number from memory.

Cursing the justice system, Bates, Dr. King, the newspaper, and himself for not being able to protect Maddy, Dexter made the call.

★ ★ ★ ★ ★

Two hours later, he and Ella perched on chairs beside Madison's hospital bed. The ER doctors had knocked her out with sedatives, and Dr. Conners, the jean-clad resident shrink, held a telephone consultation with her family physician and Dr. King's associate. They decided to keep watch for twenty-four hours.

"I must caution you about Madison's state of mind," Conners told them. "When she wakes, she could function as normal, which is what we hope for. Or, she might not."

"What do you mean, 'she might not'?" Ella asked.

"I want you to be prepared, but let's not look for trouble before we see it. We'll evaluate her condition when she wakes."

"Sorry, Doc," Dexter said. "That doesn't cut it. If there's anything we need to know, tell us now."

Conners seized a straight chair from the next bedside, turned it around, and straddled it. His curly black hair stuck out in all directions.

"Judging from my consultation with Dr. Simmons, Madison has lived in a state of angst for many years, and from what you told me when she was admitted, she has just suffered from a severe psychological shock relating to a past traumatic event."

Dexter's lips thinned to a tight line. "I'd just given her some terrible news."

Ella patted his hand. "Don't blame yourself, Dexter. There was nothing else you could do. You had to tell her. You had to tell both of us."

"The human mind is a complicated thing," the doctor went on, "and we still don't know everything about it. When she wakes, she could, as I said, be entirely normal. On the other hand, it's also possible she might suffer from a type of disassociation, even a lapse of memory. While she may recover physically, she may experience a behavior disturbance. As I said, we'll do an evaluation once she awakens."

"When will that be?"

"Oh, she should be coming around in another hour or two," he assured them. "Her own mental health doctor, Dr. Simmons, should be here by then."

"Her own doctor, Dr. King, didn't feel it was necessary to make the trip to see her," Dexter said, his irritation obvious, "so she pawned Maddy off on her associate, who still isn't here. If I were in charge, I'd tell them both to go to hell and ask you take her case. At least you seem to care."

"That can be arranged," Ella said. "I have power of attorney."

"Hold on a moment," Conners said. "I'm sure Doctors King and Simmons are fine physicians and have legitimate reasons for whatever decisions they've made. Don't be premature here. Let's just wait and see what happens when Madison wakes."

After Conners left, Dexter took Ella's hand and together they watched Maddy sleep. He thought of all the other times through the years he and Ella had taken turns sitting by her bedside after another of her nightmares.

Fat lot of good that did now. What she needed, what she had to have, was protection from Bates. And so far, he hadn't been able to do a damned thing.

"I could use some coffee." Ella rose carefully, as if each movement were an effort.

Alarmed by her evident fatigue, Dexter shot from the chair. He was such a dolt. Because he'd been so concerned about Maddy, he hadn't stopped to realize how Ella must be feeling. She had been such a rock for so many years that he'd taken her strength for granted. He suddenly realized how important she'd been, not just to Maddy all these years, but to him as well.

At the nurse's station, he explained that Ella had been ill and asked for a recliner or easy chair. When the nurse couldn't tell him where one was located, he went on the hunt until he found one tucked into a side corridor. Not wanting to scoot the thing down the hall and disturb others with the noise, he called Rico.

While waiting, he poured coffee in the nurse's station and took Ella a cup. Maddy was still sleeping, so they spoke quietly in the hushed room.

"I had the strangest feeling you knew what I was going to tell Maddy," he told her.

"When you passed up the cinnamon rolls, I knew. Human beings are funny, Dex. I've lived in fear of this very thing for years. Every time I read about a killer being paroled, my heart turned over. I hoped and prayed it would never happen, but I always knew there was the possibility. I just hoped that by the time it did, Maddy would've been stronger."

"Like you?"

"I'm not so strong. It's just that after living nearly seventy years, I've learned that things happen, and you either have to figure out how to adjust or do what's necessary to protect your loved ones. Survival, Dexter, is the key, and I intend on seeing that Maddy survives. No matter what."

Dexter had no reply, so he sipped his coffee in silence.

Rico arrived, and he helped Dexter lug the recliner to Maddy's room. Rico said the usual things one says when visiting someone in the hospital, then went silent, shifting from foot to foot.

Dexter led him to the hallway.

"How'd it go with Marie?"

"She wouldn't answer my questions or even look at me."

When a lab tech hurried past, pushing a cart loaded with small rattling bottles, some obviously filled with blood, Rico went pale.

Dexter took pity and dismissed him. This time Rico offered no argument.

Three hours later, long after the hospital staff had gathered lunch trays, Madison still hadn't awakened. Dr. Simmons hadn't arrived, and Dexter was pacing the floor.

Ella sat on Madison's bed and took her hands. "Maddy, honey, it's Gran. Wake up, now. It's time to wake up."

Madison slept on.

"Something's wrong, Dexter."

Dexter stopped his pacing and studied Madison's face. Alarmed by the stillness, he went to the other side of her bed and sat opposite of Ella.

"Wake up, Maddy." When there was no response, he commanded her again. "This is Dexter, and I'm telling you to wake up! Now!"

Still nothing.

He slapped his hands in a loud crack. Ella flinched, but Madison didn't respond, not even with the flicker of an eyelash.

"Good God!" Dexter jumped from the bed, ran for a nurse, and demanded a doctor. Immediately.

When, after a tense half-hour, the doctor still had not appeared, Ella called their family physician, old Doc Hayes.

He arrived in jeans, his white hair in a ponytail, and after exchanging pleasantries with Ella and shaking hands with Dexter, he began his examination.

He read the chart at the foot of Madison's bed, then took a flashlight from his coat pocket and directed the light into her eyes. He ran a ballpoint pen across the soles of her feet. He did as much as he could, then with a sigh, tucked the flashlight away. His expression when he looked up told Dexter the doctor was at a loss.

"I see no medical reason why she hasn't awakened," he said. "The sedatives administered in the ER wore off hours ago, and the preliminary tests show no physical abnormality." He slid onto one of the hard plastic chairs and groaned. "Lord, I wish the hospital could spend some money on decent chairs."

"They're trying to drum up business," Ella said. "After visitors sit in these things a while, they need a doctor."

Dr. Edward Hayes' blue eyes crinkled in delight.

"I'm glad you haven't lost your sense of humor, Ellie. You just may need it."

"What's that supposed to mean?" Dexter asked. "What do you think is wrong?"

"I'm afraid that's beyond my area of expertise. Didn't you say you'd called Dr. Conners? He's young, but he's a bright boy."

"Okay, Teddy," Ella said. "We realize your opinion isn't official, but you've treated Maddy all her life. Surely you must have an idea. Right now, that would be a help."

Dexter knew the story about Ted Hayes and Ella, how they'd dated long before Ella married her husband, and that, since then, he'd been the family doctor, even when Madison's parents had been alive. While he might be past the accepted retirement age, his ideas were young. He still rode his Harley, and when he didn't have the time for long jaunts, he took weekend rides up the mountain to Big Bear.

"What's been going on in her life since I last saw her?" he asked now. "Has anything traumatic occurred?"

"It's been a nightmare," Ella answered, "and it began over a week ago."

Dexter told him about finding Madison at the crime scene at Jimmy's, then about flying to San Quentin for Bates' hearing, and finally, about telling Maddy and Ella about Bates' release.

Hayes nodded. "Off the record, I'd say she doesn't want to wake up."

"Are you saying Maddy is controlling her sleep?"

"Not consciously," the doctor replied, "but in my years of practice, I've seen this before. I'm no expert, you understand, but it's as if the conscious mind is protecting itself by retreating to a safe place. Shamans believe that when we suffer a trauma, part of our soul flees, a sort of a self-protective mechanism so we can survive the pain. Psychologists call it disassociation."

"So how long will she sleep?"

"I can't say. I doubt anyone can."

"Give me your best guess."

"She could awake at any moment, or she may sleep for a month or more."

"God, no," Ella murmured.

"Isn't there anything we can do?"

"Not that I know of, but Conners would have more knowledge about medical advances in this field."

"What would a shaman do?" Dexter couldn't believe he was asking such a thing, but he was desperate.

"From what I understand, it's quite a ritual, but basically, a shaman would work to retrieve the soul."

Dexter dropped onto a chair. *Retrieve her soul?*

Were he and Ella desperate enough to try a damned fool thing like that?

CHAPTER EIGHTEEN

Two days later, Maddy was still comatose, and Dexter had to fight the urge to shake the doctors into immediate action. He knew they had ordered tests that included an EEG, an MRI, a CT scan, and even a Glasgow Outcome Scale, which adds or subtracts points during an examination of the comatose patient's eye, motor, and verbal or nonverbal responses. But none of the tests helped his frustration when he watched Maddy's pale form sink further into oblivion.

Even though Ella had power of attorney and the final decisions were hers, she always asked Dexter's opinion when the doctors suggested a course of treatment. A catheter had been inserted, and a feeding tube was mentioned. Dexter was horrified.

"You don't think she'll be unconscious long enough for that, do you?"

But it seemed that no one could answer his question. Doc Hayes explained the tube.

"Since she can't take food directly, a tube is simply a device to get nourishment into Madison's system to help her recover. The IV drip ensures she doesn't become dehydrated, but the human body needs more. If she doesn't regain consciousness by tomorrow, they'll begin treatment."

"What will that involve?" Ella asked.

"They'll try the NG tube first, as sort of a temporary measure. It's much smaller in diameter than the permanent tube." He explained the procedure. "When she recovers, the NG can easily be pulled out. It's a simple process, actually."

"You mentioned a smaller tube as a temporary measure, Teddy," Ella said, her voice as frail as she looked. "What's the difference?"

"The permanent tube requires surgery," Hayes told them, "but I don't think she'll need that. In any case, you can discuss that option with a surgeon if it becomes necessary. Let's just hope it won't be."

After Hayes left, Dexter took Maddy's hand and willed her to wake. He was alarmed not only by her continued unconsciousness, but also by Ella's failing health. How much of this stress could she take without becoming ill again?

She hadn't left Maddy's bedside and had barely eaten. He'd tried everything, including bribery, to get her to go home and rest, but she'd refused.

"I must be here when Maddy opens her eyes," she told him. "But you need some time away, Dex. Your vacation is coming up soon, isn't it? How long will you be gone?"

His vacation. Green trees, rivers, a paradise that now seemed a distant dream. One day he'd get there, but not now. Not when Maddy needed him.

"I can't leave while Maddy's so ill. I'll be right here as long as the two of you need me."

"But Dexter, you need a break."

"I'm not leaving," he said with a finality Ella must have recognized. She nodded, patted his hand, and said nothing more.

The article about Bates' parole splashed across the front page of *The Tribune*, although Dexter only read the headline. He knew he was being unreasonable. As a cop, he needed to be abreast of the news, but when it involved Maddy and Ella, the news became too personal. It still appalled him to think Marie had put her profession first, and he wondered if she had any idea what her actions had caused.

Cora, at times accompanied by Clara, spent almost as much time in the room as Ella, but while Dexter knew the sisters were fond of Maddy, he felt Cora's main concern was for her best friend.

"Ella, you haven't been eating," she said in her usual brisk tone. "Not that I blame you. Hospital food is unfit for healthy people, much less sick ones."

She hoisted a huge cloth tote bag from the floor and dropped it on a chair, and like an Army sergeant on a mission, she marched to the next bed, hijacked the tray, and rolled it to Ella's chair.

Dexter watched with amusement, thanking his lucky stars he'd never been on her wrong side. As big as he was, he was sure that if she considered it necessary, she'd box his ears in an instant.

"I've brought your favorites," Cora told Ella. "Fresh seafood salad with crab, shrimp, and rice, and fruit salad with cream cheese and walnuts."

She took a package of sanitizing wipes from her tote bag and swabbed the top of the tray.

Dexter took a helping and happily crunched on the fresh fruit and walnuts—until he noticed that Ella hadn't touched a bite. He set down his plate.

"Ella, this has gone on long enough. If you don't eat, you'll be flat on your back as well. Do you want to be in the next bed when Maddy wakes? How do you think that'll make her feel? Hasn't she lived with enough guilt?"

At Ella's wounded look, his heart turned over, but his years of training in the sheriff's department kicked in. Instead of caving, he stared her down.

152

"Dexter, you don't have to talk to her like that," Cora protested.

"Cora, I'll thank you to butt out." He ignored her quick intake of breath. He might have felt like the serial monster who'd murdered old ladies back in the sixties, but he held Ella's gaze until she sighed and reached for a plate. Only when she took a small bite of her seafood salad did he relax.

"Now chew it up, swallow, and take another bite. Repeat as necessary." He took another forkful of his fruit salad, but for some reason, it no longer tasted as sweet.

Cora scowled at him. "Really, Lieutenant," she snapped. "That wasn't necessary."

"Dexter's right, Cora," Ella said, calmly finishing her salad. "For once, butt out."

"Well!" Turning a bright pink, Cora sat up even more stiffly in her chair.

A timid knock sounded on the door, and Marie appeared, holding a bouquet of summer flowers.

"I'm so sorry," she said first to Ella, then to Dexter. "I'm sorry."

Was that a hint of moisture in her eyes? Never, in all the years he'd known her, had he ever seen her cry.

Ella took the flowers. "It wasn't your fault, Marie. I suppose it was inevitable."

"I'll take care of those flowers." Cora said briskly and left the room. When she returned with a vase, she filled it with water and the flowers, then set it on the bedside stand. "They look nice, don't they? The yellow daisies and pink roses brighten up the room."

"I can't stay long," Marie told them. "I have work to do, but I wanted to check on Madison."

"Are we intruding?" Mr. Chauncey, his white shirt and blue vest as spotless as ever, stood in the doorway. Senator Stone, in a charcoal sports coat, held onto his arm.

"Hello, Dexter," the senator said and nodded to Cora and Marie. "Ella, may we come in?"

Dexter noted the astonishment on Marie's face. He was sure she knew Ella and Maddy were friends with the senator. As a newspaper editor, she had attended a few of his dinner parties with the two women, but from the look on her face, she obviously was surprised to see him take enough of a personal interest to visit Maddy in the hospital.

With the aid of a polished wooden cane, the senator made his way to Ella and took her hand.

"I'm so sorry to hear about Madison, Ella. With the medical advances today, I'm sure it won't be long until she's back on her feet. If there's anything I can do to help, I'm at your service."

"As you always are, Senator. Thank you, I appreciate it. Please have a seat."

"Ah, yes, a seat." He took the chair Dexter had vacated. "This past year I've established a new relationship with chairs. Perhaps we can find one for Mr. Chauncey as well."

"Thank you, but that won't be necessary." Mr. Chauncey assumed a sentry position at the senator's right side.

"I appreciate your concern, Senator, and it was kind of you to make the trip," Ella said, "but how did you discover Maddy was in the hospital?"

"Oh, I have my sources," he replied mysteriously. After a few moments of silence, he smiled. "I'd love to keep all of you thinking I had special powers, but I read the article about Michael Bates in the newspaper. I was concerned. Mr. Chauncey called the newspaper, and someone on your staff, Miss Cox, I believe, told him about Madison."

Everyone's gaze went to Marie.

"I had to do it," she said, her stricken gaze moving from the senator to Dexter, then finally to rest on Ella. "The newspaper has a duty, I have a duty . . ." Then, with a muffled, "Excuse me," she hurried from the room.

Dexter felt a momentary pang of compassion for her, but his resentment won. He let her go.

Ella gazed at the doorway. "Oh dear, I do hope she'll be all right. I'll give her a call later."

"It's just like you to worry about everyone else," the senator said. "I'm sure, as a newspaper editor, she's faced tough choices before and has learned to adjust to the consequences. Now tell me about Madison."

It was almost midnight before Dexter left the bullpen and stopped by the hospital. The captain had thrown a couple of new cases at him and demanded that he and Rico spend their time and energy on them instead of chasing shadows.

Dexter knew he should arrange a lineup so Brandon Searl could observe Marie wearing a straw hat, but thinking of the endless hours she'd devoted to various functions for those in need, especially children, he'd delayed putting her through the humiliation. But the feeling that she was involved in Hawley's murder continued to nag at him. Otherwise, how could someone else, especially someone covered with blood splatters, vanish without a trace?

Hell, in his book, anyone who'd killed Hawley should be canonized for eliminating another dirtbag from society. At least with him gone, the children in his town would be safer. Still, as an officer sworn to uphold the law, he couldn't let personal feelings interfere with his duty, couldn't allow citizens, even Marie, to become vigilantes.

The hospital corridor was dimmed, a relief to his tired eyes, and hushed with only the occasional sound of a nurse's shoe squeaking on the tiled floor. From a few doors beyond Maddy's, low-volumned canned laughter erupted from someone's TV.

His steps slowed. What would he find in Maddy's room? Would there be signs of her recovery? He hoped so. He wasn't a praying man, but he prayed now. He wasn't sure he could take several more hours of watching her waste away in a coma.

Greg was sitting by her bed, holding her lifeless hand and whispering to her. His sandy hair was tousled, as if he'd run his hands through it several times.

Dexter stood quietly by the door and waited, then coughed discreetly and entered the room.

Still clutching Maddy's hand, Greg stood.

"Dexter," he said. "I came as soon as I heard." He extended his hand and Dexter took it.

In the corner, Ella was napping in the recliner, a lightweight throw tucked around her. Cora's work, Dexter thought. Instead of the harsh glare over Maddy's bed, a nightlight softened her features and threw the tubes and monitor into shadows.

"Hi, sweetheart," Dexter whispered to Maddy's sleeping form. Still no improvement in her condition. He had hoped she'd be awake, although if that had happened, Ella would have let him know.

Greg shrugged, a bewildered, helpless gesture Dexter recognized. "I can't believe this is happening."

"It's hard for all of us to take." Dexter took the other chair, an orange plastic thing so small it could've been made for an elf.

"I'm glad to see you," he told Greg, trying to keep his voice down so Ella could sleep. "Maddy could use a friend."

"I want to be more than a friend, but she won't let me. I asked her to marry me, and the next thing I knew, she broke up with me."

"I didn't know your relationship had gone that far."

"Obviously it hasn't, and that's the problem."

"Don't give up on her," Dexter urged. "She needs to start living, have a family, and after she recovers from this, I'm going to make a concentrated effort to see that she does."

"Yeah, well, I'd appreciate any help you can give, but I doubt it'll do any good. I don't know if you're aware, but under that soft exterior lies the heart of a very stubborn woman. I doubt anyone can make her do anything she doesn't want to do."

Dexter grinned. "You forget I've known Maddy since she was six. But hey, you're a smart man and a decent-looking one. You started a business in this rough economy and made it a success. Surely you can get one young woman to fall for you."

"I've tried everything, and so far, nothing's worked. When she wakes up, I'll certainly give it another try." He paused, watching Maddy breathe. Then, "She will wake up, won't she?"

"She will if I have anything to say about it."

After Greg left, Dexter took the chair next to the bed. You will wake up, he told Maddy silently, watching her eyelids twitch or a finger move. When it had first happened, Ella and he thought Maddy was waking and excitedly called a nurse, but she said it was just muscle contractions.

Now he looked at the delicate arch of her brows, the blue-veined lids over her blue eyes closed in sleep, with a sense of hopelessness. It wasn't fair. She was a beautiful, sensitive young woman, and if she didn't wake soon, her life would be over before it even began.

Ella made a sound like a long sigh and shifted in the recliner. Even asleep, her face had not lost its haggard look. How much longer could she go on before she collapsed? If she had been awake, he'd give her a hug to comfort her, to share some of his strength with her.

He sat back in the chair and leaned his head against the wall. His bones screamed with fatigue. His skin ached. For one tiny nanosecond, he longed for someone to comfort him.

Here he was, the big, strong, macho man who took care of everyone else, yet he longed for someone to comfort him. How wonderful it would be to feel a woman's soothing arms around him. Perhaps even a wife's.

But he didn't have that and it was his own fault. Sure, he'd been a good provider, always paying the bills, making sure his wife and the few women in his life could buy the things they'd wanted. But he'd never let them have *him*, not in the way they'd needed. He'd always kept his feelings locked tightly out of reach.

It had been the same with Pam. He'd known she'd loved him, but he'd blown it with her as well. Now their relationship was a friendly one, although at times he wished it were more.

The only problem was, he didn't know if he could devote the time to someone else. As he'd grown older, he'd also fallen into a comfortable rut, and now he didn't know if he could ever again have the patience to share his life with someone else.

What a waste. But he could still give it a try if he wanted. Maybe when Maddy recovered and the world was right again, he'd take a late vacation and ask Pam to go with him to West Virginia—just as a friend, of course . . .

He jerked awake to find it was three-thirty in the morning. Maddy still lay oblivious to everything. Only a few hours until they inserted the feeding tube. A feeding tube, for Christ's sake.

"Damn it, Maddy, wake up!"

He didn't realize he'd spoken aloud until Ella opened her eyes, saw him, and went back to sleep.

Perhaps somewhere in Maddy's subconscious, she could hear him too. What was it Doc Hayes had said about shamans believing that a comatose patient's soul was trying to escape? He'd also said it could be reached. Hell, he wasn't particularly spiritual, but he'd try anything to get Maddy to wake.

He leaned forward and took her hand.

"Wake up, Maddy," he whispered urgently. "You've been sleeping, but now it's time to wake up."

He watched her face for any signs that she had heard him, but she remained just as she had been. He gripped her hands and tried again.

Over the next several hours, he alternated between cajoling her to awake and demanding that she do so. The blackness at the window faded to gray and then finally gave way to the morning light. He could hear voices and the sound of metal rattling. The hospital was coming to life before the shift-change at seven.

Just as Dexter reluctantly stood to leave for work, he thought of the guilt he'd laid on Ella about not eating. Although it had been difficult for him to do, the outcome was that she'd forced herself to eat enough to regain her strength.

Would guilt work with Maddy as well?

Hell, he was desperate enough to try anything.

He sat on her bed and leaned close to whisper in her ear.

"Maddy, you must wake up now. I know you don't want to face what's happening here, but you must think about Ella. Your grandmother hasn't left your side and she's close to collapse. If you want to sleep until you die, I can't stop you, but do you want to take her with you? Is that the way to repay all she's done for you?"

He leaned back and watched her face. Were her eyes moving beneath those nearly transparent lids? Was there a slight change in her breathing?

"Squeeze my hand if you can hear me." He watched for any sign of a response, but there was nothing. If ever in his adult life he'd felt like crying, it was now.

CHAPTER NINETEEN

"So why haven't we pulled Marie Campbell in for a lineup?" Rico asked, slapping paper down on his desk. The morning's *boorah* briefing had faded into the bullpen's normal madhouse of ringing phones, clicking keyboards, and good-natured ribbing between detectives.

"If you don't want to be the bad guy," Rico pushed on, "I'll do it. I don't have a history with her."

"Can it, Rico." Dexter took a long slug of his cold coffee, his eyes scratchy from lack of sleep. He'd barely managed to stay awake through Silva's briefing. He longed to head east on the freeway and drive until he escaped ringing phones, computers, feeding tubes, and hopelessness.

"Dexter!" Silva shouted from his office door. "You and Rico get in here now!"

Christ. What now?

"Uh-oh." Chris was handing Tish a file from across her desk. "Sounds like your vacation's in danger, Dex. What have you done now?"

"Vacation's dead and buried," he told her, shuffling to the captain's office with Rico two steps behind him.

"Hey," Tish piped up, "I got the perfect thing for dead and buried. Viagra. Been on the stuff a month and Mighty Joe is alive again."

"Mighty Joe? Holy hell, now I've heard everything," Bob Frazer, fortyish and fresh from his vacation, laughed. "Shouldn't that be Tiny Tim?"

"You don't believe me, ask my wife." Tish grinned. "She's walking spraddle-legged." He rubbed his bald head. "I might even grow me some hair again."

Chris shook her head.

In the captain's office, Dexter slumped in the nearest chair.

"You look like shit, Dexter," Silva said, raking the detective with a critical gaze. "I know you've had some personal issues lately, but you're still on payroll. First-year rookies perform better than you've been doing. I've never seen you like this."

He flipped through pages of scrawled notes and blank time sheets.

"Downtown's demanding some action on our backlogs," he went on, "and accounting is on my back. Take my advice, Dexter. Straighten yourself up. Shave. Change your clothes."

"Yes, Captain."

"You better get yourself together damn fast. Downtown's heard enough of my excuses. And you, Rico, you shouldn't be tied to a sinking ship. You still want that transfer?"

Rico shot a look at Dexter.

Now he'd finally get rid of the little prig, Dexter thought. Funny. He thought he'd be happier to have that happen.

"Well?" Silva demanded. "I don't have all day."

"No sir," Rico said. "I'll stay with Dexter."

An hour later, pulling out of yet another drive-thru for coffee, Dexter popped three antacid tablets and washed them down with coffee.

"You need to eat something," Rico told him, a worried look on his face.

"I'd puke it up."

Rico sipped his hot tea and stared out the window. "I hope Madison recovers soon or we'll have to bury both of you."

Dexter slammed on the brakes. "Goddammit, Rico! Don't

ever say the word 'buried' in the same sentence with Maddy again. Do you hear?"

"Sorry."

Dexter put the car into neutral, got out, and walked around to Rico's side.

"You drive. I'm a disaster waiting to happen."

Rico took the wheel. "You want to stop by the hospital?"

"Hell, no. She'll have that thing stuck in her face and I don't want to see it. It would be like admitting it's all over."

"Where to?"

Dexter leaned his head back and closed his eyes. "You decide. Today, you're lead detective."

Just as they headed out of the parking lot, Dexter's phone rang. For the first time in his career, he didn't answer, didn't even check to see who was calling. He didn't want to hear that the hospital had successfully inserted the feeding tube; he felt too damn tired to do anything except go off by himself and die like an old elephant.

When he didn't answer, Rico's phone rang. He listened briefly, then clicked off.

"Silva said to remind you of the city council meeting today in Yucaipa," Rico told Dexter.

"Like hell."

"He said you'd object. 'It's Dexter's ballgame,' he said. 'You tell him to be there.' "

Even though it was a weekday morning, the council chamber in Yucaipa's city hall overflowed with residents, all demanding answers about Michael Bates' parole.

Mayor Goodman tried to keep order by calling one citizen at a time to the microphone, but despite his admonishment, people interrupted each other by shouting questions. Dexter was astonished. He had never seen the stately city hall so chaotic that the mayor would actually have to continually bang his gavel. Marie was snapping shots of the proceedings. Dexter found the level of tension so unbearable that he told Rico he was getting out of there.

"You can't leave me here alone," Rico hissed. "I'm not familiar enough with Bates' history."

"Improvise."

Just then, the mayor placed his microphone directly in front of the gavel and struck it repeatedly, creating thunderous bangs through the chamber. Dexter's heart slammed into his ribs. God, he had to escape this madhouse.

"Ladies and gentlemen," the mayor said as the room grew quiet, "please remember where you are. If I don't have order, I'll call the meeting to a close and no one, *no one,*" he emphasized, "will get answers. Is that what you want?"

For the first time since the proceedings had begun, there was silence, broken only by the scraping sounds made by Dexter's chair as he rose to leave the room. He had nearly reached the door when he heard his name.

"Detective Quinn," the mayor announced. "You were involved in the initial investigation that led to Bates' arrest and incarceration, and you attended parole hearings with Senator Logan Stone. Why don't you step up to the mike and answer a few questions for us?"

Oh, hell. He was trapped. Running his hands through his hair, Dexter made his way to the podium.

"Detective Quinn, please help us to understand why this has happened," a man in the audience called out. "How can a convicted killer be allowed to leave a prison and live among law-abiding citizens?"

"It's not right!" another man about thirty shouted.

"Criminals should rot in prison!" another said. " 'Do the crime, do the time.' "

The mayor banged his gavel several more times. "Gentlemen, gentlemen, please. We must keep order."

"I'd like to ask a question." A woman in her forties stood. Her blond hair was swept up and secured by one of those leather clips with a wood stick. She supported an infant on her chest in one of those strap-held carriers.

"I'm Ginny Murken. I take care of my baby granddaughter and I'm concerned about what'll happen in our community once this man is released. I won't feel good about letting my granddaughter play in my yard, or when she gets older, walk to school by herself. This used to be a safe, family community, but first we had Jeff Hawley, and now Michael Bates. How can we protect ourselves when we're surrounded by felons? How can we protect our children?"

When she took her seat, the audience broke out in applause.

Mayor Goodman banged his gavel. "Excellent questions, Mrs. Murken. Perhaps Detective Quinn can offer some explanations."

Dexter swore silently. How the hell could he offer explanations to ease their fears when he had the same concerns?

"I understand your apprehensions, Mrs. Murken, and those of everyone in the community. Frankly, I feel the same. However, according to the law, Mr. Bates has served his time and, as you know, will be released into society."

Shouts of protest rang from the audience. He even heard a "Boo," as if he were emceeing a wrestling match.

"No one wants parolees in their community," he continued, "but the fact is, you already have several. Most towns do, because short of herding them together and putting them on an uncharted island, there's not much else to do with them. The point is rehabilitation, to help them become part of society again."

"Why should my family and I be jeopardized so that felons

can live next door to me?" Dexter didn't see the woman who'd asked that question.

"Good point," he responded, "but do you have any other suggestions? As of now, our parole system, with all its flaws, is the best we've got. We have over a thousand state prisons in America, thirty-three just in California with over a hundred-seventy-thousand inmates. We simply do not have the facilities or the money required to house and feed every convicted prisoner for an indefinite length of time.

"And consider the costs involved. Do you know one report, over five years old, stated that correctional authorities spent almost forty billion to maintain the nation's state correctional system in that fiscal year? That's forty billion per year, folks."

"I say save us all some money and issue some old-time justice," someone called out. "Take 'em out and shoot 'em!"

"Aside from the controversial moral issues, executions cost taxpayers even more," Dexter replied, ignoring the jibe. "As long as people break the law, we'll have this problem."

"What can we expect once Michael Bates is released?" a woman asked.

"The county officials will be notified of the exact date of his release, and we'll keep an eye on him. In all probability, he'll be sent to the halfway house and be fitted with a GPS tracking system. If, at any time, he crosses his preset boundaries, law enforcement will be notified instantly. The tracking system is already mandatory for sex offenders, and we hope it'll also be required for other parolees as well."

When his cell phone vibrated, Dexter ignored it at first, and then, thinking it might be news about Maddy, flipped it open and read two simple words.

She's awake.

CHAPTER TWENTY

Dexter hustled down the tiled corridors with Rico at a run behind him. Not until he burst into Maddy's room and saw her up and sipping some liquid through a straw did he allow himself to breathe again.

Ella sat on Maddy's bed, helping her to eat from the breakfast tray.

"Try some of your oatmeal," Dexter heard her say. "It'll give you some strength. And for heaven's sake, have some orange juice instead of that soda. It's better for you."

"Your grandmother's right, you know," Dexter said with a big smile. "Soda will rot your insides."

"Dex," Maddy said and held out her arms for a hug.

He leaned down and wrapped his arms around her. "I'm so damned glad to see those blue eyes again. God, let me look at you."

"I . . . kept dreaming about you," Maddy said, her voice strained and weak, "a strange dream. You grabbed my hand and wouldn't let go."

Dexter felt as though his heart would explode with gratitude. "So what do the doctors say?"

"Doc Hayes . . ." Maddy's voice, already a whisper, dissolved as if she simply ran out of energy. When she lay back and closed her eyes, Ella flashed a panicked look at Dexter. Was she lapsing back into a coma?

Dexter took the cola, set it on the tray, and anxiously searched

166

Maddy's face.

"Honey? You all right?" he whispered, punching the call button for a nurse.

"I'm okay," she murmured without opening her eyes. "Just . . . tired, that's all." Without another sound, she drifted off to sleep.

"She's sleeping naturally," the nurse reassured Ella and Dexter after taking Maddy's vital signs. "The doctors will be in shortly, but I think she'll be all right now."

A text message from Marie was waiting when Dexter checked his phone twenty minutes later. Did his leaving the meeting have anything to do with Madison? If so, was there any news of her condition?

He had a few things to say to her, so he stopped by the newspaper office.

She was on the phone, her back to the door and speaking quietly, almost whispering. Yet, the intensity in her voice brought Dexter to a halt.

"That's exactly what I'm saying," she hissed. "She wanted to check my newswire service—" She paused as if to listen, then, "This is mind-boggling, but if it's true, if you're behind such a thing, you'd better end it right now. I haven't forgotten your words years ago—" Dexter must have made a slight noise because she whirred around and blanched white when she saw him.

"Dexter! What are you doing here?" Without another word, she snapped her cell phone shut.

"That sounded ominous."

"Yeah, well, you know how the newspaper business is now. How's Madison?"

Dexter brought her up to speed.

"I'm so sorry, Dexter. I had no idea Madison would have such a violent reaction."

"That's the problem with all you news people," he said, unable to control the anger he'd held in check for so long. "You just want a headline, and you don't even consider how the story affects the people involved. Did you know, after all these years, Maddy still sleeps with all her lights on?"

"Dex—"

"Did you honestly think she'd read that article and say, 'That's too bad,' as if she were reading about an inconvenient traffic jam on I-10? You people are disgusting."

Marie gazed at him with a hurt expression as if she'd been betrayed by her best friend. Then her lips thinned.

"You think cops are less intrusive? Get real, Dexter. Don't you think your personal involvement is clouding your judgment?"

"My personal involvement has kept you out of a lineup so far."

"Come on, Dex. Do you really think I'm capable of murder?"

"Anyone's capable under the right circumstances."

"Do you think I knew Hawley? That I hated him enough to kill him?"

"How the hell do I know? You won't tell me anything about that night."

"You just have to trust me."

"I used to, but you blew it. Now you're on your own."

When Madison woke that afternoon, sunlight was pouring through the window, so she knew it was afternoon. Ella's chair was empty, the other bed stripped. She was alone.

Alone. What would she do if Michael Bates walked into the room? Was he, this minute, on his way to Yucaipa to find her?

Her frantic gaze flew to the IV and to the tube leading to the catheter. Lying there, attached to so many tubes, she felt helpless, vulnerable to anything he wanted to do.

But surely, she tried to rationalize, if he were anywhere near her, if there was any way he could get to her, Dexter wouldn't have left her alone.

No one had mentioned him when she'd awakened earlier, and she'd been too groggy to ask. Was he out of San Quentin now?

When the bathroom door opened and her grandmother appeared, Madison was so relieved to see her she could have cried.

"You're awake." Ella sat beside her on the bed. She finger-brushed her granddaughter's hair back from her forehead, just as she'd done when Madison was little and woke terrified from a nightmare. "How do you feel?"

"Gran, what about Michael Bates? Is he out yet?"

Ella sighed and reached for Maddy's orange juice. "Take a sip. You need nourishment."

Madison drank. "Gran, tell me about Bates."

"He's still in prison, and Dexter doesn't know the exact date of his release yet. But the important thing is to get you well."

When Ella moved to the recliner, Madison noticed the slump in her grandmother's stance, the wrinkled navy pullover and the dirty smudges dotting her white pants. Hadn't she been home to change clothes or to have a decent night's sleep? Her face was gray, her hair matted. Madison couldn't remember a time when her grandmother hadn't cared about her appearance.

"Gran, go home. You need rest."

"I'll go home when you do."

Madison heard the firm conviction and knew changing her grandmother's mind was as likely as the Mojave Desert sprouting tea roses, so she did the next best thing. She vowed to gain strength as quickly as possible so they could both go home.

If her fears were ever to come true, she knew she'd need all the strength she could get.

CHAPTER TWENTY-ONE

Jericho welcomed each new arrival with the usual handshake. This time, their meeting featured a buffet lunch with freshly peeled kiwi, croissants, and bowls of strawberries and cream.

"How are you, Number Three?" Jericho inquired, buttering a croissant. "With all the taxes on tobacco, I'm sure you're glad you gave it up years ago."

Number Three wore his usual jeans, but today his smoking jacket was a brilliant red. He patted the pipe in his pocket.

"I am glad, but for different reasons. The day I let some do-gooder dictate what I can or cannot enjoy in my life is the day I'm ready for an old-folks home."

"Hear, hear." They all clicked their water glasses with a spoon to register their agreement.

When they'd finished their meals, Jericho picked up a file. As before, all conversation stopped.

"The scheduled date for Michael Bates' execution is approaching," Jericho told them after the servant had cleared the table and left the room, "and all systems are in place. I believe we can proceed to new business: Latisha Woodward, twenty-three years old, Bossier City, Louisiana."

Number Three gasped. *"A woman?"*

"I know it's unusual," Jericho said, setting down the file, "but times have changed."

"I'm certainly grateful for that," Number Four said, straightening her suit jacket.

"Does anyone have a serious problem with executing a woman?" Jericho asked. "If so, let me remind you that women can commit as heinous crimes as men, and as perpetrators, they must be brought to justice—in one way or another, regardless of their sex. If we can't agree on that point, there's no need to go further. I think it's time for a straw poll. Number Two?"

All eyes fixed on the bearded gentleman with the troubled eyes. He smoothed his white mustache and beard before answering.

"While I'm aware that women commit ghastly crimes," he began, "I'm also from the old school. I believe our women are the gentle sex, even the better one, and I treat them as such."

"Yes, you do," Number Four interjected. "Your courtesies remind me of my schoolgirl days and I enjoy them. But women today are heads of corporations and heads of state. We make life and death decisions, as evidenced by this organization."

"Please don't take offense, Number Four. Just because I believe women are the gentle sex doesn't diminish my appreciation of their ambitions and capabilities. That should be obvious." His eyes met Jericho's.

Number Five spoke up. "But what if a woman, such as Ms. Woodward, commits a heinous crime? Shouldn't she be punished as if she were a man?"

"I suppose so," Number Two replied. "After all, that's why we're here. I simply find the idea abhorrent."

"But can you overcome your reservations to do what's necessary?" Jericho asked.

"What has the Woodward woman done? If it's monstrous enough, perhaps I'll overcome my reluctance."

"Very well." Jericho picked up the file. "According to the police records, neighbors called 9-1-1 after hearing screams from her apartment. When deputies arrived, they found the body of a four-year-old boy, her son, unconscious, lying in a pool of his own urine. His body was covered with bruises, and he still had the imprint of a hand on his left cheek. A tiny cut was visible under his left eye. In spite of the emergency medical treatment, the child died two hours later. The coroner's report indicated a massive abdominal hematoma and numerous broken ribs. The mother claimed her son, Tommy, had fallen down the apartment stairs, but the coroner believed the child had been kicked to death."

Jericho set down the file. "Is that monstrous enough, Number Two?"

"I'm appalled."

Murmurs of agreement sounded in the room.

"Fine, then," Jericho said, consulting the file again. "It seems that the mother had never been married and had no visible means of support. She had been incarcerated numerous times for solicitation, and officers found drug paraphernalia in the home.

"At trial, first-degree murder charges were dropped when the prosecution could not prove, despite several scars, that the child had been abused. A new trial on child neglect resulted in Ms. Woodward's eight-month incarceration. However, she's now back in her apartment, watching her neighbor's three-year-old toddler, who, unfortunately, just happened to fall down the same stairs as her son. The child survived, but is currently hospitalized with several fractured ribs. Ms. Woodward is expecting her second child, and she's due to deliver any day." Jericho paused long enough to meet each member's eyes, then proceeded.

"We all agree, do we not, that if an infant is orphaned, that child would have an excellent chance of being adopted by caring parents?"

After the members agreed, the vote was taken, the decision announced, and the members retired to the leather chairs for a bit of socializing before leaving. Jericho, along with Number Two, pulled Number Six to the side.

"I have a bit of other business I'd like you to execute."

"I'm ready to hear about Michael Bates now," Maddy told Dexter. Snugly wrapped in a soft afghan Ella had knitted years ago, she sat on her grandmother's porch overlooking the sparkling lights of the city below. Ella rested in the patio chair beside her, her feet propped up on the ottoman that Dexter had hauled from the living room. He sat on the lounge chair between them, his long legs stretched in front of him, happy that Maddy was finally out of the hospital. In the kitchen, Cora and Clara were helping Greg with dinner.

"I'm sorry I reacted so horribly when you tried to tell me before," Maddy continued, "but if you'll give me another chance, I'm ready. I need to know."

"You just got out of the hospital today." Dexter hedged, reluctant to talk about anything that might spoil her recovery. "Let's just enjoy the fresh air, the company, and the good food."

The screen door opened. "Am I interrupting something?" Greg wiped his hands on the towel slung over his shoulder.

"Nothing that can't be discussed later," Dexter replied, glad for a reprieve.

"But Dexter," Maddy started to protest.

"Let's have a nice dinner and celebrate your homecoming. Then we'll talk about it. Tomorrow might be good. Okay, Maddy?"

She nodded, but Dexter could tell from her expression she wasn't happy.

"I can delay dinner a few minutes," Greg suggested, looking from Dexter to Madison, no doubt sensing the tension. He had stopped by with a pot of fresh stew and had taken over Ella's kitchen to prepare a salad and bake the corn muffins he'd pre-mixed.

"Of all the nerve," Maddy had said when Greg carted his pots and pans into the kitchen. Ella had been delighted and had ignored Maddy's scowls. Cora and Clara followed to help him prepare dinner.

But even though Maddy frowned and grumbled, barely answering whenever Greg spoke to her, Dexter noted that she watched him intently whenever he came into view.

"We're fine," Dexter told Greg. "Now, how about dinner out here?" He threw his legs over the side of his chair and carefully rose from the low chaise. "Now that the sun's down, there's a nice breeze, and after a week at the hospital, the outside air feels wonderful."

"I'll set the patio table," Ella said and went inside.

Twenty minutes later, Maddy sat back from the table, most of her stew still in the bowl.

"What's the matter?" Greg asked with a frown. "Didn't you like it?"

"It was delicious, but I couldn't hold more than a couple of bites. I'll save the rest for lunch tomorrow."

"Good idea," Ella said, finishing her small helping. She buttered her second muffin. "You must give me the recipe, Greg."

Dexter ladled another helping of the stew. "Sure beats a burger joint or frozen dinners."

"Now wait a minute." Greg set down his spoon. "Not that I'm fishing for compliments, but that's not saying much. Can't I get some raves here?"

"Sounds like fishing to me." Maddy gently dabbed her mouth with the napkin, as if she were seated at a formal English tea, then set the cloth next to her plate.

Ella nearly rolled her eyes. "I think dinner was fantastic, and I don't mind buttering up the cook. Thank you, Greg." She leaned over to give him a kiss on the cheek. "I hope you'll do it again sometime. Anytime."

Maddy threw a scorched look at her grandmother, and Ella simply shrugged. Dexter watched with amusement and took a sip of coffee to hide a grin. If he knew Maddy at all, he'd swear, no matter how she might protest, that she was smitten.

"It was delicious, Greg," Clara said. "And the muffins were the best I've ever had."

Cora glared at her sister. "They were tasty, I admit, but the best? I always thought you liked mine."

"I do. It's just that Greg's were sweeter, more like cake."

Cora sniffed. "If I'd wanted cake with dinner, I'd have baked one. True cornbread is never sweet. It's crusty. All you young people think you have to pour sugar into everything. What's happened to good, old-fashioned cooking?"

Forks froze in midair. All eyes went to Greg, whose face had that deer-caught-in-the-headlight look. Dexter felt sorry for him.

"Of course you're right, Cora," Greg managed to say. He even smiled. "I bet you make yours the best way, the way my mother and grandmother taught me—the unsweetened batter poured into a hot iron skillet to form a crust and then baked in the oven. There's nothing like that first crunchy bite dripping with fresh butter. But it is nice to occasionally try variations of our favorites, isn't it?"

"I suppose variety can be a good thing—in moderation, of course."

"If you'd be willing to share your recipe," Greg told her, "I'd love for you to supervise a special cooking session at my restaurant. At your convenience, of course. We'll name the cornbread after you, announce it to the customers, and add it to the menu."

For a moment, even Cora seemed speechless. "I think that

could be arranged," she finally said before calmly returning to her meal.

Everyone breathed again. Strike a hundred points for Greg, Dexter thought.

Ella fixed her granddaughter with a glare. "It wouldn't hurt you to say something nice. He spent a lot of time that night at the hospital."

Greg's face turned a slow pink. "You were asleep, weren't you?"

"Of course—most of the time."

Dexter enjoyed the silent play between Maddy and Greg and knew he would be a perfect match for her. He was a hard-working, determined young man, and Dexter knew, from the moment he'd overheard Greg talking to Maddy at the hospital, how much he cared. She needed to open her heart, but after what she had already been through, not to mention what was coming up with Bates' release, that would take some effort. He just hoped Greg had a lot of patience.

After dishes were cleared and all six relaxed on the porch, the conversation drifted to the shooting at Jimmy's.

"Have there been any leads on the woman in the straw hat?" Greg asked Dexter.

"Sorry, can't talk about it."

"I've been curious. I haven't seen anything more about it in *The Tribune*."

Dexter shrugged.

"Well, here's something you can discuss," Maddy said. "Tell us about Bates."

"Wouldn't it be better to wait for this discussion after you've had a good night's sleep? Or until we're alone?"

"Everyone here is quite aware of what's happening. Besides, I have to know, and we might as well get it over with. Is he out yet?"

Dexter was cornered. "Okay, honey. If that's what you want, we'll discuss it now." He sat back in his chair.

"My contact says that it might be another week before Bates will actually be released. Like most state agencies, they're short on staff and behind on paperwork. It all takes time to process."

"Only a week," Maddy said softly, "then that monster will be loose. I thought it would be longer. But go on. I want to know everything."

Dexter wondered if the determination to talk about Bates signaled a change in her attitude, a willingness to finally face her past. He repeated the information about Bates going to a halfway house. "That'll give everyone some time to adjust," he added.

"No one should have to adjust to a murderer in the neighborhood," Cora snapped.

Dexter was tempted to remind her that, although some things shouldn't happen, it didn't mean that they would not.

CHAPTER TWENTY-TWO

Madison's first thought on waking the next morning was that today was one day closer to Bates' release. She had to keep her determination to get strong, and after she had breakfast, she'd go for a walk to build her stamina. It was surprising how several days in the hospital had sapped her strength.

Usually she was so groggy from the lack of sleep that she couldn't eat until lunchtime, and then only a snack. But while she'd had a few moments of anxiety last night, the medication she'd taken must have put her immediately to sleep. Whatever the reason, the thought of her grandmother's Swedish pancakes, the special delicate crepe treats her grandmother made when Madison needed extra cheering, pushed thoughts of Bates aside.

But because she wanted Ella to rest today, she dug out the recipe card, gathered the ingredients, then put bacon on to fry.

"That smells wonderful, honey." Ella entered the kitchen and poured coffee. "But don't overdo today. You need to rebuild your strength."

Madison greeted her with a kiss, but couldn't help noticing that, although her grandmother had paid attention to her hair and clothes, she moved like an old woman. And an ill one.

She added a pat of butter to the sizzling skillet and poured the batter. Instantly, the scent of vanilla filled the kitchen.

"I'll do the cooking for the next couple of days. I'm not the only one who needs to rebuild strength," Madison said, turning the crepe.

Ella nibbled on a small bite of bacon. "I am tired," she admitted.

Now Madison was really alarmed. She couldn't ever remember her grandmother admitting to fatigue.

"More reason to let me pamper you a bit."

"But you're the one just out of the hospital."

"Look at all the rest I got. Now don't argue, Gran. I'm going to wait on you for a change."

When the first two pancakes were done, Ella pronounced them delicious and ate two bites before setting down her fork.

Madison piled three pancakes on her own plate. Her grandmother smiled

"Glad to see you finally have an appetite. Greg's a good cook, isn't he?" Ella couldn't hide the twinkle in her eyes. "He's quite a catch, you know."

"Now don't start. I don't want to talk about him."

"He's a fine young man, and it would do you good to see him."

"I did see him last night."

"A date, dear. You know, those things where a young man and woman go to fun and exciting places and get to know each other. And on a regular basis."

"I'm not ready to see anyone on a regular basis," Maddy said, carefully wiping her mouth, "but I have decided to do something about my life. I'm going to start walking."

"Walking's good. But why the sudden interest?"

"Something happened in the hospital that I didn't tell you about. One time I woke and I was all alone in that room. You were in the bathroom, but I didn't know it. All I knew was that I was alone, hooked up to tubes, and all I could think of was how helpless I'd be if Michael Bates walked into the room."

"Oh, honey, I'm so sorry."

"You have nothing to be sorry about. I'm glad it happened. It made me realize that I have to get myself in shape so I won't ever feel that helpless again. First thing is to build my stamina, and I can start by walking the hills behind your house like I used to do. And later today, I need to check my apartment and get my mail."

"Cora's been picking it up for you. It's on the buffet. She's a bit overwhelming at times, but her heart's good."

"Yeah, she is pretty overwhelming."

"Greg handled her pretty well. Shows he's sensitive to others and he can think on his feet. And don't forget, he's an excellent cook. All great qualities in a man, don't you think?"

"Gran, quit pushing it. If you keep it up, I'll recuperate at my apartment instead of here. Actually, it might be better that way. At least you'd get some rest."

"That's a terrible idea. I'd worry all the time. At least here I can see how you're doing. Promise you'll stay right here. Promise, Maddy."

Madison smiled. "I promise. But no more talk about Greg."

After clearing the dishes, Madison headed for her room, pulled on socks and her old Nikes, tied her hair into a ponytail, and dug her frayed red Disneyland ball cap from the closet.

"You're not going to overdo, are you?" Ella asked when Madison returned downstairs.

"I know my limits."

"Wear your boots, honey. It's the season for rattlers."

"You're always saying that, and I haven't seen one in years."

"Let's keep it that way."

Behind her grandmother's two-story home, several miles of brush-covered rolling hills climbed toward the San Bernardino Mountains, and Madison could see the rooftops of scattered homes nestled in the trees in the higher elevations.

Growing up, she'd always thought her grandparents' home was in a perfect location: separated just enough from the city to have the open feeling of country living, yet only minutes down the hill to Yucaipa.

About half a mile to the north, the Oak Glen Road led to the scenic apple-growing community at five-thousand feet, a place of apple orchards, family restaurants, and specialty shops. And less than four miles north from the Oak Glen Road, Highway 38, a two-lane winding road, climbed to Big Bear, a resort town sitting at seven-thousand feet.

On winter weekends, Madison's grandparents used to gather her, along with her friends, and take the winding road up for a day of snowboarding or skiing. And in the summer, they loved fishing at the lake. Now she simply took her grandmother into San Bernardino or to one of the casinos for an excellent Friday night seafood buffet.

Madison headed behind the house for her favorite childhood haunt, a hollow surrounded by trees a few-hundred feet from Ella's back door.

Years ago, Dexter had helped her grandfather clear the brush and gather rocks for a circle of three fire pits, and Madison had joined them to scour the area for larger boulders to use as seats. Her grandfather said he'd rather she and her school friends spent their evenings in their personal campground than hot-rodding on the freeway.

Although she hadn't visited the area in several months, Madison still loved it. She brushed the dirt from her favorite white boulder that had a perfect dip in the middle, and sat, reminiscing about all the evenings spent with friends and dates around the campfire roasting hot dogs and making s'mores. Everyone told her how lucky she was to live in the hills. Most of them lived in Yucaipa or Calimesa in a normal neighborhood of residential streets lined with houses.

Her own parents had lived on a street like that, although, she'd realized later, a little more upscale, located in a subdivision close to Crafton Hills, a two-story brick home on a three-acre lot with a swimming pool. Sitting now on one of the dirty-white boulders, she thought about her former home, torn down about ten years ago because no one wanted to live in the house where two people had been brutally murdered.

Had her parents been wealthy? she wondered now. Was that why Bates had chosen her family? Her grandmother had never talked about family wealth or spoke as if they had money. Certainly her grandparents had never exhibited signs of wealth, and Madison couldn't remember feeling privileged as a child. Her parents had never lacked for necessities and even had some of the luxuries such as a nicer car, the latest TV, and had taken trips to Disneyland and the San Diego Zoo a couple of times a year, but her parents and grandparents had never acted like the rich people she'd seen on TV. Perhaps one day, if she could stand facing him, she'd ask Bates if he'd thought they'd had money in the house. Was that why he'd murdered her parents?

Birds chirping in the distance and squawking crows captured her attention, and she looked around, savoring the breeze rustling through leaves on the fir trees and the canyon live oaks. A clump of three aspens shaded her favorite boulder, and Ponderosa pines stood as sentinels bordering the hollow. San Gorgonio peak, or Old Greyback as it's locally known, stood in the distance, its elevation of nearly twelve-thousand feet providing a bit of heaven right in southern California.

Madison lifted her face to the puffy clouds. Was there such a place as heaven? If so, were her parents there now, watching over her as she used to believe? She had felt comforted in that belief, but now she didn't know.

But that uncertainty wasn't what haunted her. What alarmed her more than anything was that she had forgotten how her mother had looked. Madison could see her outline in her memory, but her mother's features were blurred. All she could distinctly remember was the sound of her mother's screams that night, the one thing she constantly prayed to forget.

Just thinking about them triggered the agonizing sound in her mind. She tried to think of something else, anything else, but the screams built in intensity just as they had that night. She covered her ears with both hands.

No! She didn't want to hear that sound!

She had to do something, anything, to push it from her mind, so she grabbed a slim aspen branch and swiped furiously at the ground leaves, sweeping them from the clearing, and when one branch snapped under her frenzy, she grabbed another and another.

But no amount of sweeping could erase the memory of that night. She relived it, waking to the horrible sounds, lying in bed terrified, every instinct urging her to run to her mother, yet the sounds of her screams so terrifying that Madison felt frozen to the bed—until sudden silence smothered the house, a silence so terrible that she forgot to breathe. She had lain listening intently to the unnatural sound until she heard the soft creeping footsteps in the hall, the sound her parents made when they wanted to check and make sure she was sleeping.

But that night, the footsteps were different, and they were creeping closer to her door.

What should she do? Pretend she was asleep? Her frantic pulse pushed her out of bed, and like a threatened animal, she ran to the only dark place to hide, the dark corner of her closet.

Panting, she peeked through the louver slats. The door knob turned. She crouched down. He entered her bedroom, looked under the bed.

"Are we playing games?" He grinned, then raised the corners of her rumpled sheets.

She tried to hold her breath so he wouldn't hear her.

"I'm gonna find you," he chanted in a horrifying singsong

voice. And with that evil grin, he looked directly at her through the closet door.

Now Madison swept the twig furiously around the boulders, fighting the memory and nausea that weakened her knees, jabbing in between to make sure no rattlers had nestled, hoping, praying she could forever erase that night like a bad movie on a video tape, when suddenly, her twig hit something solid.

Like a blessed miracle, her memories dissolved as she jabbed the twig again and again until it snapped. Whatever was between the two boulders was solid, so it wasn't a snake, a rabbit, or any other living creature. She grabbed a larger twig, crept closer, and jabbed harder to push the item, inch by inch, into the open.

When it emerged, she stared at a crumpled blood-splattered straw tote.

CHAPTER TWENTY-THREE

The tote was a two-handled flowered straw, smeared with dirt and splattered with rust-colored stains, and it lay crumpled and torn between the boulders where it had been stuffed. Ants were crawling over it as well as on the flannel shirt spilling out of the top. It too was spotted with the stains.

Next to the shirt, the muzzle and barrel of a small, black handgun spilled from the top of the tote. She recoiled as if it were ready to fire. Could it be connected to the shooting at Jimmy's?

She prodded the tote with her twig to make sure a rattler hadn't found a home in its depths, then pulled her cell phone from her jeans, called Dexter, and described what she'd found.

"Don't touch it," he instructed, as if she needed reminding. Years of listening to him talk about crime scene contamination taught her enough to stay clear.

The line crackled and she heard sounds of scraping chairs.

"Come on," she heard him say to someone, then to her, "We're leaving now. Don't let anything happen to it before we get there."

Madison glanced in the direction of her grandmother's house, at the rooftop barely visible behind trees and felt a creeping anxiety. If she were gone long, Ella would worry. She could call, of course, but what if her grandmother was napping? It would only take a minute to check.

She took off running and burst through the back screen door.

Ella was on the porch watering her pots of burgundy and yellow coleus plants.

"Look, Maddy," she said. "They're going to live after all. I thought the lack of water while I was at the hospital would kill them, but see? They're springing back." She turned to Madison, who was leaning against the door frame. "You're panting. Are you all right?"

"I'm okay," Madison managed, "but Dexter's on his way. I found something out back in the campground, and I have to get back. He wants me to stay and keep watch, but I wanted you to know where I was."

"Oh, Jesus," Ella murmured and seemed to shrivel before Maddy's eyes. The watering can slipped through her fingers.

Madison grabbed her and eased her onto the porch chair. Alarmed, she unbuttoned the top buttons of her grandmother's blouse, terrified it was a heart attack.

"What is it? Are you having pains? I'll call the doctor."

"No, don't bother," Ella said, breathing easier. She pushed the cell phone away. "It's just the heat. Let me rest a few moments."

"I don't know, Gran." Madison noted the ashen color of her grandmother's face. "I'd feel better if the doctor checked you."

"Don't make a fuss. Just get me some water and I'll be fine."

Her voice did sound stronger, so against her better judgment, Madison got the water and stood by while her grandmother drank.

"Come on," she said. "I'll help you to the sofa."

The sound of Dexter's SUV heading up the hill alerted them to the police's arrival. A patrol car followed the SUV, and a crime scene van trailed close behind.

"I'd rather stay out here in the fresh air," Ella said. "You go on and meet Dexter."

Reluctantly, Madison walked down the steps.

"Why didn't you stay by the straw bag?" Dexter greeted her. Without waiting for an answer, he dashed around the side of the house and disappeared through the trees. Rico didn't even try to catch up. One uniformed sheriff's deputy exited his patrol car, and from the van behind, two crime scene techs in navy jumpsuits, field kits in hand, hurried toward them.

"And he says I need to learn manners," Rico said to Madison with a wry smile, "but I guess you're used to him. Since he's disappeared, would you show us the way?"

By the time they made it to the site, Dexter was kneeling in the dirt by the tote, a flashlight in one gloved hand and holding the top of the tote open with an oak twig in the other. He was peering inside. Rico, pulling on gloves, skirted the outer edge of the campsite to join him. The young deputy walked the perimeter, stringing yellow crime scene tape to trees surrounding the area.

"Finally, we have a break," she heard Dexter say. "Hey, Joe, how about some close-ups?"

"You got it." His long dark hair brushing his shoulders, Joe Morales took close-ups of the tote, the gun, and the boulders around them before snapping several photos of the general area. Tony, the other tech, unloaded plastic bags, manila envelopes, and evidence boxes from his case.

The uniformed officer, a blond surfer-type, finished with the tape, and after a lingering glance at Madison, hustled over to the detectives to crouch down beside them.

"Standard Glock 26 subcompact pistol, semi-automatic, matte black finish." He pulled a pencil from his creased uniform pocket to insert it, eraser-end, into the gun's barrel.

Rico knocked his hand away.

"Are you some kind of rookie, for God's sake? Didn't you learn to never use a pencil?"

The young officer flushed and glanced at Madison. Embarrassed for him, she dropped her gaze.

"Don't you know the metal below the eraser can add scratches inside the barrel?" Rico said, his voice scathing, "and totally screw up ballistics?"

By now, the officer's face was deep crimson, and Madison thought Rico had a lot to learn about discipline. It was never a good idea to criticize anyone in front of other people. Dexter must have had the same reaction.

"It's okay, Williams," he told the officer. "No harm done. Hey Tony," he called to the other tech. "how about doing a spiral search for footprints? We could get lucky and find something before it all gets trampled."

Footprints? Madison's heart took a plunge and she felt sick. After all the times Dexter had helped her, she'd had one chance to help him. And she'd blown it.

"Dexter," she said, her voice a whisper, "I've walked all over the area. You won't find anything now."

"What, honey?" he said, obviously distracted. He'd pulled a writing pad from his pocket and was making notes. "You go on back to the house, and I'll stop by when I've finished here." He rose. "Take a look at the tote, Joe. It's shiny, so the manufacturer may have used a compound to preserve the straw. I don't want to risk losing any prints, so let's superglue it and the gun before we try to move them."

"You won't get any footprints, Dexter," Madison said so loudly that everyone stopped what they were doing.

"I ruined the campsite for you. I swept it with a branch before I saw the tote." She pointed to a forked aspen branch on the ground, and five pairs of male eyes looked. Most of the leaves had been scrubbed off, but it was obvious that each end of the forks had held clusters of leaves.

No one spoke. Finally, Dexter stepped around the circle and gently took Madison by the arms.

"Why would you do that, Maddy?"

She refused to meet his gaze. Everyone was watching her, waiting for her answer. "I needed some exercise, so I decided to walk behind Gran's and wound up here. I'd stopped to rest, and I . . ." She broke off, aware that her cheeks were burning. She couldn't tell Dexter about reliving that night, not in front of everyone.

"I haven't been down here in months, and . . . before I sat down, I wanted to make sure there were no rattlers hiding under the leaves and rocks." Feeling more miserable under Dexter's concerned gaze, she rambled on. "You know how Mojave greens are."

Rico looked up from labeling the evidence bags. "How are they?"

"You must not be from the desert area," Tony said, unloading casting materials. "They're a greenish rattler, and they're bad-tempered mothers." He glanced at Madison and flushed. "Sorry. My brother got bit several years ago and nearly died, and that was in the hospital after several anti-venom injections. His doc said they're about sixteen times deadlier than a typical rattlesnake. Their venom paralyzes you so you can't breathe."

Rico stood very still. "Where's that stick Madison used?"

"I'll protect you," Dexter teased.

"Who'll protect you?"

The techs laughed and even the deputy broke down. Madison could feel the tension ease.

Dexter grinned. "Rico, you just might make it after all."

"Make it where?" Madison's grandmother asked, picking her way through the underbrush to the site. Panting heavily, she reached for Maddy. "Give me a hand, will you?"

"You shouldn't be down here." Madison took her grandmother's arm.

"I just wanted to see what was going on." She let Maddy lead her away from the secured area. Sitting down on one of the rocks, she and Madison watched the tech secure a plastic tent over the tote.

"Is that what you've been looking for?" she asked Dexter.

"I hope so. You shouldn't be here, Ella. We're going to use some chemicals, and you don't want to be breathing them."

"Chemicals? What for?"

"I'll talk to you both when we're through. Go on home, and don't argue with me. We have work to do while we still have daylight, and we don't need the distraction. Rico can help you."

"I got up here on my own steam, and I'll get back the same way."

Although Ella sounded strong, Madison didn't like the way she was breathing or her pallid color. "Oh, Gran. I wish you weren't so stubborn."

Dexter watched the two women disappear through the brush, concerned because neither of them had looked well. He made a mental note to take them to dinner to make up for being so brusque. If, that is, he could contain his excitement about the tote long enough.

He wiped the sweat from his face, took off his tie, and stuffed it in his pocket. Even though the foothills were several degrees cooler than the entire Inland Empire, the weather was still in the high eighties. Perhaps, when this case was solved, he'd take a couple of days and rent a cabin in Forest Falls, just ten miles up Highway 38, but an entirely different world in the forest. It even had a waterfall. If things had worked out differently, he'd be fishing in a Blue Ridge Mountain river right now, but not even snagging a prize rainbow trout could compare to the elation of finding the straw bag.

Ballistics should prove that the gun was the same one used to kill Hawley; he just hoped they could pull some prints from it.

He'd bet his entire career that the blood spatters from the man's shirt would prove to be Hawley's.

He carefully tucked the shirt and the washcloth into evidence bags and labeled them. No signs of gloves. He carefully extracted a single sheet of paper embossed with the name, The Ruby Red Society. Something was printed underneath, but blood streaks had obliterated it.

"Anyone hear of the Ruby Red Society?" he asked.

"Not me," Rico said, and the others shrugged or shook their heads.

Dexter carefully placed the envelope and note into an evidence bag.

"Madison did a good job of sweeping," Joe told him.

"Let's hope we can pull something from the gun and tote. And the boulders. You think we can get some prints from them? The perp might have touched them while hiding the tote."

"We can try."

Dexter observed the techs working together like a well-rehearsed, skilled team to assemble a small plastic tent, each anticipating the needs of the other, and he felt lucky to have both. If it were possible to lift prints from an impossible place like rocks around a campsite in the foothills, they were the ones to do it.

"I'll get the propane burner from the van," Tony said, taking off through the brush.

"Plastic?" Williams stood next to Dexter, arms crossed, watching the process. "And a propane burner? What's up? I don't have much first-hand experience in forensics."

"Superglue fuming," Rico piped up, his voice smug as he helped Joe assemble the glue and chemicals for use on the rocks.

Dexter sighed. Rico and his one-upmanship again, but for once, he seemed to have a willing pupil.

"Fuming is a good method for cementing prints on a

nonporous surface," Rico explained. "Too often we smudge or lose them when transporting items to the lab. Fuming might take a while, but we have a better chance of preserving prints."

When Tony returned and the techs treated the tote and gun, all three officers observed the process. Tony set an aluminum saucer on the burner, poured water into a Styrofoam cup, and placed it inside the plastic tent. He turned on the heat. Once the dish was hot, Joe covered the top of the dish with glue, and when it began to fume, he stood the tote by the burner and sealed the plastic.

"Humidity from the water helps the glue to vaporize," Rico informed Williams, "and it reacts with acids and proteins in a latent fingerprint to form a powdery substance on the ridges. If everything goes right, we'll have prints that can be photographed and preserved. Only then can we safely transport the items. Of course it's all more complex, but at least now you know the basics."

Williams was taking it all in, Dexter observed. Guess he truly wanted to learn. But from Rico? If anyone could strut while standing, it was Rico. But he had to admit his partner knew his stuff.

"Now we wait to see if we can get anything."

"How long?" Williams asked.

"Could be ten minutes to two hours," Dexter answered, every nerve in his body fixed on that plastic tent.

Would fuming on the site with crude equipment result in anything? If the fates were kind, they'd get nice, white prints that would lead them to the straw-hat lady and, he was sure, Hawley's murderer.

Since the fuming might take a while, Joe and Tony began the process for lifting prints from the two large rocks that had concealed the tote.

"What can I do to help?" Dexter asked.

"Just stay out of our way," Joe told him. "On second thought, how about taping around the bases? It would save some time if we find anything."

Dexter took the tape Joe handed him and ran it around the base of the two rocks, each about the size of a living room ottoman. Both were fairly smooth, with a slight indent on the top, which was why he and Ella's husband had chosen them.

"After dusting first, they'll use a casting silicone to lift any prints they find," Rico continued, obviously reveling in his role of instructor. "And the tape is to catch the excess that may run down the stones. While it may be messy, it's the best material to use on curved or rough surfaces."

"Hey guys," Dexter called to Joe and Tony, "before you start dusting the rocks, how about checking the tote? Is it time yet?"

He, Rico, and Williams silently watched while Joe and Tony carefully opened the plastic tent. Would it show any prints?

Dexter moved in closer, and when he saw the tote, his heart sank. There was no powdery substance anywhere on the tote.

Nothing.

His questioning gaze flew to each tech, and Tony shook his head.

"Sorry, Dex. She probably wore gloves. Or maybe the straw had some kind of preservative that worked against us. Hard to say, but we may have better luck with the gun." Tony glanced around the site. "We have to get this right, so help me find a couple of twigs to prop it off the ground."

All five men scoured the area for the right three twigs, and Joe used a pocketknife to trim them into long forks, which he then used to prop up the gun inside the plastic tent. Again they started the fuming process, and again, Dexter gritted his teeth with anxiety. Would it work this time?

"We'll give it a bit longer," Tony said, "just to make sure."

Joe had begun dusting one boulder and Tony worked on the

second. Each used a dark powder to better see any prints on the light-colored boulders.

"Anything yet?" Dexter moved closer, checking the dusty surfaces.

"Yeah," Joe said. "Hundreds of prints, all smudged. They could be weeks or months old. No telling who has walked around up here and taken a break on these rocks."

Damn. "How about the gun?"

Again they carefully checked the tent, and again, no signs of fingerprints.

Dexter felt like kicking something, but he wasn't ready to give up yet. Not when they had their first solid clues. But what could he do? Eyeing the boulders, he suddenly had an idea.

"Let's try something." He glanced at Rico. "You're shorter. Come over here and pretend you're a woman stuffing something between the rocks."

Rico flushed, but squatted down and did as Dexter asked. Then he placed his hands on the boulders to brace himself.

"Tony, dust there on each rock, right where Rico's hands were." Dexter watched the techs dust each boulder. The first one revealed nothing, but with the second, he moved in closer, almost nose-to-rock, and even to the naked eye, the outlines of one lone palm print, complete with two fingers, became visible.

CHAPTER TWENTY-FOUR

Once they were back at the house, Madison settled her grandmother on the chaise on the porch and retrieved a lavender afghan from her bedroom.

Ella kicked it off. "Too hot," she murmured, sounding as if she were out of breath.

"Gran, is there anything I can do?" Madison asked, almost wringing her hands with worry.

Her eyes still shut, Ella shook her head. Madison was horrified to see tears rolling down her cheeks.

"I don't know what to do for you," she said. "You're not well and you won't see a doctor."

"What's going on here?" Cora asked, approaching from the top of the stairs. "There's a police car and a van parked in front, and isn't that Dexter's SUV?"

In her concern, Madison hadn't noticed or heard Cora's car, but she was so glad to see her grandmother's friend that she could have kissed her. If anyone could override Ella's stubbornness, it was Cora.

"You're both obviously alive," Cora said, striding over to look down at Ella, "although I must say you look like death warmed over. And Madison, you don't look much better. What's happened here?"

Ella said nothing, didn't even look at her friend.

My God, Madison thought. Was Cora right? Was her grandmother showing signs of Alzheimer's?

"I'll get some cold drinks." Madison motioned for Cora to follow her into the kitchen. "Sit down, and I'll tell you what happened." She prepared a tray of lemonade and brought Cora up to date. "Maybe you can convince her to see her doctor. I certainly can't."

"I'll see what I can do, but don't let her know you're worried."

But when Madison handed a glass to her grandmother, Ella frowned. "I know you two were talking about me," she said, "and I appreciate the concern. But I'm feeling much better. I just need some rest without all this jabbering. Quit your worrying and go do something useful. Take some cold drinks to Dexter and his men. They must be parched."

Exasperated, Madison headed back to the kitchen, this time letting the screen door slam behind her. It was perplexing how Ella seemed all right one minute and on the verge of collapse the next. She'd take drinks to the campsite, then check online for symptoms.

Fifteen minutes later, Madison was handing out cold glasses to the men at the campsite. They were so preoccupied with their work that they barely acknowledged her presence. The sun was going down, and a breeze from the higher elevations was whipping up the dirt. Shadows from the trees were growing longer, and Madison could see that the men were hustling to complete their investigation. She left them to their work and returned to the house and her laptop. She had some investigating of her own to do.

She entered "Signs of Alzheimer's" into the search engine, praying she wouldn't recognize any of them. Several sites came up. She clicked on the first one and began reading.

Symptoms of the disease included forgetting names of those close to the patient, decreased interest in activities. The signs continued over several pages. Most Madison could explain as normal signs of aging, but when she read one, her blood went cold.

Unpredictable mood changes.

God. She sat back and stared at the screen as if willing the words to disappear. Then she read more, learning about the three stages of the disease. Shaken, she sat back.

Could she afford to quit work and spend some quality time with Ella? There were so many things she'd always wanted the two of them to do, so many places to see. Would they have time before the disease took control?

She didn't know how long she sat there before she heard the screen door shut.

"It's past suppertime, Madison," Cora said, "and Ella seems stronger. I'd like to take you both to dinner."

"Look." Madison motioned to the computer screen and pulled out a chair.

"I don't know to operate one of those machines," Cora told her, "and I don't care to learn."

"Just read."

With an exasperated frown, Cora sat close to the screen and peered through her bifocals. She silently read, then sat back. "Oh dear."

"Maybe you can help me convince her to see her doctor," Madison said. "Maybe he can give her something that'll help it from progressing."

"I've tried, but she won't listen to reason, not even from me."

With Cora's help, Madison put together a dinner of salad and pasta primavera made with veggies in the fridge, and wondered how to get her grandmother to talk to Doc Hayes. She called Dexter about joining them, but he wanted to stay with the evidence.

After the meal, Cora settled on the sofa with Ella and they began their ritual of arguing about programs to watch. Madison took the opportunity to check on her condo and pick up mail, more clothing, and personal items.

From the street, her place still looked as if she had just stepped out for a moment. The lights were blazing, and when Madison opened the door, she could hear the radio softly playing an instrumental.

Moving through the rooms, she decided to put it up for sale and move in permanently with her grandmother. If Ella had Alzheimer's, Madison wanted to spend every moment she could with her, and even though she'd have the trust fund her parents set up for her, the extra money from the sale could go toward a trip for two to a place Ella had always wanted to see. Perhaps Scotland, and then, if her grandmother's health allowed, Egypt. Ella had always dreamed of sailing up the Nile and touring the pyramids.

Madison checked her mail, and it was the usual bills and advertisements, although she had a handful of get-well cards for her supposed bout with the flu. One from Marie included a personal note and said not to worry about returning too soon, that she'd cleared two weeks' sick leave.

Nice of her, Madison thought, stuffing the mail into her handbag. She checked her plants, adding water to the glass vase of leafy bamboo shoots over the kitchen sink, and stood gazing out the window to the mountains beyond.

It was too dark to see anything but their faint outline, but her grandmother had always loved them, and she'd passed that love to Madison. Not only had they all enjoyed the campsite when her grandfather was still alive, but she and Ella, sometimes Dexter when he had the time, would walk the foothills and occasionally drive the winding road up the mountain.

While packing some clothes and gathering toiletries, Madison thought about her grandmother's deterioration, and knew she had to do everything she could to make whatever years Ella had left comfortable.

But, an inner voice nagged, how was she going to help her grandmother when she couldn't even help herself? She still cowered and shook every time Bates' name was mentioned. What would happen when he actually lived in the same town, if she actually spotted him in the grocery store or even on the street?

Suitcase in hand, she flipped off the switch that controlled the living room and hallway lights, stepped out and locked her door, then, although she fought the familiar urge, hurried back to switch the light back on.

One thing was for sure—she'd better figure out something to help herself, and she'd better do it fast.

"Senator Stone called," Cora said as soon as Madison walked through the front door. She and Ella were still on the sofa, although the TV was muted. "He called personally to remind Ella about the garden party tomorrow, and he invited me as well. Clara too. What a nice man."

"I'd forgotten all about it." Madison hid a smile. Even though Cora hadn't raised her voice, her excitement was evident.

"I'm not sure we should go," Madison told her.

"Not go?"

"Nonsense," Ella said. "You all should go. Don't let an old woman's ailments keep you from an enjoyable afternoon."

"I can't go without you," Cora said.

Shaking her head, Madison headed for her bedroom and put her things away. Back in the living room, Ella and Cora were still arguing—or discussing, as her grandmother would say.

"All that fuss . . ." Ella grumbled, sitting back with her arms crossed. Madison knew that look. Ella had made up her mind, but which way?

It was after two in the morning when Dexter passed a female

driver on the I-10 East and realized she or any of the other drivers could be the straw-hat lady.

Where was she? he wondered. How could anyone manage to murder someone in a public place and disappear so completely? That took a hell of a lot of luck. Or careful planning. A washcloth to wipe away blood pointed to meticulous planning. But no one was perfect. Leaving the tote where it could be discovered was certainly an error in judgment. If *he'd* committed the murder, he would have taken a harbor cruise and dropped it into the Pacific.

When he passed a Denny's off I-10, the thought of bacon, eggs, and butter-drenched pancakes made his mouth water, and he realized he hadn't eaten since breakfast. He'd love something hot, but every muscle in his decrepit body ached, and stretching out on his bed was his highest priority. He might have some cheese in the fridge. If it wasn't moldy.

What a frustrating evening. He'd spent over an hour trying to get a lab technician to stay late and process the prints. No one wanted to put in the extra time on such a low-priority case, and when he'd finally found a willing young woman, no amount of processing produced more prints on the tote, the gun, or even the plastic bag holding the bloody washcloth. An analysis of the blood on the cloth and the man's shirt could take weeks, but he wasn't concerned about that. He was sure the blood was Hawley's.

The biggest disappointment was the handprint. A check with IAFIS, the Integrated Automated Fingerprint Identification System maintained by the FBI, revealed a match to Madison, obtained, no doubt, when she purchased her .38 handgun. She could've left the prints when she had pushed the tote from between the two rocks, or it could've been made months ago. With the small amount of rainfall in the area, the print could've lasted for months.

Once again, he was right back where he started, and he felt like a dog chasing his tail. Even if ballistics matched the bullet to the gun, he still wasn't any further ahead. If he couldn't find something soon, Hawley's case would go into the cold file, and that grated. In all his years of service, no case of his had gone unsolved, and he wasn't about to set a precedent now.

Perhaps the straw-hat lady had slipped up somewhere else, and if she had, there was more evidence. He just had to find it.

Something had to break soon.

CHAPTER TWENTY-FIVE

"I'm so glad to see all of you." Senator Stone, elegant as usual in a finely tailored suit, along with Mr. Chauncey, assisted the four ladies from Cora's Mercedes.

"You're riding in style," he said and Cora beamed. "And how lovely you all look," he added.

Ella wore a long sapphire dress cut in a shirtwaist style with a two-pointed collar, fitted waist, and buttons running all the way to the floor-length hem.

Madison's dress was one she'd chosen a few years ago for a friend's wedding, an elegant gown with its white top cut in a V neckline, Empire bust, and a black skirt, which flowed around her ankles. She had tucked her hair into a low chignon and completed her look by wearing her mother's Swarovski crystal and onyx necklace.

Cora wore a tuxedo-style pantsuit, and Clara's buttercup dress reminded Madison of a long-ago southern belle.

The senator held out each arm for Ella and Madison and led them through the side garden to the back lawns. Behind them, Mr. Chauncey escorted Cora and Clara.

White roses bloomed along the gravel walk, and pink cyclamens, white lilies, and fan palms surrounded a koi fish pond. In the distance, Madison could hear strings of a live quartet and the buzz of conversation.

The manicured grounds of the back lawn were filled with about three-hundred elegantly dressed men and women who were active in politics or the social scene from Redlands and the Inland Empire. Madison even recognized several of the senator's colleagues from Washington as well as executives from Fortune 500 companies. Six party tents provided shade for the linen-covered buffet tables and seating areas. Two fountains were bubbling.

"I wasn't sure either of you felt strong enough to attend," Senator Stone said, "but I'm glad you did. I've arranged special seating under the tent," he added, leading them to a table near the front of the center tent. "I regret that Dexter was unable to get away from work. I would have enjoyed seeing him, but he called with his regrets. Whatever he's working on, it must be important."

"It's the straw tote and gun," Madison said. When he looked puzzled, she told him about finding the tote at the campsite, and how she'd ruined the area for footprints.

"You couldn't have known," he replied, "but what a terrible thing to find so close to your grandmother's home. Are you certain they were from the Yucaipa shooting?"

"Dexter seemed to think so. There was a gun and everything."

"Let's hope that puts an end to the violence in the area. And now, if you ladies will excuse me, I'll see to the other guests. Please help yourselves to the buffet, and most of all, enjoy yourselves."

When the senator and Mr. Chauncey were several feet away, Madison said, "Oh, I forgot something," and hurried to catch up.

"I need to talk to you about a private matter," she whispered to the senator.

"What is it, my dear?" He motioned for Chauncey to continue on.

Madison explained it all, her concerns about her grand-mother's health and how her trip to San Diego had been cut short because of it, adding details about the decline she'd noticed in her general well-being after the tote had been found at the campsite.

"And when Gran showed up at the campsite to watch them search for prints, she looked terrible. And later, she didn't even make sense. I'm concerned about early Alzheimer's. Cora mentioned it earlier, but now . . ." Her words trailed off and she fought tears.

"Cora knows about all of this?"

"She and Gran are best friends and they share everything."

"Of course. Well, Cora's right. No matter her protests, you need to get Ella to a doctor. It's amazing what they can do when they catch diseases in the early stages. I'd be happy to recommend someone, a local man and the best in the field. I'll give him a call, and if Ella still refuses to go, let me know. I'll call her tomorrow to check on her."

Thank God, Madison thought, feeling a measure of relief for the first time. Both she and Ella had such regard for the senator that surely her grandmother would listen to him.

After two hours, Madison suggested they leave. Not only was she exhausted, but so was her grandmother. She had nibbled on a finger sandwich when Madison insisted she eat something, but even then didn't finish it. By the time the senator had stopped by to check on them, Ella had withdrawn so completely that she wouldn't even look at him.

Neither Cora nor Clara protested. One look at Ella was all it took to know that something was wrong.

Nothing about Charles Bartrum attracted attention. When he exited the Greyhound bus in Shreveport, Louisiana, he appeared a bit thin perhaps, even skinny, but his light pullover and jeans permitted him to blend in with everyone else. Even after the seventeen-hour trip from El Paso, he looked neat and clean with his long gray hair pulled into a ponytail and his beard carefully combed.

It was only after he took a paper sack from the terminal locker and changed clothes in the men's room that he looked like a street bum. Splotches of white paint were splattered across the front of his T-shirt, and his knees stuck out of his ragged jeans. As for his hair, freed from its ponytail, it hung in his face

When he boarded a city bus to cross Red River for Bossier City, he hoped he wouldn't get stopped for vagrancy before he reached his destination. If he were picked up, not only would the drugs in his pocket cost him his freedom, but he'd fail in his mission. He didn't want that; even though the Society would assign someone else to do the job, his own petition would go unfulfilled.

When he hit the sidewalks at Bogalusa Avenue and Pecan, he double-checked the address inside the Ruby Red Society engraved envelope and took off in a northerly direction.

Overhead, the sun blazed until he felt as if he were walking in a steam bath. Once away from the main drag, he stopped and wiped the sweat from his face and gulped a long, thirsty drink from the water bottle he'd stuck in his pocket.

He hadn't been prepared for the cloying heat. It had to be a hundred degrees, and though he was used to the scorching sun of west Texas, walking in the thick soggy air of Louisiana felt as if he were moving underwater. Thank God the housing project wasn't too far from the bus stop.

The shabby three-story building looked as though it must have been built shortly after the Civil War. The crumbling bricks had long since faded to a rusty brown, and each building had one main door. Children of all ages and races played in the patch of dandelions in the triangular courtyard, and women, most of them dressed in shorts and tank tops, stood in clusters watching them.

But in the midst of shabbiness and neglect, he could see traces of beauty. Two ancient live oak trees shaded part of the courtyard, and wisteria and honeysuckle vines climbed the fences between the projects, adding their sweet scents to the air. Huge huckleberry trees stood next to magnolias, and blood-red pomegranates bloomed next to fig trees. He made a mental note to visit the area with his family once his contract had been completed.

He scanned the brass numbers and found the one he wanted. When he slipped on latex gloves and entered the building, no one looked his way. Inside, a dark hallway led to several doors on the first floor, and a scuffed wooden staircase led to the second. An infant cried. When he knocked on the numbered door, the baby's cries rose to screams.

Finally, a young petite woman in a dirty bra and panties opened the door about halfway and scowled at him from half-closed lids. Her long ebony hair hung over her face and she pushed it back.

"Wha' tha fuck you want?" Her slurred words indicated that she'd either just been awakened or she was high. Or both, he thought. Despite the infant's screams, she continued to ignore the noise.

"You Latisha?" he asked.

"So?" Her eyes narrowed suspiciously.

"Wanna score? I got some good stuff, and I heard you can be grateful."

When he pushed past her, she didn't try to stop him.

Inside the tiny space, the smell of dirty diapers and rotting food hung in the musty air. The kitchen counter was cluttered with fast-food containers, and roaches fed on bits of a burrito and taco. A stained mattress lay on the floor next to an LCD TV, and in the corner, a dirty white crib held the screaming infant.

Every instinct urged him to go to the tiny girl, to hold and comfort her, but he had to bide his time and set the stage. But maybe he could get the woman to check on the baby.

"Can't you do something about that kid? That racket's giving me a headache."

"It's a'right," she said, shrugging. *It,* she'd called her daughter, as if her child wasn't even human. "What you got? I ain't got no money, but I can take care o' you."

She smiled and unhooked her bra. Her small breasts spilled free. Her body was needle thin and covered with a rash. He wasn't about to touch her.

The baby still screamed. He hurried the process now, digging in his pockets for the marijuana and meth crystals.

"Oh," she cooed, her smile growing wider. "You got ice."

She eagerly watched as he ran some water and prepared the meth for shooting up. Either she didn't see or didn't care when he added a couple of drops of another liquid.

When it was ready, she tied her arm and held it out for the injection. While he pumped the syringe into her vein, her first reaction was to close her eyes and sigh. But soon after she began to choke and gasp for air, then lost consciousness and sank to the floor. Stepping over her body, he hurried to the crib, changed the infant's soaked diaper, and picked her up.

"Soon, baby girl, you'll have a new home and parents who'll take care of you," he crooned.

The baby stopped crying and her brown eyes turned in his direction.

He carried her to the fridge for a bottle. Not finding one, he wrapped the baby in her grimy blanket, stepped over the dead woman, and slipped out the door.

CHAPTER TWENTY-SIX

Back home from the garden party, Madison helped her grandmother into her comfortable robe.

"I'm so sorry I spoiled it for you, Maddy."

"You spoiled nothing. With everything that's happened the past month, I'm surprised either of us is still standing. But I'm making a doctor's appointment for you as soon as Senator Stone calls."

"Senator Stone?" Cora appeared in the doorway to the bedroom holding a tray with Ella's teapot and cups. "What does the senator have to do with a doctor?"

"Oh, Maddy," Ella sighed, "you didn't burden him about this, did you?"

Madison related her conversation at the party. "He's going to personally call a specialist, which was more than I'd hoped for. Now let's get you settled on the porch for some tea. And I don't want to hear any more about you not seeing someone."

By the time Cora and Clara rose to leave, they'd had the satisfaction of hearing Ella finally agree to see a doctor.

"We'll be going now, Ella. You need to rest, and I want out of this ridiculous costume."

Ella took her hand. "You're a good friend, Cora, and I've appreciated your help. You too, Clara."

"What are you talking about? Of course we're friends. It's not like you to sound so maudlin, Ella."

"Just know that I love you."

Cora frowned. "Oh for heaven's sake. I'll call later tonight." After a worried glance at Madison, she ushered Clara down the stairs.

Madison tried not to panic, but her grandmother had sounded as if she were going somewhere and not expecting to return.

What in God's name was wrong?

She'd make Ella comfortable the rest of the day, then, if she hadn't heard from the senator about the specialist by tomorrow morning, she'd call Doc Hayes. Nothing mattered as much as her grandmother, not even Bates.

After preparing a dinner of grilled cheese sandwiches and tomato soup, she and her grandmother, a bowl of popcorn between them, settled down to a DVD of one of their favorite romantic comedies.

Suddenly, Madison sensed a sound so slight that she shouldn't have heard it over the TV, but something made her look at her grandmother. Even though Ella was staring at the TV and made no noise, tears were rolling down her cheeks.

"What's wrong, Gran?" she asked, slipping one arm around her grandmother's shoulders. "What has you so upset?"

"I love you so," she said, the tears still falling. "Your welfare has always been my main concern."

"I know that, and I love you too. But something's wrong. How can I help if I don't know what's going on?"

Ella looked miserable, as if the weight of the world had been on her shoulders and it had become too much to bear. "I've let you down."

"Nothing you could ever do would let me down," she crooned, suddenly noticing how thin her grandmother felt. She knew her appetite had waned considerably, but Ella actually felt thin, something she'd never been as long as Madison could remember. And she'd become so frail.

She rested her head next to Ella's, remembering what she'd read about Alzheimer's, wondering if she were strong enough to care for her grandmother if she was, indeed, suffering from the disease. No matter what it took, she vowed, she had to be strong enough.

An hour later, Ella fell asleep almost as soon as Madison pulled up the sheet on her bed. While nights in Yucaipa cooled several degrees from the summer heat, it was still too hot for a blanket. One of her grandmother's knitted throws would be perfect.

Rummaging in the cedar chest at the foot of the bed, she found the special one, embroidered with roses that Ella had made for her daughter, Susan, Madison's mother. As she pulled it out, a piece of paper fell to the floor, a torn airline ticket stub or boarding pass.

It had to be an old stub, a trip that Madison had long forgotten, Madison thought. The name of the ticket holder was gone, but she could make out part of the round-trip schedule, a same-day flight dated around the time Ella had driven to San Diego with Cora and Clara.

Well, that was impossible. It had to be a misprint. But what was it doing in her grandmother's cedar chest?

Then she read the destination:

Depart: San Diego, CA

Arrive: Yuma, AZ

Depart: Yuma, AZ

Arrive: San Diego, CA

Stunned, Madison sank to the floor. Her grandmother had gone to Yuma? Why? What possible reason would she have to make a trip to Arizona when she was already on a trip with Cora and Clara?

But if Ella had made the reservation, had Cora or Clara known? Surely her grandmother hadn't actually taken the flight, because if she had, Cora and Clara would have said something. They'd all been together and they would have known—unless they'd all gone together.

But why would they do that? Had they discovered something special in Arizona that they didn't want to miss? If so, why hadn't they mentioned it?

And then a sudden thought sent her running to her laptop. Sure enough, the date of the Yuma murder was the same as the date on the ticket.

The same date as the ticket.

No, no, no! Her grandmother couldn't have had anything to do with the murder. She couldn't even think such a terrible thing. Ella had trouble getting rid of the occasional mouse when, in winter, one wandered into the basement. She'd wanted it captured alive and released back into the hills.

Besides, she'd been ill in San Diego and the three women had returned early. It had to be a mistake. Bewildered, she stuck the paper into her pocket.

She paused while covering her grandmother with the throw. What was it that Cora had said? The *Do Not Disturb* sign had been on Ella's door all day.

Her knees went weak. So it had been possible for her grandmother to leave the hotel without Cora and Clara knowing.

Madison staggered to the living room sofa. If, just if, it were Ella who'd made the reservation, it must have been during an irrational moment, a manifestation of early Alzheimer's. Was that possible? And if she'd actually boarded the plane to go, could the disease drive a harmless person to commit murder? And if she'd actually intended to commit a murder, what bizarre thought process could cause her to pick someone in Yuma? Despite the impossibility of it all, Madison still wondered if her grandmother had actually taken that flight to Yuma.

Dexter could check. Madison reached for the phone to call him, if for no other reason than to put her mind at ease, but just as she picked it up, she hesitated. As much as she loved him and as close as he was to the family, did she really want to tell him what she'd discovered? If it turned out that Ella was involved in a murder, Dexter was still a police officer, and she'd hate to make him choose between protecting them and upholding the law.

So what should she do? She had to find out what happened in Yuma that day. There had to have been something else going on in Yuma that Ella felt she simply couldn't miss. She could use Marie's computer. Checking the newswire service for other events that day was the only way to allay her fears—and suspicions. And, if she found out the worst—no major events except the murder—she had to know. It was the only way to protect her grandmother.

But how could she use Marie's computer when she'd been refused access to the service? She certainly wasn't going to tell Marie anything. Arousing suspicions in a newspaper editor's mind wasn't what she needed now.

There was only one way. She had to break into Marie's office.

After work, Marie felt wrung out and in no mood to go home and face a house full of company, even if it was her brother and his family. Since her divorce three years ago, she'd lived alone and had grown accustomed to quiet in the evenings. Today, with two employees out with the flu, she'd been so busy that now she desperately needed peace and serenity. She called her brother and told him she was working late, that she wouldn't be home for dinner.

And no matter how often she told herself she was only doing her job, she couldn't shake her guilt over Madison's hospitalization.

After making a stop at the Chinese take-out, she took Highway 38 to her favorite lookout spot in the hills above Yucaipa, wishing she had time to drive on up to Big Bear Lake or even to Forest Falls.

She pulled onto the narrow dirt road about four miles up the canyon, just past the point where the brown hills and scrub brush gave way to pines, firs, and oaks of the San Bernardino National Forest. She turned off the air conditioning and lowered her window, still amazed at how dramatically the temperature lowered just a few miles above the city.

A winding dirt road ended at a bluff overlooking the valley below. While it was much better in the evening with all the lights twinkling, the spot was still her favorite.

Directly below the ledge, a steep gorge plunged a thousand feet, and since the turnoff to the spot was only a narrow dirt road, there were seldom other cars except on weekend nights when teens used the place as a make-out lane.

She had just finished her dinner and was loading the bag with little white boxes when she heard another vehicle approach. Damn. But, she reasoned, it was getting late. The first star was becoming visible, so she should be heading home to her company.

Strange, though. The other vehicle didn't pull up beside her, yet she could hear the engine clattering like a diesel. Oh well. Perhaps it was kids and they'd changed their minds about parking after seeing her.

She didn't want to crane her neck like a nosy old lady, so she pulled down the visor mirror and saw a black pickup, a Dodge Ram, she thought, idling almost on her back bumper.

Why did they pull up to her car? There was room for at least three vehicles on the lookout point. And why were they just sitting with the motor idling? Were they trying to scare her for some reason?

But no. It had to be thoughtless kids. Now she'd have to get out of her car and ask them to back up.

Annoyed, she grabbed the door handle, and just at that moment, she felt a thump on her back bumper.

What the hell?

She turned around to look, but another hit threw her head backward and jarred her teeth. Before she could recover, she felt her car moving forward.

Oh my God, they were pushing her over the cliff! She stomped on the brakes. The car lurched sideways, but kept moving forward.

Gravel crunched.

Marie pounded the brakes, but the car didn't stop. Now her front tires were at the edge.

She had to get out of there, now!

She opened the door to jump, but her seat belt was still locked. She fumbled with the catch, but it wouldn't release. She glimpsed the dry creek bed at the bottom of the gorge.

She clawed at the lock, but it wouldn't give. Two nails broke and bled, but she didn't feel them.

The car was tipping over the edge. She grabbed the steering wheel to hold on. It hurled downward, picking up speed, mowing scrub brush, crashing through gullies. Sky melted into ground when it took to the air, crashing on the large rocks below. It burst into flames.

Madison waited two hours after her grandmother fell asleep, two hours of watching the clock, of pacing in her bedroom, willing the hands to move forward more quickly.

Tonight was the night. She was going to break into Marie's office. She'd never done anything immoral or illegal in her entire life, not the petty theft some of her classmates in school thought was such a lark, and certainly not experimenting with the drugs that were so popular. She figured the prescription drugs from her shrink were enough to float away any rebellion she might feel about anything, but the main reason, she knew, was her grandmother. Ella had suffered through enough, and Madison didn't want to be the cause of more pain.

Tonight, if she were caught, she'd certainly upset Ella. And Dexter would be mortified. But she had to look for possible reasons why her grandmother might have made a fast round-trip to Yuma that day. She still wondered if Cora and Clara had accompanied her. She'd called the airlines and asked, but they'd refused to give her the information.

Perhaps she'd get lucky and find Marie's office open. As editor, she often worked late, so if this were a night when she'd stayed on after hours, she might have been too tired to lock the door.

At midnight, the upper end of Yucaipa was void of traffic except for an occasional vehicle pulling into the brightly lit convenience store off of Bryant. On Yucaipa Boulevard, streetlights cast a yellowish glow on the deserted city blocks.

She pulled into the parking lot beside the newspaper building, but instead of parking where she could be seen from the street, she pulled around back and edged as close to the building as she could get. Then, because her car was white, she covered it with a navy-blue bedspread she'd brought from home.

Glancing over each shoulder like a criminal, she used her key to open the front door. Inside, she maneuvered past the reception area and desks outlined by the faint glow from the streetlight. She tried Marie's door. Locked, just as she thought.

Okay, this was it. If she turned around and left now, she'd still be a law-abiding citizen, but the mental image of her grandmother's weakened condition pushed her to the point of no return.

She glanced over her shoulder, then pulled out a flexible

credit card, hoping she'd remember the steps Dexter had once demonstrated when trying to convince Ella to change her old locks for deadbolts. Aiming her flashlight at the lock, she slid the card between the door and the frame where the latch was located and wiggled it.

Nothing happened.

She inserted it again, thanking the fates that the inner door frame wasn't lined with molding, and that Marie never bothered to replace the old lock. She wiggled the card and pushed, trying to get that wedge to slide back, and each little metallic jiggle sounded as if it were connected to an amplifier. Surely the police would hear and come running. It was taking too long, and if it didn't give soon, she'd have to leave.

Sweating now, she glanced over her shoulder. No cop cars, no spotlights aimed at the office, yet, but it was taking too much time.

She reinserted the card one last time, wiggled it, this time remembering to bend it in the direction Dexter had shown. Just as she was ready to give up, she heard the click. The door popped open. She was in.

At Marie's computer she booted up. Then, as the screen lit up, she set the flashlight aside and moved the frog from the keyboard.

She tried several times to log onto the newswire service, and each time she received an error message. What now? Sweat dotted her forehead and under her arms. She listened for any sound from the front door. Nothing. She was safe—for the moment. She'd try once more, then she'd have to get out of there.

What password could Marie have used? Madison tried several variations of Marie's name, the newspaper, her grown children's names, and still, the error message.

Just as she was ready to give up, her glance fell on the stuffed frog, a sign that Marie had a fantasy streak inside that gruff, no-

nonsense exterior. *Kermie,* she called him. Suddenly, she knew. She typed "Kermie."

Suddenly the screen changed and she was in. With a self-satisfied sigh, she entered Yuma, AZ, and the date on the reservation and watched articles fill the screen. One major news event dominated the headlines: the death of William "Willy Boy" Martin, age twenty-seven, of Yuma, Arizona. He'd been observed talking to a *senior* person, the article said, who had subsequently fled the scene.

Madison felt sick. Ella couldn't be guilty of such a crime, not her gentle, loving grandmother. Could she? But it would explain so much. And if some aberration did cause her to commit murder, why this man? What caused her to fly to a different state and choose him? What connection was there between them?

With only more questions instead of answers, Madison printed out the pages and tucked them into her bag. Driving home, the questions haunted her, although now she wasn't sure she wanted the answers.

CHAPTER TWENTY-SEVEN

After the morning briefing, Captain Silva called Dexter and Rico into his office.

What the hell had he done now? Dexter wondered.

"Thought you'd like to know. Missing Persons took a report about the Yucaipa's *Tribune* editor. Seems she's gone missing."

Dexter grabbed a chair. "Marie Campbell?"

"She didn't show for work this morning, and when someone called her home, her brother said she hadn't been home all night. While missing persons isn't our department, I figured you know her, Dexter. Is she the type to disappear for a day or two? You know, for one of those little quickie trips to meet someone for an unscheduled vacation?"

"Not Marie. She's as straight an arrow as anyone could be. Besides, last I heard, she wasn't seeing anyone."

"Maybe that's changed. Look. We don't have the manpower to do an all-out search, but you might nose around when you're in the area. If she doesn't show by tomorrow, we'll make it official."

Dexter took I-10 east to Yucaipa. From the passenger seat, Rico made several of those long-suffering sighs. Dexter tried to ignore them but his grip tightened on the wheel. When Rico expelled the next long, drawn-out breath, Dexter exploded.

"What the hell's your problem?"

"You're on your way to the newspaper office, aren't you? We're homicide detectives, not babysitters if someone wants to take a powder."

That did it. Dexter swerved to the shoulder on the Crafton Hills incline just before the Yucaipa Boulevard exit. Cars and eighteen-wheelers whizzed by. Fighting the urge to knock Rico's teeth down his throat, Dexter reached past him and threw the passenger door open.

"Get out."

"What the hell?"

"You listen and listen good, because I'll only say this once. I'm the senior officer here, and if you don't like what I'm doing, you can get your ass out of my car. I've known Marie for twenty years, and if she's in trouble, I want to know about it, and I don't give a flying fuck what you think. Now make up your mind. Stay or go? And make it quick. I'm not going to waste time arguing with a prick like you."

Rico shut the door very carefully. "Jesus, man. I was only—"

"Shut up, Rico. I don't even want to hear your voice."

At the *Tribune*'s office, Dexter and a sullen Rico questioned employees. Marie hadn't checked in, and no one had any idea where she could be.

"We were supposed to go over notes from the council election this morning," Steve said. "It isn't like her to not show."

Dexter's guts were tightening, just like they always did when something wasn't right.

At Marie's home, her brother's wife, Sara, acting as if she were hostess at a social event, seated Dexter and Rico in the living room with a tray of coffee and cookies. Marie's brother, Julian, was so agitated that he couldn't sit still. At the living room window, he pulled the drapes aside and stood gazing out the window.

"I just don't understand it," he said. "She didn't come home at all last night, and that's not like her. Especially when we're only going to be here a few more days." He turned from the window. "We're from Cleveland, you know."

"If you ask me," Sara said, "she hasn't tried too hard to be here so far. It wouldn't surprise me if she breezed in with some excuse or another."

"Sara, don't start."

From rooms down the hall, Dexter could hear a boy and girl arguing. Outside, a little dog yapped.

"That's Pixie, our toy Yorkie," Sara told him, excusing herself to open the sliding doors to the patio. Soon a brownish-blond lump of fur with a pink bow perched between its ears trotted into the living room and jumped onto Marie's sofa. It sat and barked at the detectives.

If I were Marie, Dexter thought, I'd want to escape this madhouse too. But he knew she'd let someone know.

Walking toward his car, Dexter called Madison. "Have you heard from Marie?"

Maddy made a sound like a gasp. "Why? Anything wrong at the office?" She sounded breathless.

"Honey, you okay?"

"Uh, yeah. Sure. Why are you asking about Marie?"

"She didn't show for work today and everyone's concerned. Just wondered if you had any idea where she could be."

"Oh. I haven't talked to her lately. I've been too concerned about Gran to think of anything else."

Dexter frowned. It wasn't like her to brush off concerns about Marie or anyone else.

Something besides her grandmother must be going on with her. He'd make a point to stop by as soon as he could.

When Dexter called to ask about Marie, Madison had been certain that someone had discovered she'd broken into her office last night. Thank God it had been a false alarm. But what she'd said was true. Her grandmother seemed to occupy all her thoughts now.

After a late breakfast, Ella seemed a little stronger physically, although she was listless and had no interest in doing anything other than sitting on the porch. Mornings usually found her bustling about the house, straightening this or that, preparing something wonderful for dinner, or puttering around her flowers. In the dry heat, flowers didn't last long without water, so Madison made a mental note to water everything that evening.

"Gran, I made an appointment for you with Doctor Hayes, and he can see you tomorrow morning."

Her only reaction was a slight nod.

"And when the senator calls with a referral," Madison added, "we'll go there as well."

This time there was no response. Her grandmother stared into the distance as if in a world of her own.

"I need some things from my place," Madison told her, fighting tears, "so as soon as Cora gets here, I'll leave."

"For heaven's sake, Maddy, I don't need a babysitter. I won't set the house on fire while you're gone. I'm a little down, not mindless."

Wishing that were the case, Madison pulled out of the driveway, drove around the curve, and waited until she saw Cora's car before heading down to Yucaipa.

Instead of heading for her condo, she drove to the doctor's, hoping it was one of the days he opened the office. The lights were on and she asked Jenny, the part-time receptionist, if she could speak to him. "It's urgent."

Twenty minutes later, she took a chair in his office.

"I'm so happy to see you up and about," he told her. "You had us all worried, you know. But you're looking pretty robust now."

"Thanks, Doc, but I'm here about my grandmother." She

brought him up to date on Ella's condition while he quietly listened.

"Cora mentioned Alzheimer's, and I've gone online to find out as much as I can, but I need more information. Can the disease cause a person to do something rash, something totally out of character?"

"We don't have all the answers, Madison, but we can start testing in the morning. To what specific signs are you referring?"

"Oh, making a reservation at a swanky hotel in Paris, for example, or hopping on a plane for a quick trip to Las Vegas. Just something Gran wouldn't normally do."

Dr. Hayes smiled. "Making impromptu travel plans would certainly be interesting, but unfortunately, the disease usually manifests in other ways. Typically, the person withdraws and loses the ability to remember things. While any of us may temporarily forget where we've placed our car keys, the Alzheimer's patient forgets how to drive. They may have periods of lucidity, but the ability to remember continually fades. I'm curious. Did Ella decide to book an exotic vacation?"

"Not exactly," Madison replied, unwilling to mention the Yuma trip.

"Too bad. She deserves to do something special, although she wouldn't go without you, you know. Your welfare has been her purpose in life, and I think that's why she's been so healthy all these years."

"Until now," Madison said in a whisper.

"Let me ask you this." Dr. Hayes stepped around the desk to sit beside her. "When did you first notice the decline?"

Madison gave it some thought. "I'm not sure, but it's been in the last several weeks."

"Has anything happened that would precipitate a loss of mental faculties? An unresolved stress, perhaps—other than your hospitalization?"

She wished she could tell him what she'd discovered, desperately needed to confide her suspicions, but she didn't dare. She'd heard about doctor/patient confidentiality, but since there was the possibility of murder, she didn't know if it would apply.

Instead, she answered in a vague way.

"You know Gran. She's always been strong, always faced life's curves with determination."

"Give it some thought, Madison, and see if you can think of anything that might have triggered her condition. While technology has progressed beyond all expectations in the past century, we're still learning about the effects our emotions have on our bodies.

"And," he continued, "I'm a firm believer in things not classified as science—yet. Ella may have something on her mind that she's not sharing with you, something affecting her physical health. If you can find the problem and solution, we'd have a better chance of helping her."

"You think it might be emotional rather than physical?"

"I can't say until we do a series of tests, but I've been your grandmother's physician and her friend for more years than you've been alive, and I've never known her to be seriously ill. Oh, her blood pressure is higher than I'd like, but we keep that under control with medication. I can say that if her problem is emotional, once the issue is resolved, her health may be fully restored."

"I hope that's true," she said, "but you know how stubborn she can be. How can I help her if she refuses to tell me what's bothering her?"

"Then, my dear, you'll just have to find a way."

Heading for her condo, Madison prayed Doc Hayes was right. She tried to remember when she'd first noticed the change.

Had it been after the trip to San Diego? But no, it had been the day after the shooting at Jimmy's when they were going to visit the senator. Madison had asked about the friend she'd met at Ella's house the night before, and her grandmother had difficulty remembering Adelle's name. And it became worse after the San Diego and Yuma trip, if, indeed, she'd gone to Yuma.

Of course it would get worse after that, Madison thought with a sense of the absurd. Committing a murder would have an adverse effect on a person.

Her grandmother a murderer? Madison couldn't accept that. There had to be another answer.

Or was all this about Michael Bates? Madison was astonished to realize that, after years of barely living her life for fear of him, she hadn't thought about the man for several days. She knew she'd have to deal with him when he was released, and how to do that, she had no clue.

But right now, her first concern was for her grandmother.

Inside her condo, Madison opened the drapes to let in the sunshine. She even cracked open the window over the kitchen sink for some fresh air, then checked her voice mail. Most were employees from the newspaper letting her know about Marie's disappearance.

Where could she be? In the several years Madison had worked at the newspaper, she'd never known Marie to disappear for even an afternoon. Had something happened to her?

With a chill, Madison realized that too many things were happening, that her carefully ordered world was falling apart.

"We have a crisis," Jericho told the assembled members. "Otherwise I wouldn't have insisted on this meeting." There was no buffet, no chafing dishes holding delicacies to delight faded taste buds, no servants to attend to every wish. Carafes of hot coffee and tea were the only refreshments.

"We realize you're not a frivolous person." Number Five tried unsuccessfully to hold back a yawn. "Pardon me, but my old bones are no longer accustomed to so much activity."

"I understand and I appreciate your cooperation."

"It's the Woodward operation, isn't it?" Number Three said. "I knew there would be repercussions after eliminating a woman."

"Actually, that execution went as planned," Jericho assured him, "and you'll be gratified to know that the infant child is in safe and caring hands. You will receive a full report at our next scheduled meeting. But right now, we have an urgent matter to discuss. We had a breakdown in procedure. Evidence has been found near a contact point."

Other than a gasp from one member, the room went silent. Each person fixed his or her concentration on the chairperson.

Number Two spoke. "What was the evidence, and in what state was it found?"

"California, and it was the bag and weapon, which are now in police custody, from the Hawley execution. Luckily, the executioner wore gloves, so I believe no prints were discovered."

"I'm afraid I don't understand the crisis," Number Five said with a frown.

"The problem is not with the executioner," Jericho replied. "It's with the contactee. The subject provided shelter according to her contract, even transported the visiting executioner to the airport. However, she failed to properly dispose of the evidence. Rather she 'ditched' it, she explained, where it was later discovered. That's a severe breach of protocol. And she recognizes that. But there were unexpected events that distracted her. And, to her credit, she did carry out the requirements of her contract. However, the fact remains that, because of her negligence, the evidence from the Hawley execution is in police custody. She's been under surveillance since, and it ap-

225

pears that she's under a severe strain. I'm concerned that if she's questioned at any length, she could break and put the organization in jeopardy. That, my friends, cannot be tolerated." Jericho paused and looked around the room. "Therefore, we have a decision to make."

"What are you suggesting?" Number Three asked with a frown. "Surely you're not thinking of eliminating a member, are you?"

"I'm afraid we must, unless you have another solution."

Number Two spoke. "I can't be a party to that. That's not what we're about. The very idea is unconscionable."

"I agree. But look at what's at stake. Not only is our organization in danger, but each of us, professionally and personally, could be indicted. We could face prison terms and execution as well. Are you willing to die to save one person?"

"I cannot be party to murdering an innocent person."

"That sounds very noble," Jericho replied, "and I'm sure we all feel the same way. But consider this. Look at all the good we've done over the years, the countless perverts we've eliminated from society and kept from further violence. With the justice system overworked and understaffed, the overcrowded prisons, countless criminals are freed each day, free to walk the streets, free to prey on innocent people, and that cannot be allowed. We must not let someone's negligence bring us down."

Number Three frowned. "Didn't the submission process reveal this possibility?"

"Unfortunately, no. The psychological profile suggested a strong personality, one capable of overcoming unexpected events."

"That should be a lesson for us in the future."

"If we have a future, Number Three. At present, we're in danger of discovery, and the longer we allow the subject to continue, the more risk we take. We must resolve this problem immediately. Today. Number Two, who in the area could eliminate this issue for us?"

"I don't like this . . ." Number Five's mouth curled down, the winkles folding in on each other. "Our entire purpose is to uphold justice, to execute those who committed heinous crimes and escaped the law. We simply cannot execute someone because they're a danger to us."

Number Six said nothing.

The discussion continued for another half-hour, and although Jericho's solution was abhorrent to the members, it was with the assurance that they would see the necessity of such action that he circulated the ruby bowl for their votes.

When the meeting adjourned, Number Six tipped over his glass of water, then dabbed the liquid with his napkin.

"My shaky hands," he apologized to the departing members. When everyone else had left, he stood.

"It's done, Jericho, although I must say I didn't want to be a part of it. I only commissioned it because of our long friendship. But her vehicle lies crushed at the bottom of a ravine."

Jericho nodded. "As distasteful as it was, it was necessary."

"I'm concerned about the Society's future. I fear you may be venturing too far into a gray area."

"That *gray area* will ensure the Society's future, my friend. We will return to our agenda as soon as we complete one more course of action."

CHAPTER TWENTY-EIGHT

With Rico beside him, Dexter pulled onto the hillside street just as Madison was backing Ella's Hyundai out of the driveway. He pulled alongside, put the Tahoe into park, and approached the driver's side.

"I'm taking Gran for a checkup," Madison told him.

"Have you heard from Marie? Rico and I are checking it out."

"I hope she's all right. I never knew her to take time off, not even when she was too sick to work. It's just not like her."

"That's what I'm concerned about. We'll be around for the next hour at least. Any idea how long you'll be? I thought I might take my special ladies to a late lunch, early dinner, but if—"

A faint sound interrupted him, a sound recognizable on a visceral level, dangerous enough to make a man's heart race.

He froze.

"Shhh," he said to Maddy. They both went quiet, listening intently, then he heard it again, the unmistakable sound of an angry rattlesnake.

Maddy must have heard it as well because her face went white. Trying not to move his feet, he looked around, not sure where the sound came from.

When it rattled again, Dexter glanced over his shoulder to the edge of Ella's lawn. No snake. He took two cautious steps backward.

"Maddy, turn off the engine. You too, Rico," he said in a slightly louder voice.

"Dex—" Rico began.

"Just do it, for Chrissakes."

Once everything was still, he heard the rattle again. This time the sound didn't stop. It seemed to come from the Hyundai. Without moving, he bent down to check under the car. Nothing. He visually inspected the tires, then cautiously walked around to check from the other side. Still no snake. On the passenger side, he stepped toward the car.

The rattle was louder.

"Oh, my God." Madison barely breathed, her eyes huge with terror.

"Maddy," Ella whispered, her posture rigid, "don't make any sudden moves. I think the snake's in here. We have to get out."

Dexter peered through the closed back window. A rattlesnake lay curled on the back seat, triangular head reared, tongue flicking, poised and ready. And it was in striking distance of the two women he loved most of all.

"Ella," he said, his voice steady, his eyes on the reptile, "stay calm and don't you or Maddy make a move."

When he stepped slightly to the left, the snake's head swiveled to follow. It appeared to be at least five feet long and bore the typical diamond-shaped markings of a rattler with one major difference: its color had a distinct greenish tinge. With a sickening realization, he knew

A Mojave green, which, with its strong neurotoxin venom attacking the central nervous system, was the deadliest rattlesnake in the States.

"Ella," Dexter said, "do exactly as I tell you. When I give the signal, I'm going to open your door and grab you. Just let me lift you out. Madison, very carefully, slowly, ease your hand to the door handle. When you hear the signal, open your door and jump out. Got it?"

Without moving, both women acknowledged his instructions with a breathless "Yes."

"Don't move until I tell you." He swayed slightly to keep the snake's attention. "Rico!" he yelled. "Get over here! Now!"

Rico hustled over to Dexter, then watched him sway. "You've finally flipped your cork. I knew it was going to happen."

"Shut up and listen carefully." Dexter swayed and kept his eyes on the snake. "There's a Mojave green in the back seat. You stand right here and do exactly what I'm doing, and when the snake's focused on you, I'll grab Ella. As soon as Madison jumps out, go around and shut the door. Got it?"

Rico turned a little green himself, but he took Dexter's place at the back window and swayed slowly from side to side.

"Good," Dexter said, watching the snake's head follow Rico. He slowly, carefully reached for the front door handle.

"Steady, don't move yet," he told Ella and Madison, praying his strategy would work. "Rico, see how far back you can get it to turn."

Rico eased to the left a little more, making sure he was still in the reptile's line of sight. Tongue flicking, still curled, the snake turned slightly to follow the movement.

"Now!" Dexter shouted and suddenly everything happened at once. He flung open the door, grabbed Ella under her arms and yanked her out of the seat. Rico dove to slam the passenger door shut. Madison opened her door, jumped out, and slammed her door.

"It's okay now," Dexter said, holding Ella so tight he could feel her heart racing. "You're safe."

"Madison," she gasped. "Is she all right?"

"I'm fine, Gran," Maddy answered, holding onto Rico's arm. "Thank God Dexter pulled up when he did." Dex lowered Ella to the ground, and Madison dropped down beside her and took her hand.

"I wonder how that thing got in a locked car?" Dexter said, pulling out his cell phone to call Animal Control. "It was locked, wasn't it?"

"Of course," Ella said when she caught her breath. "It's been sitting out of the garage, but I keep the windows rolled up and it's always locked." She shuddered. "Could it have crawled up from underneath?"

"Makes me hesitant to get into a car again," Madison said, shivering.

"I doubt a snake can get inside a locked car," Dexter said, punching in another number on his cell phone, "but I'll check with Hunt's Garage to make sure." He waited, then told Ken, his mechanic, what happened. "Is it possible for a snake to crawl inside a locked car?" He listened, then said, "No, it's less than five years old." Then, "Thanks, buddy."

"Ken said that unless the car is old and rusted out with holes in the floor," he told Madison and Ella, "there's no way a snake can enter a locked car, especially with the windows rolled up. Not even from underneath. He said a car's cabin is sealed as a safety issue to protect the occupants against exhaust fumes and other odors.

"That snake did not get into your car by itself. There has to be another explanation."

Another explanation, Dex had said, and that phrase ran though Madison's head while he drove them to Ella's doctor appointment. Doc Hayes ran a series of tests, and they could do nothing but wait for the results. Ella had been cooperative, almost subdued, yet when they returned home a couple of hours later and Madison settled her on the porch, she felt drained and longed for a nap. Dexter made sure both women were all right, then he and Rico left.

What explanation could there be? A deadly snake in a locked car was a strange, freakish occurrence, something that had never happened before. Oh sure, in all the years Ella had lived in the foothills, they'd seen snakes. Everyone in the area had. But contrary to popular myth, snakes avoided contact with humans, only striking if threatened. Madison's grandfather had taught her years ago to slowly back away if she came across a snake at her campsite or while hiking in the hills.

Once, when Dexter had joined them to scout for large seating rocks, they'd found the perfect one about three feet in diameter. The problem was, a large brown Western Diamondback lay right on top sunning itself. When they got too close, the snake coiled into a defense posture and rattled furiously.

She remembered how her grandfather had taken her by the hand and told her to back away slowly. And when they had done this, the rattling had stopped. Then, when they made no aggressive moves, the snake uncoiled and slid into the brush. It was a lesson she had never forgotten.

But the most poisonous of the species in her grandmother's locked car? How was that possible?

Suddenly their lives seemed to be filled with strange occurrences. The campsite and the tote. Marie's disappearance. The snake.

But the strangest of all was Ella's mysterious trip to Yuma followed by her sudden lethargy and maudlin behavior. And it seemed to have started about the time of the shooting at Jimmy's.

Something was definitely wrong.

She'd first thought it was Alzheimer's, but now she was beginning to wonder.

Another explanation.

Could it be that all the events were somehow connected? If so, how?

She'd come right out and ask her grandmother, but Ella was already weak, and she didn't want to upset her further. Madison knew firsthand how sudden upsets could affect someone.

One thing was clear. She needed to do another search on the newswire service.

She had to get back into Marie's office.

"Keep watch for Marie's 4Runner," Dexter told Rico, heading east on Oak Glen Road. "We'll scout Oak Glen, then, if we still have some light, we'll check a few miles up Highway 38 toward Big Bear. When Marie felt stressed, she liked to drive in the forest."

In less than two miles past the Bryant Street intersection they were in open country. A few upscale housing subdivisions thinned to houses scattered here and there, some with horse corrals, until the ascending road reached the Y cutoff by one of Oak Glen's apple orchards. The heavily treed shortcut led to the small community, and they checked the parking areas around the free-standing restaurants dotting the curved, forested road, then the gift shops, campgrounds, and even the old stone schoolhouse and museum, searching for any possible place Marie might have driven for some tranquility after work. They found no sign of her. They continued on the two-lane road around the canyon, then took the Wildwood Canyon cutoff back to Yucaipa.

"I don't get it," Dexter said, heading north on Bryant to Highway 38. "Something's off-kilter here. Yucaipa's always been a quiet, family community, and suddenly strange things have been happening, especially to Madison and Ella. Now Marie's disappeared. I don't believe in coincidences, so that suggests another answer. I just can't figure what it is."

"Before the snake episode, I'm not sure I would've agreed," Rico said, scanning the rolling hills, "but now, I don't know."

By the time they turned northeast on Highway 38 and began the climb up the canyon road, the setting sun had dipped below the horizon. Dexter drove a couple more miles, but shadows made it too difficult to see.

"I'll pick this up tomorrow," he told Rico. "I wouldn't want to waste any more of an important homicide cop's time, so if you'd rather ride shotgun for someone else, go for it."

Rico flushed. "Cut it out, Dex. I'll be there."

This time, breaking into Marie's office was a snap. Just like a pro, she thought, moving quickly to the computer. She didn't even feel a prickling of guilt.

The digital clock on Marie's desk glowed an amber 12:13 A.M. when Madison placed her flashlight next to the keyboard. And since she knew the password to the newswire service, she wasted no time logging on.

First she ran a search on California murders with the words "senior" or "senior citizens," and similar to her own computer, the results listed page after page of crimes committed against senior citizens.

How else could she word it? She didn't have the time to follow each headline. What if Ella woke and discovered her gone? What if someone happened to see her small light and called the cops?

Not knowing exactly what she was looking for, she searched for the Yuma story again. Perhaps something there would trigger something else. When she found it, she scanned the basics on the William Martin murder, then did a search on the victim. Other newswires revealed astonishing additional facts such as that Martin had previously been arraigned and released on second-degree murder charges relating to his wife, Sharon, and

234

their infant daughter, Jennifer.

So he killed his wife and daughter, then he was killed. Madison sat back in the chair. Just like the Yucaipa murder, she thought. Hawley had been paroled after serving years for the murder of a child, and in both stories, a senior person had been standing by.

Was that the connection?

She did another search, this time entering murders committed against felons and was astonished at the results. Page after page of results in all states, dating back at least ten years. And the percentage of stories mentioning a nearby senior person was more than coincidental.

Her mind spun with possibilities, wondering if the police had made a connection. If so, were they investigating? Was her grandmother, at this moment, under investigation? And if no one had made the connection, what then? She certainly couldn't bring the articles to anyone's attention, not when Ella would somehow be involved.

Madison logged off and left the office like a sleepwalker. Something was going on, something involving seniors and murder.

But what should she do about it, and what, for God's sake, did her grandmother have to do with it?

CHAPTER TWENTY-NINE

When Madison walked into the kitchen following an afternoon nap, Cora and Clara were mixing shrimp salad for a light dinner.

"Where's Gran?" she asked, yawning.

She had called Cora after breakfast, asking if she'd spend the afternoon with Ella so she could nap. After returning home from Marie's office at nearly three in the morning, she'd spent the rest of the night unable to sleep.

Could it have been her grandmother in Yuma? As improbable as it sounded, she had to face the possibility. Had she actually killed someone? And, if Madison discovered that she had, what should she do with the information?

Even after a nap, her bones still felt as mushy as Ella's cooked cereal, and it took all of her energy just to stand.

"Cora shooed Ella out of the kitchen after she dropped an open jar of pickles on the floor," Clara said, chopping celery and carrots for the salad. Cora was toasting sourdough bread. "I think she's on the porch."

What wonderful friends Cora and Clara were, Madison thought. She'd always considered Cora as Ella's friend, that Clara tolerated her because of that friendship, but on the phone, she hadn't even asked why Madison asked her over. She just agreed.

When the phone rang, Madison almost let it go to voice mail, but the ID showed it was from the senator.

Madison longed to tell him everything she'd discovered, to take advantage of his years of wisdom and knowledge of the law. Or perhaps to simply talk it over with a good friend and discuss the options.

But she hesitated. As much as she admired and respected Senator Stone, she'd rather talk to Dexter. She did, however, tell him about the snake, and he was horrified. They briefly discussed the possibilities of Marie's whereabouts, then the senator gave Madison the information about the doctor.

"I'll be going out of town for a couple of days," Madison told him, surprised that had popped out. She hadn't planned on going, hadn't even thought about it, but there it was. Decision made. "To Yuma. I have some personal business to attend to."

Both sisters turned to stare at her, silently watching as she hung up.

"Yuma? Arizona?" Clara echoed, as if she'd never heard the name.

"I hope you're free to stay with Gran," Madison said. "If not, I'll take her with me, but I must go."

What a miserable waste of a day, Dexter thought, throwing down his pen at his desk. It had been glued to his hand for so long he was surprised he could even let the damn thing go. Administration had finally nailed him on paperwork, and Captain Silva demanded he get it done. To make sure, Silva actually stood watch most of the day, even ordering in lunch.

At three, Dexter ducked out the back door and was just turning the ignition on his Tahoe when Rico caught up with him.

"Want me to drive?" he asked with a snicker. "I imagine your hand's too cramped to steer."

"Go fuck yourself."

"If you'd just get organized and take a few moments each day, it wouldn't pile up."

Dexter stopped the car on Arrowhead Avenue, right in the middle of traffic, and reached over to throw open Rico's door. Honking horns blasted the air.

Rico exhaled one of his long drawn-out sighs and calmly shut the door.

"That's getting old, partner. You need to find a better way of expressing yourself." He rolled down the window. "Sorry, folks," he shouted. "My partner's facing a mid-life crisis."

This time it was Dexter who sighed.

Ten minutes later, they cut to Lugonia Avenue, which turned into Highway 38 once through the small town of Mentone, and then steadily ascended past homes and vegetable stands to open arid land before hitting the San Bernardino National Forest canyon. After all his time in California, Dexter was still amazed at how one minute he could be in the midst of town, and the next, be surrounded by rocky canyons and a heavily treed forest.

As he drove, he scanned the hillsides for a sign of Marie's SUV, looking for anything that stood apart from the landscape. He pulled over and parked on the gravel next to the dry creek gully on Rico's side, and they walked in opposite directions, scouting the bottom just in case, hoping they wouldn't find her 4Runner down there.

"You might have to face the possibility that she simply took off," Rico said back at the car. Dexter ignored him. Rico wiped sweat from his forehead with his handkerchief, carefully folding it before putting it in his pocket.

Dexter gazed up at the mountains, turning to look in all directions.

"If she's up here, if she's had an accident and can't get out, I just hope she has some water with her."

"Maybe she is up there and doesn't want to be found—at least not yet. Maybe the pressures got to her and she felt she had to get away from it all."

"Shut up, Rico."

Back in the car, they took the highway at a snail's pace as it slowly climbed the mountain, occasionally pulling to the side to let faster traffic by. Another frustrating half-hour went by before Dexter suddenly remembered Marie mentioning a favorite spot, a look-out point several hundred feet back. He scouted for a turn-around point, but finding nothing, he stuck his emergency light on the roof, pulled to the side to let the immediate traffic by, then swung around in a U-turn on the narrow highway. His tires hit the edge of a steep slope, shooting dirt and gravel down the gorge.

"*¡Válgame Dios!*" Rico clutched anything he could grab. "Are you trying to get us killed?"

"Get out and walk if you don't like my driving."

"God. I'm partnered with a nut case." Rico made a big show of pulling out his handkerchief and wiping his face.

Dexter ignored his antics as long as he could, but finally glanced over and chuckled.

"It's easy for you to laugh." Rico shifted positions. "You're not sitting in wet shorts."

Dexter howled.

Ten minutes later at the end of the deeply rutted turnoff, all laughter died as both men spotted the two sets of tire tracks, the fresh skid marks and deep gouges at the edge of the cliff. Years of investigating tragedies had left their mark, and Dexter dreaded what he knew he'd find.

There, at the bottom of the gorge a thousand feet below, was the burnt and mangled shell of Marie's 4Runner.

"Of course I'll stay with Ella," Cora said, washing the dinner dishes, "but why on earth would you go to Arizona? Is it business related?"

"I'm going for the newspaper." Although Madison trusted Cora and Clara with her life, she was reluctant to discuss her suspicions with anyone other than Dexter. "They want more information about a recent incident at a food bank," she said, drying the last cup and placing it in the cupboard.

The sound of glass shattering caused both women to spin around. Behind them, Clara stood staring at the shattered remains of Ella's heavy glass pitcher on the floor, her soft features so stricken that Madison felt sorry for her.

"I'm so sorry," she said, her voice wavering. "It just slipped out of my hands."

"Here, let me help." Madison tossed the dish towel on the sink and hurried to the back porch for a broom and dustpan.

"That was one of Ella's nice pitchers," Clara said, nearly in tears. Cora scowled, one of the few times Madison had ever seen her show displeasure to her sister.

Madison swept the smaller fragments into a pile. "I'd consider it a big favor if neither of you mentioned my trip to Gran. I haven't told her yet."

Just then, the kitchen door swung open and Ella walked in. "Is anything wrong?" She saw the broken glass on the floor and immediately helped to clean it up. She kept assuring Clara that the loss of a pitcher wasn't worth such concern.

Fifteen minutes later, Madison served strawberry ice cream, her grandmother's favorite, at the table. After making sure she finished her helping, Madison, carefully keeping her tone casual, mentioned her trip to Yuma.

"What?" Ella went ashen. "You're going where?" Her spoon clattered into the bowl. Madison rose, concerned that she was going to pass out.

"I'm okay, Maddy. Finish your ice cream."

"Gran, are you sure?"

"I'm okay, for heaven's sake. Don't fuss." She took a drink of water. "But why on earth are you going to Arizona?"

"The paper. They want to see if I can handle some minor investigative reporting," she improvised. "I'll only be gone a day, two at the most. Cora and Clara will stay with you."

"But I don't understand. I thought you didn't want to be a reporter."

Madison shrugged. "Things change."

The glowing crimson sun hung just above the purple horizon as Dexter waited for the rescue team. An evening breeze had chased the haze away from the Inland Empire, and the first stars twinkled in the sky. It was going to be a beautiful evening, one Marie would have loved. Every spare moment had found her hiking her beloved mountains, glorying in nature's beauty.

As much as he wished he could avoid it, he glanced down again at the wreckage. He'd tried to scramble down to her vehicle, but after several stumbles on the steep cliffs, he gave up. The recovery of her vehicle might have to wait until first light the next morning, but at least the coroner would get her out of the car.

His cell phone rang and it was Madison. Ah, hell. Why now of all times? The last thing she needed was more bad news. "Hi honey. What's up?"

She needed to see him ASAP, she told him, and no, it wasn't health related. She'd made a decision and wanted to discuss it with him. "Can you stop by?"

"I'm going to be on a call until late," he told her. "How about in the morning?"

"I plan to be in Yuma in the morning," she told him.

"Yuma? Christ-all-Friday, what for?"

"That's what I want to talk to you about. Please, Dex, meet me at Denny's when you're through, no matter how late."

★ ★ ★ ★ ★

It was nearly midnight before Dexter left the scene of Marie's death, and every fiber of his exhausted body screamed for rest. He'd stayed long enough for the coroner to recover Marie's charred body. Because of the condition, official identification would have to be done later during autopsy, but in his heart, Dexter knew it was Marie. He felt sick, but at least they got her out of there, and in a few days the family could have a service.

Now, the last thing he wanted to do was to meet Madison, but she'd said it was urgent, something about Yuma.

His steps dragging, hoping the urgency wasn't anything he couldn't handle with a few suggestions, he shuffled into the Denny's on Yucaipa Boulevard.

CHAPTER THIRTY

"Then I found this." Seated at a booth next to a window overlooking Yucaipa Boulevard, Madison handed Dexter the ticket stub for a round-trip flight to Yuma.

Dexter examined the stub. "You're saying Ella took that flight to Yuma?"

"I can't prove it was her, but Dex, it was stashed in her linen chest, and Cora said Gran had the Do Not Disturb sign on her door all that day. She could have gone anywhere and no one would have known."

"Why would she do such a thing?" Dexter checked the date on the stub against the newspaper clipping, hoping they'd miraculously changed in the short time since he'd first read them, but again they matched.

"This is preposterous. Ella couldn't commit a murder. It's against every principle she's ever held. And what motive could she've had? No, there has to be another explanation for her making this trip."

"What, Dex? What could possibly make her suddenly take a trip to Yuma, of all places, spend a couple of hours there, then return on the same day?"

Perplexed, Dexter sat back in the booth. At almost one in the morning, the coffee shop was nearly empty except for one elderly man at a front booth. The server ran the carpet sweeper near the cashier's station before disappearing behind the counter. Dexter thought about more coffee, but his insides were already churning. And he still hadn't told Maddy about Marie.

"Look at this." Madison pulled more papers from her briefcase. "These are just samples of what I found when I broke in."

"Wait a minute. You're saying you broke into Marie's office to get this information?"

"I had to. She wouldn't give me access."

"Christ-all-Friday, Maddy. I'm an officer of the law. I can't hear this."

"Forget that for a moment, and look at what I found."

"Forget it? You've admitted you've committed a crime, a serious crime, and I'm looking at the evidence. Aren't you aware of that?"

"Dex. This is my grandmother we're talking about. I can't worry about anything else right now." She took a page from the pile. "Just look at this. This man in Yuma dropped dead while talking to someone they called a senior person, and the man I interviewed at Jimmy's mentioned a senior woman with Hawley the night of the shooting. Both victims had a criminal past. And look at this." She pointed to sections she'd highlighted on the different newswire articles. "*All* of these victims across the country were felons, guilty of committing heinous acts."

Against his better judgment, Dexter scanned the articles, his fatigue forgotten.

"I don't know what's going on or what it has to do with Gran," Madison continued, "but look at all these stories. And think about what's been happening to Gran and me. Something's screwy here."

"I don't know, Maddy. It could all be coincidental."

"I don't believe that for a moment, Dex, and you don't either. I see it in your eyes. Look. All I care about is Gran, so I have to find out if she was involved. I'm going to take her photo to Yuma and question the witnesses."

"Good God, Maddy. Are you out of your mind? You're not a cop. You can't question witnesses."

"Nothing is stopping me from knocking on their doors and asking as a private citizen. Go with me, Dex. Find out if the Yuma police know anything."

"Christ. Give me a minute to think." He flagged the server for a milkshake to coat his fiery stomach.

As preposterous as it sounded, he had to admit he had the gut feeling that everything Madison had shown him was somehow connected. He didn't know how, but he was intrigued enough to do a little investigation.

But *Ella?* Maddy's conjecture would be easier to swallow if the perpetrator had been anyone but Ella Osborne.

"First, let's find out if she was on that flight." Dexter picked up his cell phone and called the airlines. After identifying himself, he gave the ticket confirmation number and waited while the agent checked. He then turned to Maddy, his expression troubled.

"Well?" Maddy asked, leaning forward.

"She, or someone using her name, traveled to Yuma that day."

"That does it. I'm going."

"I'll contact Yuma PD and let them know we're coming."

Dexter squinted at his bedside clock. Just past four in the morning. Christ. He'd planned to pick up Maddy at seven-thirty for the flight. If he got to sleep now, he could still get a couple of hours.

He rolled over, punched his pillow, and closed his eyes, but he kept seeing the articles Maddy had found, all murders with offenders as victims. Were they connected? And were there more? He hated to even think the word, but the evidence all smacked of vigilantes at work.

If that wasn't bad enough, the articles came from all across the country, so what did that mean? Was someone traveling the country, mowing down perps like the guy in *Death Wish*?

But some of the articles were dated from years ago. Whoever was doing the killings would have to be old by now—unless more than one person was responsible. How could that be?

And what the hell did senior citizens have to do with everything?

Cold dread forced Dexter up. How did Ella fit into it all?

A half-hour later and in no mood to socialize, Dexter entered the bullpen through the back door. Although it wasn't surprising to see other detectives at that time in the morning, he'd hoped to avoid anyone he knew, and grunted without making eye contact in response to a vice officer's surprised greeting.

After leaving a voice mail on the captain's phone about taking a sick day, he logged onto the CLETS database, and sent a request for info about murdered felons. He was astounded at the results. Most were unsolved cold cases. Then he did the same search on NLETS, the National Law Enforcement Telecommunications System, which operated similar to CLETS, only it went beyond the state level and exchanged information with federal and international law enforcement agencies. This time, gazing at the results, chilled dread prickled the back of his neck.

Then he narrowed the search with the words "senior" and "witness," and again, the number of results was astounding.

He stared at the screen. What the hell? Something was up; he just had no idea what it all meant. He hoped Yuma would be the first link to finding some answers.

The Yuma International Airport sat on a stretch of sandy desert south of the city, and when Dexter and Madison walked outside to pick up the car rental, a hot breeze slammed gritty dry heat into their faces. It had to be over a hundred and ten, Dexter thought, loosening his tie. Thank God he was living in an age of air conditioners. The roar of an airplane caught his attention. Overhead, a military plane was descending to land at the nearby Marine Corps Air Station.

They took the broad avenue into town, and sand and brush slowly gave way to landscaped lawns and trees.

Maddy stared out the window. "I keep expecting to see Russell Crowe and Christian Bale gallop by."

After a bit of zig-zagging, they soon pulled into the Yuma Police Department, a stucco and glass building landscaped with four palms on one side and two on the other. Dexter convinced Maddy to wait in the lobby and made his way to Lieutenant Ed Banners' office in the Investigations Unit.

"So why the interest in a shitbag like Willy Martin?" Banners asked after they shook hands. His neatly trimmed white sideburns and thick gray mustache with a slight upward curl on the ends reminded Dexter of Buffalo Bill Cody. With his white, almost platinum, hair pulled back into a ponytail, he could've been near retirement age, but he was lean, his movements quick, and Dexter felt his steady blue eyes missed very little.

Dexter told Banners about Hawley's homicide in Yucaipa. "I'm playing with a theory and want to compare notes with William Martin's murder."

"Whoa," Banners interrupted him. "We're not classifying that death as murder, Detective. There were no visible signs of foul play, and we don't have the lab tests back yet. I doubt he's even been autopsied. Backlog, you know."

"Can you find out?"

"Is it important?"

"Both vics were felons, and they could be connected. I'd like to know the toxicology results."

"Hell, if someone took Martin out, more power to him."

Dexter recognized that attitude. *He got what he deserved, and no one's in a rush to investigate,* an attitude Dexter had never endorsed.

"So what's this theory you're playing with?" Banners asked, a hint of amusement in his eyes.

"A witness mentioned something about Martin talking to an older person right before his death. Do you have any information about that?"

Banners shrugged. "All ages are in those food lines, Detective. These are hard times."

"Have you heard of anything similar regarding another death?"

"Sorry, can't . . . wait a minute. Now that you mentioned it, Taylor, that's my cousin, said something at the last reunion about a strange case, something about a child molester getting whacked. And I think he did mention something about a senior citizen on the scene."

Dexter forced himself to remain calm. "Any arrests?"

"Can't remember, Detective. Last time I saw him was at the family reunion a couple of years ago."

"In Yuma?"

"Taylor was the deputy sheriff in Spokane."

"Would you mind giving him a call?"

"Wish I could, but he was killed last year in the line of duty. Parolee shot him."

"I'm sorry," Dexter said.

"That's a chance we all take."

"Mind if I have a copy of the list of people in that food line with Martin?"

"You want to waste your time, no skin off my ass." Banners checked the computer, then after hitting PRINT, he handed the sheets to Dexter. "Anything else?"

"The autopsy."

Banners picked up the phone and called the medical examiner.

"Just as I thought," he said after a brief conversation. "They haven't gotten to Willy yet. You know how it is—hot weather, hotter tempers, a surge in deaths. Willy's packed in a cooler. He'll keep."

"It's just odd that a young man in his twenties would suddenly drop dead while waiting in line at a food pantry."

"Have to be careful in the summer heat here," Banners said. "It's deadly."

After three hours of hitting a wall with the list of names, Dexter and Madison had one more to check. Christina Sanchez.

They were pulling up to a taco stand when Dexter's cell phone rang, the fifth time that day. Once again the ID showed Captain Silva, and without a second thought, he let it go to voice mail.

"Will you get into trouble at work?" Maddy asked, getting out of the car.

"Won't be the first time."

After placing their orders, they found a table inside. Dexter nearly emptied his water glass and Maddy was working on her soda.

"What a frustrating day." She blotted the sweat from her face and neck with a napkin. "All this time and we haven't found out anything."

"Not necessarily. It looks like something similar happened in Spokane. I don't remember seeing it in the printout, so it makes me wonder just how big this thing is and who's behind it all. It has to be well-organized or we'd have a record of arrests."

After Dexter brought their tray to the table, Maddy picked up her taco and studied it as if she'd never seen one before. "Gran couldn't be involved in something like that, could she? I would've known."

Dexter nearly devoured his taco in one bite. "I can't imagine her doing anything violent, but at this point, I just don't know. Something strange is going on, but whatever it is, I want you to stay out of it." She opened her mouth, but before she could say anything, Dexter continued.

"Maddy, if this thing is as big as I'm beginning to think, it could get dangerous, and I don't want to worry about your safety."

"I'm already involved," she told him. "You know that rattler didn't get into Gran's car by itself. If she's involved in this, this *vigilante committee,* someone's after her for some reason, and I can't stand by and do nothing. God, Dexter, I can't believe this. It all sounds like a grade B movie, but it would explain so much about her moods."

"I can't keep watch over you twenty-four hours a day, but at least promise me you won't do anything without talking it over with me first." When she made no reply, he demanded, "Promise, dammit."

"All right, I promise. But that doesn't mean I'll stand by quietly while you do your own thing."

"Maddy, I'm a cop, for God's sake. I'm trained to 'do my own thing' without interference from outsiders."

"I'm not an outsider, Dexter. Someone made it personal when they tried to kill Gran with that snake."

Something in her tone made Dexter take a long look at her. The set of her chin and the determination in her eyes was very different from the frightened girl he'd always known, and he was astounded. When had this change taken place?

"We only have a couple of hours until our flight," he said, checking his watch, "so let's hope Miss Sanchez has some answers."

"I'm praying she doesn't recognize Gran's photo."

Twenty minutes later, they pulled up to a barren three-story apartment building, a boxy sandy-colored walk-up sitting on a concrete lawn. Sanchez's door was, of course, on the third floor.

The plus-size young woman in shorts and a halter who answered the door could have been attractive, but the hopelessness in her brown eyes dulled any spark she might have possessed. From inside, a baby cried.

Dexter flashed his shield. "We'd like to speak to you about Willy Martin's death."

"I already told the cops everything." She stepped back to shut the door, but Dexter stuck his foot on the frame before it closed.

"Please, Miss Sanchez," Madison said, "all I want is for you to look at a photo."

"We're not here officially," Dexter told her, "but you could be a big help."

"Why should I help you?"

"This is why." Madison took a bill from her handbag and tore a fifty into halves. She handed one to Sanchez. "You'll get the other half if you'll let us in and look at the photo."

Astounded, Dexter stared at Maddy. She smiled sweetly when, suddenly, the door opened wide enough to let them in.

"I watch TV," she whispered, then entered the apartment.

They took a seat on the sofa, which was half-covered in laundry. Miss Sanchez picked up the clothes and dropped them into a cardboard box on the floor. The baby, about a year old, Dexter guessed, sat up in an old-fashioned playpen and stared at them curiously. The smell of urine in the small room was overpowering.

Madison handed a photo of Ella to Sanchez. "Do you recognize this woman?"

Sanchez glanced at it and shrugged. "Who's it supposed to be?" The baby started crying again, and Sanchez put down the photo, grabbed a bottle from the floor, and gave it to the baby.

"Miss Sanchez, if you want the other half of that fifty, you'd better take a better look. Otherwise, I'm leaving."

Good God, Dexter thought. Is this *Madison?*

Sanchez snatched the photo, and with a disgusted saunter, took it to the window. "Kinda looks like that old broad, maybe if she had on different clothes."

Madison went pale, and Dexter slid an arm around her. "Are you certain?" he asked. "Look again. It's important."

With a sigh longer than Rico's ever was, Sanchez moved closer to the sunshine. "Yeah, it's her. Look, do I get the money or not?"

On the flight home, Maddy stared out the window and said little. Dexter fought to keep his eyes open. He still hadn't told Maddy about Marie, and he wanted her to know before they arrived in Yucaipa.

But she was clearly already devastated. How could he tell her about another tragedy?

He hadn't talked to Maddy about what the witness' ID meant; he needed some time to decide on a course of action. Even though Sanchez identified Ella, he still didn't have proof that Ella had killed Martin, or that his death was due to anything other than natural causes, and he wouldn't have until the autopsy proved otherwise. And he wasn't sure that Lieutenant Banners gave a shit.

But first things first. He had to tell Maddy about Marie.

Just as he was about to tell her, bells dinged in the cabin and the Fasten Seat Belt sign lit up. Dexter could feel the plane slowly descend. He caught sight of city lights below and knew they were getting close to the airport.

Damn. He'd waited too long again. But in a way, he was relieved. Maybe it would be better to tell her on the drive to Yucaipa. Maybe they could stop and get a hot meal, and maybe by then, she'd take the news a little better.

Although they managed to get into one of their favorite restaurants before closing, he knew it would take more than good food to make Maddy want to hear what he had to tell her.

CHAPTER THIRTY-ONE

Dexter stood next to Maddy and held her hand during the graveside service. Ella had wanted to attend, but because of her weakened condition, Cora advised her to stay home. To his surprise, Rico had insisted on attending even though Dexter had told him over and over that his attention would be on Maddy.

"We're partners," he'd said, "and even though you haven't fully realized that yet, it means I'm concerned, in one way or another, in everything that concerns you."

The man was like a pit bull; he locked his jaw and held on. Dexter hated to admit it, but his respect kept growing.

Maddy squeezed his hand. She seemed all right. Tearful at times, but strong.

As for him, Dexter felt sweat running under his arms and wished for a breeze. At least two hundred people dressed in their finest had gathered at Desert Lawn to honor Marie, and the blazing noon sun was wilting everyone. He hoped the minister would cut the service short.

He scanned the desert cemetery, glad there were a few trees to offer a cooling effect in the brown sand. Under one leafy tree, a section of small crosses marked The Garden of Angels, a special area where abandoned or unclaimed babies were buried. Because of the concern of a Yucaipa housewife, legislation was now in place that would make it legal for the mother of a newborn to surrender her baby within three days of birth without questions or prosecution. The woman had begun the process by burying the first abandoned newborn, a baby boy, in the cemetery. Knowing that some people placed this special value on life gave Dexter hope.

He was feeling as drained as Maddy looked when the minister concluded the service.

"You want to stop by your parents' graves?" he asked, taking her arm. "They're just over there, aren't they?" He indicated a southeastern direction with a nod.

"No. Thank you, but I can't face that today." Maddy kept her head down and urged him toward his car.

Would she ever recover from feelings of guilt? he wondered. He wished he could help her, but he was at a loss.

A thin woman about forty approached them. He'd hoped to escape without having to stop and socialize, but when she called his name, he had to respond.

She was a faded blonde dressed in wrinkled slacks and a sleeveless blouse, and was so lean she appeared almost emaciated.

"You're Dexter, aren't you? Marie told me so much about you. She loved you, you know, in her own way. She said you were a 'pain in the ass'—her words, not mine," she said with a grin, "but that you were honest and decent, and that if I ever needed something she couldn't handle, to contact you. Well, thanks to Marie, I don't need anything. I just wanted to meet you."

"Were you on one of Marie's committees?"

"Heavens, no. She helped me escape from my husband. He abused me, and told me if I ever left, he'd kill me. Marie got me into a safe house, then she helped me find a small apartment for me and my kids. She also set up some interviews for a job. I start next week at Clark's."

"I'm glad to hear such good results. I hope your new life is a happy one."

"To think that such a tragic night for someone else was a night of freedom for me."

"Tragic night?"

"Yeah. The night that guy got killed at Jimmy's."

Dex was so taken aback that he barely spoke. He went through the motions of nodding and smiling to the woman, but all the while he felt like he'd been punched in the stomach.

Pulling onto the I-10 West on-ramp, he thought about his conversations with Marie. Why hadn't she told him about the abused woman? Almost immediately, he realized. Since California had no waiting period to act on a missing person's report, he would have been morally conflicted if the husband had filed. Remembering how he'd almost hauled Marie to the station for suspicion of murder, he felt like shit.

But conflicted? He couldn't have been more so than he was right now.

He glanced at Maddy, sitting quietly in the passenger seat, staring out the window at the scorched land. They hadn't talked about Yuma since getting home, both stunned, he was sure, by what they had discovered, both trying to decide what to do with the information.

He'd been checking NLETS again, and NCIC, the FBI National Crime Information Center, nosing around every other place he could think of to get a handle on what was happening. The information had been staggering.

Someone, he was convinced, was going around the country knocking off perps who had, due to some glitch, either escaped punishment for heinous crimes or had served a light sentence.

And more than one person had to be involved since the victims lived in various states. Each time, the killer or killers escaped the murder undetected, so the system had to be highly organized.

And Ella? How did she fit in? If indeed she had killed Martin, which was still beyond belief, why would she have done so? Dexter had never heard her mention him before, so what was the motive?

And if she had killed him, had she been involved in the other murders?

He laughed at his own suspicions. Ella a gun-toting senior? Ridiculous.

"What's so funny?" Maddy asked.

"Just thinking about your grandmother. You know I have to act on this information, don't you?"

"Dex, please, don't do anything yet." She turned to face him. "I'm begging you. You said yourself that Yuma hasn't classified it as a murder, so what's the harm in waiting?"

What *was* the harm of sitting on it, Dexter wondered, just until he decided what to do? Ella couldn't have been responsible for all those murders. Not only hadn't she taken a trip out of state since she'd assumed care of Maddy twenty years before, but she'd been with friends the night Hawley was murdered.

So who *was* responsible? A murderous group of senior citizens? He didn't have it together yet, and he needed a concrete theory before he talked to Silva. Otherwise, the captain could laugh him off.

And, Dexter wanted to talk to Ella first. He should have done so before, but with Marie's accident, he just couldn't bring himself to cause her more anxiety

And that was another thing. Marie's accident didn't sit right. She was so familiar with that parking spot, had gone there often. How could she have driven over that ledge? Had she accidentally pressed the gas instead of the brake? But the deep gouges indicated that she'd braked hard, and there were signs of another vehicle behind her, a big one. He'd talk to CSI again after their investigation. So far, the results were inconclusive.

257

He kept thinking about the last time he had seen Marie and what an asshole he'd been. Even while berating her, even threatening her for running the story about Bates, he'd known she, like himself, had brass to answer to and had only been doing her job.

Still, that didn't lessen the crushing guilt that lay heavily on him, preventing him from drawing a deep breath.

Now, as he seemed to do a lot lately, he wished he had someone to come home to. Ella offered comfort, of course, with her warmth and food, but he needed someone closer, craved loving arms to hold him, to soothe him. But he had no one—except Pam. He always felt better after spending time with her.

He picked up his cell phone, and just before he punched her number, he hesitated.

Because he did think so highly of her, he couldn't call, not when he had nothing more to offer than a single night. Pam deserved more, more than he could give. She deserved someone who could be there every day, to offer love and support as well as receive it. And he wasn't that man—at least not yet. If ever.

Cora and Clara had a light lunch prepared, and after asking for Ella's approval, Dexter had asked Rico to join them. They could barely eat for all the phone calls, including one for Maddy from Greg.

Dexter noticed how pink her cheeks were when she returned from taking the call in the living room.

"Well?" he asked.

"He offered condolences," she said, keeping her head down to spear a lettuce leaf.

"That's all?"

She flushed. "He asked to see me."

Cora helped herself to macaroni salad. "He seemed like a nice enough young man," she said, passing the bowl to Clara.

258

"It wouldn't hurt you to get a life."

"I've been trying to tell her that for years," Ella agreed. It was the most she'd said all day.

When the phone rang again, Maddy sighed and picked it up, only to return moments later with her face ghostly white.

"It's the senator. He's not very happy right now. I told him I've decided to go to San Quentin and talk to . . . to that man as soon as he's released, and now he—"

Dexter sprung to his feet. "You decided *what?* You're going to meet Bates?"

"Don't argue with me, Dex." To Ella, she said, "He wants to talk to you, Gran, but you can tell him that my mind's made up. I just have to find out the actual day he'll be released."

Everyone at the table stared, dumbfounded, at Maddy. Gran looked stunned, but she rose and took the receiver.

"Of course she mustn't go," Dexter heard Ella say. "This is the first time I've heard about it. Yes, I'll call you later."

"Honey," she said, walking back into the kitchen, "you—"

"Before you lecture me," Madison interrupted, "please hear me out. Cora's right. I do need a life. You've been telling me that for years, but it took Marie's death for me to realize that every minute's too precious to live in fear like I've done most of my life. It's time I did something about it."

"Are you out of your mind?" Dexter asked. "You can't go to San Quentin."

"I certainly can. Dexter, Gran, please understand. I have to do this, I have to face him. It's the only way I can go on with my life. Look." She smoothed her napkin, taking pains to fold it without wrinkles, taking her time, Dexter thought, to gather her thoughts.

"We're all family here," she finally said, "at least that's how I feel about all of you—except for you." She smiled at Rico. "I haven't known you long enough, but you're a friend of Dexter's and that's enough for me."

Rico said nothing, but he took her hand and kissed it in an old-fashioned gentlemanly way.

"You all know Michael Bates has governed my life," she went on, "even when he wasn't physically here. Because of him, or my fear of him, I've led a quiet, *safe* life, hiding away, living in shadows, terrified that he'd show up.

"Well, I'm not living that way any longer. I want a husband and children, and until I can face my fears and put the memories of that night into perspective, I can't have any of the things I want. So I'm going."

"Dexter," Ella said, her face stricken, "don't let her do this."

"She's a grown woman and I don't know that I can stop her." Seeing the determined lift of Maddy's chin, he knew she'd made her decision.

"If you insist on doing this crazy thing," he said to her, "I'll go with you."

"No. This is something I have to do myself. And when I get back," she eyed him pointedly, "we'll discuss that other matter."

CHAPTER THIRTY-TWO

For two days Dexter tried to talk Maddy out of her insane idea, but there was no changing her mind. As much as he'd hoped she'd put the past behind her and go on with her life, he never expected her to do a damn-fool thing like meeting Bates face to face.

But no matter what he or anyone else said, she stubbornly refused to change her mind, insisting that she was going to go alone. Although he continued to worry about her, Dexter had to admit that underneath, he felt proud. At last she was taking control of her life.

One thing was certain. He had to find a way to go with her, or at least follow her to San Quentin. But he had to be discreet—not only because of her, but Captain Silva hadn't been pleased with his sick day before. At his age, he couldn't afford to risk his pension, so he had to come up with something. He needed to know exactly how long he had, so he called Josh with the parolee board.

"He'll be released in three days," Josh told him. "The paperwork's in order, so he's set to go." Christ-all-Friday. Dexter felt sick.

And when Dexter called Senator Stone, he found that Ella had already talked to him.

"Dexter!" Silva yelled. "Get in here!" Everyone in the bullpen recognized the captain's tone and froze. "Move your ass!"

Ah, shit, Dexter thought. He did a slow shuffle toward the office, hoping the summons was about skipping out on the rest of his paperwork, or a rehash about his day off. He wasn't in the mood for anything else.

"Close the door." Silva stood behind his desk, hands on his hips. With one glance at the captain, Dexter knew he was in deep shit. In all the years he'd known the captain, he'd never seen that shade of red.

"What the hell's going on?" Silva demanded, his jaws clinched so tight that Dexter wondered how he managed to speak. "I just got a call from a Lieutenant Banners with the Yuma PD." The captain almost spat out his words. Oh, Christ, Dexter thought, here it comes.

"He says you made inquiries about a Willy Martin and he had some results he thought you'd be interested in. 'What inquiries?' I had to ask, so this cactus puller from Arizona thinks I'm some hayseed from San Bernardino because I don't know what my detective is doing in his town. How many shades of dumb do you think I felt?"

"Christ, captain, I'm sorry—"

"If this happens again, if you go into another city, state, or country without telling me first," Silva said, his voice rising a full octave, "you'll find yourself working as a crossing guard on the midnight shift. Now what's this about?"

"Captain, I need tomorrow off."

"You need what?" Dumbfounded, Silva stared at him. "I didn't hear right, did I? You didn't just ask for time off."

"Something personal I have to do," Dexter said in a low voice. "It's important."

"You take tomorrow off, and while you're at it, take the next day too. Matter of fact, I don't ever want to see your sorry ass here again. Is that clear?"

Silva took his seat behind his desk and turned his attention to a manila folder in the center of his desk, closed it, and tossed it to the side.

"Before you throw me out," Dexter said, "did Banners' call reference Willy Martin's autopsy? Was it a homicide?"

His jaw muscles working furiously, Silva stared at Dexter. After a few long moments, he seemed to come to a conclusion.

"They found a pinprick in his side below his right arm. Toxicology reported traces of sodium thiopental, pancuronium bromide, and potassium chloride."

"Christ-all-Friday, that's a lethal injection cocktail."

"Instead of administering the drugs into an IV bag one at a time, the perp stuck Martin directly with one large syringe, possibly a horse syringe." He referred to his notes. "Used a large-diameter eighteen-gauge needle. Killed him within seconds."

Dexter nodded. He'd held the small hope the death was due to natural causes, but he'd known in his gut it was murder. Now he had proof.

Ella had killed Willy Martin.

But why?

"What's this about, Dexter? Don't you think I should know?"

Was it time to spill it? One thing was for certain. People were dying, and no matter if the victims were scum, vigilantes weren't the answer. No way could breaking the law ever be condoned.

But to point to Ella? A woman who'd taken him in over the years, who'd comforted him when his own parents died? Even though she was only ten years or so older than he, she'd mothered him when he'd needed it and he was damned grateful. How could he turn her in? He couldn't, he knew, at least not without talking to her first and giving her a chance to explain.

He'd tell Silva everything, except her part in it.

"Well?" Silva said. "My patience is running thin."

"I'm on to something, Captain, and it's explosive. But I didn't want to bring it to you until I had proof."

Silva's eyes leveled on Dexter and a long minute passed. The red faded, and Silva sat back in the chair and folded his arms over his chest.

"Let's hear it," he said slowly. "And it better be damned good."

Over the next hour, Dexter brought Silva up to speed, even fetching paperwork from his desk, all the while ignoring Rico's curious gaze. He also scrambled to come up with an excuse why he'd found the cases in the first place. No way did he want to involve Maddy or Ella.

"Is Rico on this too?" Silva demanded.

Christ, there it was again. Dexter shook his head.

"Get him in here."

An hour later, Rico helped Dexter hang the last of the info on a large board in the bullpen, including histories of all the victims and photos from all the various law-enforcement agencies they could think of, local and national. The data filled the board and overflowed onto the walls.

"My God, this is incredible," Rico said to Tish and Chris, his wounded feelings obviously forgotten. Silva had called a special briefing and all his detectives crowded around the board.

"And these are just the cold cases who mention an older person near the victim?" Silva asked, studying the board. "Who knows how many there are that don't include that bit of information. I agree, Dexter. There are too many to be coincidental."

"You suggesting the perps are all pistol-packing senior citizens?" Chris's voice was incredulous. "If it weren't so deadly, it would be comical."

"But it's ingenious," Tish said. "Think. They're the perfect assassins. No one would suspect them, I know. Since hitting sixty, no one sees me as a person anymore, not until I pull my shield."

Chris glanced from Tish to the board. "I know one thing," she said. "I'll never look at a senior citizen in the same way again."

"This is nationwide," Rico said, his voice hushed, "and it goes back at least twenty years. We have to notify the feds."

"We don't have enough information to make a case," Silva said, "no proof of anything. We don't even know how it works. Do they have a trained force to travel to different cities, or are there enough assassins who live in each city? But that doesn't make sense, does it? Just how the hell do they make it work?"

"And who," Dexter said, his eyes on the board, "is behind such a massive operation?"

"Do you really think it's possible?"

"If I didn't," Dexter said, "I wouldn't have risked my career because of it. That's what I did, and you know that, don't you, Captain?"

San Quentin looked nothing like Madison had expected. After taking Main Street off Interstate 580, she headed west on a two-lane open stretch of road that skirted San Francisco Bay. A grassy ledge dotted with trees and an occasional building, probably government-owned, separated the road from the water, and on her right, a brush-covered hillside gradually gave way to older houses.

She rolled down the window and stuck out her hand to test the temperature. The air felt mild, soft almost, and her skin drank in the moisture. She clicked off the air conditioning. The traffic was light, and she could have been on a Sunday drive.

She passed one stop sign, then a second one, which ended at the prison gate.

Even that didn't look particularly menacing. She wasn't sure what she'd expected—iron spiked bars enclosing the entire prison, she supposed, and dead trees filled with vultures. Certainly not the brown and white walls with a small section of sliding gates. Even the guardhouse looked like any government building. One-storied with several doors and a window, it even provided an outside pay telephone, a vending machine, and a water fountain. Behind it, Madison could still see the Bay.

She rolled her neck to ease the cramped muscles. After leaving Ella's house at five that morning and driving straight through, she felt exhausted. Yet knowing she was finally going to face the source of all her nightmares filled her with nervous energy, and she knew she couldn't rest until the meeting had taken place.

She pulled onto the parking area on the right, and glancing into her rearview mirror, she spotted a late model blue sedan pulling to the curb by the post office just outside the prison gate.

It looked familiar. Hadn't it pulled behind her when she'd stopped for coffee?

Her cell phone rang and it was Ella. Again.

"Are you all right?" She asked for the twentieth time since Maddy had left home.

"I haven't fallen into the Bay, haven't had a blowout and gone skidding off the freeway. Call Cora and go shopping. Do something, anything, because I'm not going to answer your calls for the next couple of hours."

As soon as she got off the line, she made her way to the guard station. Through the closed iron gate with a large red stop sign across the middle, she could see outbuildings, parking areas, and even more trees standing in front of the huge prison.

Two white turret-style buildings, each three stories high, with long, narrow gothic windows, the tops forming two arcs meeting at a point in the middle, were connected by a smaller main entrance.

At the guard shack, she inquired about Bates.

"His parole officer is supposed to pick him up," one guard said, checking the schedule, "but so far, he hasn't shown. Bates is a high-risk offender, so he'll be watched pretty closely."

If he was curious about her relationship with Bates, he gave no sign of it.

"So what will happen if the parole officer doesn't show?" she asked. "Will they drop him off at the gate?"

"No, ma'am. We transport newly released prisoners who don't have anyone to pick them up to the nearest bus station. Watch for a white van."

Madison waited in her car. Ten minutes went by, fifteen, then twenty, and the longer she waited, the dryer her mouth became. When she reached for her bottled water, she noticed her fingers were trembling.

Run! Her instincts screamed. Get out of there! After all the years of living in fear, after all the nights sitting guard with a gun, did she really want to go through with seeing the man who had savagely murdered her parents and threatened to return for her?

Dexter was right. This was an insane idea. What had she been thinking?

Heart pounding, she was about to turn on the ignition when she hesitated.

It didn't matter what she wanted, she realized. She had no choice but to finally face this man and put an end to the fear that had governed her life.

The clang of the gate opening caught her attention, and a white van eased through. It stopped at the guard post.

This was it, Madison knew. Even though every instinct screamed for her to run, she couldn't allow herself to do it. Too much depended on her confrontation with Bates, not only her future, but of the people she loved as well.

Concerned that Maddy might spot him, Dexter had pulled his rental car to a vantage point beside the post office and waited.

She was actually going through with it. All during the trip, he'd hoped and prayed she would change her mind and turn around, but stubbornly, she'd stuck to her plan.

If he weren't so exhausted, he'd be proud of her. He hadn't known when she'd planned on leaving, so he'd been on stakeout at Ella's home since late afternoon the day before, catnapping when he could, sure the sound of her car would wake him.

It had, at five that morning.

He needed go-juice, so he sipped stale coffee from his thermos.

Only two people knew he'd followed her: Ella and Senator Stone. Three, actually. Rico had threatened to walk if he didn't spill. Even then he wouldn't have let Rico know, but he'd grown used to the little shit's ways. Besides, it took too much energy to break in a different partner.

Ella had called in a panic, urging Dexter to talk Maddy out of a confrontation with Bates.

"You mustn't let her get anywhere near him," Ella had said, her voice holding an urgency Dexter had seldom heard.

Well, he hadn't been able to change Maddy's mind, but, he'd assured Ella, he'd be with her all the way.

"That's not good enough," she practically screamed. "She must stay away from him!"

He'd finally calmed her down, then, knowing he wasn't going to stop Maddy, he finally cut her off.

"I'm hanging up now. I'll let you know when it's over."

Now he scanned the lot in vain for Josh Gidding's Honda, although Dexter knew he might have parked inside the gates.

He'd like to get out and check, but he didn't want Maddy to see him. She had to feel she was doing this on her own, and actually she was. He only wanted to make sure that nothing happened to her in the process.

Finally tired of waiting, Dexter called the parole officer and discovered Josh was in the hospital's maternity ward. His wife was about to give birth.

"Jones was supposed to fill in for me," he told Dexter, "but I haven't heard from him."

After offering congratulations, Dexter was worried. Since Gidding hadn't heard from this Jones, it was unlikely he'd show. That meant Maddy would be facing Bates alone. Thank God he'd followed her. Whether or not he'd let her know, he hadn't decided.

It all depended on Bates' reaction.

He was just replacing the thermos lid when the gate opened and the van slid through.

Now, Dexter thought, taking a deep breath, it would begin.

Three men exited the van, and none bore any resemblance to the man Madison remembered. To make sure, she checked the newspaper file photo she had of Bates, struck by the absurd notion that she might miss him. Once she saw him up close, once she'd looked into his eyes, she'd know him, no matter how many years had passed.

Each of the men, two white and one black, were met by someone, one woman holding a small girl's hand.

The van moved on, heading down Main Street.

Madison ran to the guard shack. "What happened to Michael Bates?" she asked. "Wasn't he released?"

"They're taking him to the bus station." The officer pulled out a map with directions. "See? It's circled right here."

Back in her car, Madison swung around and followed the van

onto Interstate 580 West. Not long after the freeway merged with Highway 101, the van exited the freeway. Madison followed it to the station, but it pulled into a section with several covered platforms marked "Buses Only."

She found a nearby parking area, then hurried across Third and made it just in time to see four men exiting the van. She stood next to a bench under the closest sheltered platform and watched.

All four were dressed in jeans and blue chambray shirts, prison-issue, she assumed. The first one wasn't Bates—too young with light hair. The second wasn't him either, but when she caught sight of the third man, her heart skipped a beat. He was about six feet tall, muscular build, and still wore a mustache and beard.

Just to make sure it was him, she cut across the drive, moving closer. He turned and happened to look in her direction. When those dark eyes leveled on her, the shock of recognition nearly left her breathless.

It was him.

Forcing her feet to move, she ran, hurrying to catch him before he boarded a bus.

CHAPTER THIRTY-THREE

He sauntered in the direction of a Greyhound bus parked about twenty feet away, pausing here and there to look around.

"Michael Bates!" she yelled. "Stop!"

He glanced back at her, frowning, then, when he got a look at her, he turned around and grinned.

"For you, doll face? Anytime," he said with a leer. Madison felt sick. Didn't he recognize her?

"My name is Madison Young. You were in prison for killing my parents—"

"Ah, fuck." His grin dissolved into disgust, and he turned and headed back in the direction he was going.

She ran ahead of him and stopped, barring his way. People stopped to watch. His eyes narrowed.

"Get the fuck outta my way," he snarled, pushing past her.

"Look. I just wanted to see you, to ask why my parents? Why did you choose them?"

"This man bothering you?" a security guard hustled up to them.

"She's bothering me!" Bates said. "Get her outta my face."

"Just answer my question!"

"You really want to know, doll face? Your place was the only one I could get in to."

Madison was stunned. Could it really have been that simple? Had he really chosen their home simply because he could pick the locks? And all those years of nightmares, all the years of thinking he was plotting to come after her for some personal vendetta against her family or because she could recognize him, all for nothing. He hadn't known her family, hadn't even recognized her. She stared at him, barely able to comprehend what she'd just heard.

Just as he was turning away, an explosive crack echoed through the station, sounding as if someone slammed two boards together. Two more cracks immediately followed. Before Madison could react, blood exploded from Bates' neck and chest, and he collapsed on the street. His eyes stared vacantly at the sky.

The smell of burnt gunpowder hung in the air. Around her, people were screaming and hitting the ground, but she stood frozen, hearing nothing but a roar in her head, seeing nothing but Bates, lying on the ground in a pool of blood.

A blue sedan screeched to a stop beside her. Dexter jumped out and pushed her into the passenger seat. Tires squealing, he peeled out.

"You okay?" he asked, careening around corners, catching the on-ramp to the freeway. She heard his voice, but the words didn't register.

"Answer me, dammit! Are you all right? You didn't get hit, did you?" His voice cut through the roaring in her head. She blinked.

"He's dead, Dexter. Someone killed him."

"I know, honey."

They were exiting the freeway, and he drove the streets until he saw a market with a large parking lot. He pulled in and twisted in his seat to face her.

"What are we doing here?" she asked, looking around, her voice higher than normal. "Shouldn't we be at the bus station? Won't they need witnesses?"

"Look at me, Maddy." He took her chin in his hand. "Listen

carefully. Neither of us saw anything other than Bates go down, so we couldn't offer anything for the investigation. We'd be stuck there until they were satisfied, and we don't need that now. Look. I'll turn this car in and I'll take us home in yours."

"Where is your car? And what you are doing here?"

"I couldn't let you face him alone, could I?"

After Dexter turned in the rental car, they were back on the freeway, heading home in Madison's Saab. She stared out the window at the passing landscape, trying to absorb everything that had happened.

"I wanted him dead, Dexter. Over the years I actually wanted him to die. But like that and right in front of me . . ."

"Honey, listen to me. You didn't kill him. Even wishing him dead doesn't make you responsible. I wish you hadn't seen it happen, but you have to know you're not at fault."

"But—"

"Maybe you should make an appointment with a therapist to help you, a new one. Will you think about it?"

"As if I weren't neurotic enough before," she murmured.

Her cell phone rang, and it was Ella.

"Maddy! You're alive!"

"I'm fine," Madison said, putting strength into her voice for her grandmother's benefit. In response, she heard nothing but silence, then a muffled sob.

"Gran? What's wrong?" She glanced at Dexter in alarm. "She's crying."

"Thank God, thank God," Ella finally managed. "Bates' death is on the news, and I was so worried . . ."

"I'm okay, Gran. I'm with Dexter, and we'll—"

"Dexter was there?"

"I'll explain when I get home." After hanging up, Madison suddenly felt so exhausted, so drained of energy that she could barely keep her eyes open. She yawned.

"Tired?"

"You wouldn't think I would be, but I'm exhausted."

"It's the letdown after all that adrenaline. Relax and go with it. Take a nap. It'll be several hours before we get home."

She lay back and let her heavy eyelids close, just a nap, just for a minute or two . . .

When Madison woke, they were swinging onto the Live Oak Canyon Road exit from I-10. Yawning, she sat up. Outside the car windows, the black night was broken only by an occasional traffic light. She saw one other car and checked the dashboard clock—nearly two in the morning.

"We're almost home. I can't believe I slept after all that happened."

"You needed the rest."

She said nothing, only stared absently through the window. She kept seeing Bates as he hit the ground. And all that blood. She must have made a sound because Dexter asked if she were all right.

"He's dead, Dexter. After all the years of thinking about him, he's dead. I must be a ghoul because I'm not sorry."

"Honey, make an appointment with a shrink if you think it's going to bother you, but it's only natural you'd feel that way. And if it makes you feel any better, I'm sure as hell not sorry either." Dexter took a sip from a Styrofoam cup, then offered it to Maddy. "Want some?"

She sipped, but made a face. "It's cold. And full of grounds." She noticed a half-eaten muffin in the center console and realized she'd slept through his pit stop.

He pulled onto Yucaipa Boulevard near the Von's shopping center. All the businesses, even McDonald's, were closed in the strip malls on both sides of the boulevard. Only Denny's was open. Maddy's stomach growled, and she realized she hadn't eaten since the day before, and that was only a quick donut on the way to San Quentin.

"I'm starved."

"I was going to stop at Denny's after I got my car, but you want to have something with me?"

After ordering, she told Dexter about all the calls her grandmother had made during her trip to San Quentin. As protective as Ella had always been, that was taking it to a different level.

"That's Ella for you. Always concerned and ready to fight your battles."

"Guess it's time I fought my own."

"You did that, Maddy. You actually went up to Bates and talked to him. I never thought I'd see that day. You should be proud of yourself, honey. I certainly am."

"I wasn't sure that once I saw him, I'd be able to go through with it. But I did, didn't I?"

"It was a damn-fool stunt to pull, but I'm still proud of you."

She nodded, too much on her mind to do anything but accept his comment.

"He didn't know us, Dex," she finally said. "The only reason he chose our house was because he could get in. That's incredible, isn't it? My parents were slaughtered simply because they didn't have good enough locks."

"A lot of crimes are senseless, Maddy. I'm so sorry it happened to you."

She had no response to that, so she stared out the window onto the boulevard, trying to reconcile all the years of fear, all the nights standing guard against his return for her. What a waste of years, she thought. In the end, he hadn't even recognized her.

When the server brought their meals, the Lumberjack Slam for Dexter and a veggie omelet for Madison, she mentioned her grandmother's calls again.

"She called at least six times after I got to San Quentin."

"Guess it's true what they say," Dexter said, spearing a sausage link with his fork. "No matter how old your children get, you never stop worrying about them."

"She's always been concerned, but never this obsessive, not even when I was a child." Madison munched on an English muffin, then washed it down with a diet cola. "It's almost as if she expected something terrible to happen. But how could she have known? One thing's for certain. She didn't shoot Bates. She was home.

"Besides," she went on, "Gran couldn't kill . . ." Maddy stopped cold and met Dexter's eyes.

He took a drink of coffee, then carefully set down the cup. "The tox screen came back positive on Willy Martin," he said moments later. "It looks like Ella killed him."

"I don't understand, Dex. Why would she do it? She's never mentioned his name, so she'd have no reason to kill him. None of this makes sense."

"I'm not sure all murders do."

"But Gran a killer? Dex, you know how she was when I was growing up, all the special things she did for me. I doubt I ever went to bed without her preparing a glass of warm milk and honey for me. She and I loved to cuddle together, share a bowl of popcorn and watch movies. And you remember all the times she'd encourage my friends to come over and have cookouts at the campground. She always did the work, always baked cookies. How could someone that loving kill someone?"

"Beats me, honey, but not only did she kill him, the manner in which she did it was unusual, to say the least." He briefly explained.

"But where would Gran get the chemicals? And how could she get them on the plane? I don't know, Dexter. It all seems so complicated, too much so for a woman who might be exhibiting signs of Alzheimer's. She's frail in every way. You know that."

"I don't have the answers, honey, but it fits with everything. Think about it. Hawley's murder at Jimmy's, all the info you gave me from the newswire service. No one's been arrested for any of those crimes. It's as if the killer swoops in for the kill, then disappears. Maybe Tish is right about senior citizens. If they are the assassins, maybe they get away because no one suspects them."

"It sounds preposterous."

"But it's perfect, Maddy. What about the night Hawley was shot? Could Ella have done it?"

"She was home that night, even had company. Cora was there, Clara, and a woman I'd never seen before, Adelle something. I can't remember her last name. Gran said it was an old friend from her school days."

Dexter sucked in his breath. "Think carefully, Maddy. Did this woman have a straw tote with her?"

"I didn't see one, but . . ." She stared at Dexter, her eyes widening. "You think she's the one who killed Hawley?"

"I don't know, but that tote was found on Ella's property. It's a damn good lead, the first one I've had."

"Gran was acting funny that night. Nervous, edgy. She even dropped her whipped cream." She stared at Dexter.

"I have to talk to her."

"She hasn't been doing well, Dex. You can't accuse her of anything right now."

"Christ-all-Friday, Maddy. Do you think I want to? That woman's been like a mother to me, always there after my own mother died, welcoming me into her home, offering love and support all these years. Do you think I want to question her like a common criminal?

"But what else can I do? She could be the key to this entire thing. It could take years, perhaps, to track down all the victims and question witnesses. In the meantime, whoever's behind all this is still killing."

Madison was silent a long moment. Then, "Is it really necessary to stop them? All the so-called victims were deviants, weren't they? Maybe this organization is doing all of us a favor."

Dexter stared at her. "Can you hear yourself? Do you realize what you're saying? How can you condone someone outside of our system of justice deciding who's to die?"

"But Dexter, look at Bates. I can't be a hypocrite and pretend I'm not relieved he's dead. I'll never have to be afraid of him again."

Dexter reached across the table and took her hand. "I understand, Maddy, but you faced him. *You're* the one who took away the fear, not some assassin."

"But—"

"Look at it this way. I have no idea who shot Bates, but suppose it was this organization, and let's suppose, for instance, they decide they don't like the way you dress or the way you drive your car. Suppose they go after you for some reason. Or Ella, or Cora, or . . ." Frowning, he trailed off, obviously thinking.

"What?" Madison asked.

"They did go after Ella. That snake in her car wasn't an accident."

"God," Madison breathed, remembering the terror she'd felt when she heard that rattle. What would she and her grandmother have done if Dexter and Rico hadn't been there?

"And there's Marie."

"That was an accident, wasn't it?"

"From all appearances. But Maddy, Marie knew that spot. I can't think of any way she could *accidentally* go over that ledge. There has to be more to it. Too many strange things happening, and I'm not a believer in coincidences."

Maddy was silent again, her expression thoughtful. "I get it, Dex, but you just can't arrest Gran. Not Gran."

"As much as I love her, I'm still an officer of the law. Maybe she'll get a lighter sentence because of her deteriorating mental condition, or maybe I can swing a deal for clemency if she turns state's evidence, but I have to talk to her."

"Give me a day or two, please. Let me make sure she can handle it. You owe her that much."

"Christ."

The server refilled Dexter's cup and left the check.

"Then help me, Maddy. Who would Ella know who could be behind all this? I need a list."

"A list?"

"People in her local organizations, her women's clubs, her friends."

"She hasn't attended any of her meetings in quite a while, and as for friends, about the only close friendships she's kept up is with Cora and Clara." Her mouth flew open and her eyes met Dexter's.

"Cora," they said at the same time.

"She's perfect," Dexter said. "Cool, logical, and a formidable figure. She could easily command the kind of organization we're talking about."

CHAPTER THIRTY-FOUR

Ella an assassin and Cora the mastermind? Madison thought it too preposterous to believe, yet the clues seemed to point to that conclusion.

She dropped Dexter at his Tahoe just as the coming dawn was pinkening the eastern sky, and she felt too restless to go home. Besides, she didn't want to disturb her grandmother. She decided to check her condo and pick up her mail.

Could Cora be behind everything? Someone she'd known all her life and fondly thought of as the stern old maid?

Cora had been at Ella's the night Hawley had been shot, so it would fit. She had acted as if she hadn't known Adelle, but that could have been a pretense. And she could've covered for Ella in San Diego for the trip to Yuma. But if she had supplied the chemicals, where would she have gotten them? All the details needed to pull off such a feat were overwhelming—and that was just for one job.

Job? Hit? Target? Whatever it was called, Dexter was right. It was still murder.

How could she come to terms with such a thing? Dexter had wanted her to act as if nothing were wrong so he'd have time to investigate, but how could she act normal with Ella when nothing was normal?

And she still wondered *why*. Why would her grandmother be part of such a thing?

Yucaipa Boulevard was nearly deserted, so within minutes,

Madison pulled up at her condo.

After picking up her mail at the outside lockbox, she stuffed the envelopes into her handbag. For the first time that she could remember, she felt completely safe returning home alone. The living room lights sent a soft yellow glow through the closed drapes, and when she unlocked the front door, she could hear the soft instrumental strains from her radio.

She watered the lone plant on her kitchen sill and snapped off the radio. Walking toward the front door, she flipped off the hall lights, and before leaving, she firmly snapped off the living room lights and closed the door.

Dawn had brightened the sky by the time Madison tiptoed into her room at Ella's and crawled into bed. She fell asleep wondering how to ask her grandmother if she were a killer.

Even though he was so exhausted that every muscle ached, Dexter couldn't sleep. Images of Ella and Cora strapping on gun belts and mowing down criminals ran through his mind, and no matter the evidence, he still had trouble believing either woman was capable of cold-blooded murder.

He punched down his pillow and rolled on his side, but now he faced the window, and a sliver of light from the breaking dawn peeked through a gap in the blinds and pierced his eyes. Annoyed, he rolled over again, but the more he tried to sleep, the more awake he became.

Finally giving up, he checked his computer for info on Cora and Clara Barton, only to find, as he'd expected, that neither woman had even received a traffic ticket. Always the quiet ones, he thought.

Their home was off Wildwood Canyon Road in upper Yucaipa, and Dexter realized that in all the years he'd been acquainted with them through Ella, he'd never known, or cared, where they lived. He decided to check it out.

After throwing on jeans and sandals, he grabbed his keys. On his way to the garage, he left a vague message on Captain Silva's voice mail saying he was following a lead.

It was going to be another blistering day, Dexter thought, slipping on his sunglasses. Already the streets were crowded with early-morning commuters. He pulled into a fast-food place for coffee and a sausage biscuit and headed for the Barton home.

He took Wildwood east toward the mountains. Once past Bryant Street, the homes grew farther apart as the road climbed to over thirty-eight-hundred feet. Checking his notes, he took a side road just before the intersection at Wildwood and Oak Glen Road where the only home on the dead-end lane sat on a small mesa overlooking the valley below.

Dexter pulled to the side of the graveled lane under the shade of a live oak and stared at the mansion ahead. He thought he'd seen everything in his years of service, every race and class of human being, every style of home from a hovel inhabited by illegal immigrants to a mansion worthy of the Rockefellers.

But he'd never seen anything like the Barton home in this area, had never realized how wealthy the Barton sisters were.

Sure, he'd seen Cora's Mercedes, even lusted after it and knew such a car had probably cost more than he made in a year, and he'd heard Cora occasionally refer to their father's orange groves. But still, he hadn't been prepared for the home before him.

The block-long home, build in the Southwestern style, was a two-story earth-toned stucco with a ceramic tile roof. An arched portico with stone detailing and a bubbling fountain surrounded by potted palms shaded the front entrance. He could see the roof of a second building several feet in back of the main house, but he didn't want to get too close. How would he explain his presence if spotted?

Two gardeners were working on the front lawn, mowing and pruning, and while he watched, a uniformed butler stepped from the front door to speak to one of the gardeners. Not wanting to be spotted, Dexter eased his car back a few more feet.

He stared at the house. All the years he'd known Cora and Clara, he'd had no idea of their background. Certainly the wealth behind such a home could fund the kind of organization he believed was behind the assassinations. Hell, that kind of wealth could fund a small country.

He hadn't planned on what to do once he got to Cora's, but now that he was there, he decided to tail her for a couple of days and observe. He had no proof of anything, so he couldn't make himself obvious. She knew his Tahoe, so he called Rico.

"I'm doing some scouting," he said, not ready to tell his partner everything, "and I need your car. How soon can you be here?" He'd almost disconnected before he realized he'd never seen Rico's vehicle, didn't even know what he drove. "What do you have?"

"A BMW," Rico answered.

Something showy, Dexter thought. It figured.

After disconnecting, he turned around and drove to another side road a hundred feet down the canyon, far enough away so he wouldn't be spotted, yet close enough to watch if Cora left. He finished his biscuit and coffee and waited.

About forty minutes later, Dexter heard the low roar of a motorcycle. Rico pulled in beside him and whipped off his helmet.

"Got here as soon as I could. What's up?"

"A *motorcycle?*" Dexter got out of his car and walked around the maroon BMW. "Why the hell didn't you tell me?"

"You didn't ask." Rico tried to hide a grin. "You ever been on one?"

"A long time ago in a galaxy far away. Today my ass needs comfort."

Laughing, Rico climbed off to retrieve another helmet from the left saddlebag.

"Take it for a spin. You'd be surprised how comfortable it is."

"Absolutely not. No way." Dexter opened his front door and was ready to climb in when he saw Cora's Mercedes stop at the end of her driveway and turn toward the Oak Glen intersection.

"Let's go," Rico said, sliding his helmet over his head and climbing onto the driver's seat.

Dexter hesitated, glancing first at the BMW, then at Cora's car as it turned south on Oak Glen Drive toward Beaumont.

"You want to lose her?" Rico revved the engine to a loud roar. "Come on, Dexter!"

"Get off."

"What? Are you crazy?"

"I'm not sitting behind you on that thing. Now get the hell off the bike. Now!"

Rico moved slowly, like an injured party, and Dexter tossed his keys at him.

"Use the Tahoe till I get back."

Cursing under his breath, he swung his leg over the bike and roared away. He didn't look back, but he could picture Rico staring after him.

Getting used to the bike was something else. Even though he'd ridden before, had even had his own in his younger days, the newer bike took some practice to handle. Thank God the road wasn't heavily populated, and after a few miles, his choppy ride began to smooth.

He followed Cora down the hillside into Beaumont, a desert town about twelve miles southeast of Yucaipa.

Once a rest stop for train passengers from the Mojave Desert to Los Angeles, the town had withered in the heat for years until a boom of upscale senior communities brought new housing, golf courses, and big-box stores to the area.

Cora pulled up to a frame house in the older section and picked up a white-haired Hispanic man in worn jeans and a plaid short-sleeved shirt.

What the hell was she doing? Dexter wondered, following the Mercedes onto I-10 West. He squirmed and tried to ease into a better position. While he had to admit she would never guess he was the one on the bike following them, he wanted off the damn thing. He wanted to stretch his legs and rest his ass. He was used to a big, soft, leather seat that had molded over the year to the contours of his particular ass. But there was no time to stop, so he gritted his teeth and followed two car lengths behind.

The Mercedes slowed and took the Ontario Airport exit, and when Cora pulled up to the loading zone at the Delta Airlines terminal, Dexter pulled into the lot across the street. Watching the car, he called Rico.

Soon Cora's passenger door opened and the elderly man exited, putting something, a piece of paper, Dexter thought, into his wallet. Was she doing a nice favor by giving someone a lift to the airport, he wondered, or sending another assassin on a kill-mission?

He had to know.

Cora waited until the man entered the terminal, then she pulled out into traffic.

Dexter whipped off his helmet and dashed across the street. "I'm following that guy," he told Rico.

"What about my motorcycle?"

"Get someone to bring you down."

Dexter followed the Hispanic man to the airlines counter, watching as he checked in and, ticket in hand, followed the agent's directions to the gate. Dexter cut in front of the line, ignoring the irate looks from other passengers. He whipped out his shield.

"Get your supervisor."

"I'm Mrs. Tannenbaum. Can I help you?"

"The Hispanic man, what's his destination? I'm on official business and I need to get on his flight."

The agent studied Dexter's shield, then glanced at a nearby security officer, obviously undecided what to do.

"Hurry!" Dexter urged. "I can't lose him."

"Let me check." Tannenbaum stepped to the agent who'd issued a boarding pass to the Hispanic man and minutes passed as they conferred and checked the computer. Dexter tried to be patient, but he wanted to jump over the counter and shake both agents.

"His destination is the Akron-Canton Regional Airport in Ohio," the supervisor finally said, "with a two-hour layover in Atlanta, arriving in Canton this evening at seven. He returns tomorrow, arriving back in Ontario at eight."

A one-day round-trip to Ohio? Dexter doubted the guy would book a long flight to visit family or friends for just one day.

"Can you tell me who paid for the trip?"

"Sir, we're not allowed—"

"If you prefer, I can get a warrant and make all these nice people behind me wait while several detectives do a search."

With a scowl, Tannenbaum checked the computer. "The passenger's name is Jose Sosa, and the flight was booked by the Ruby Red Society."

The Ruby Red Society? Where had he heard that name? Then he remembered. It had been printed on the card in the tote bag behind Ella's. Like a bloodhound, he knew he had the scent.

If he were right, Sosa was headed to Ohio to commit murder.

The next thing Madison heard was the sound of pans banging

together in the kitchen, and the delicious scents of cinnamon and yeast filled the air. Ella was making cinnamon rolls! And the time? Good Lord, it was nearly eight in the evening. She'd slept all day. Hustling out of bed, she grabbed her robe and joined her grandmother in the kitchen.

"Sorry to wake you," Ella said, innocently spreading icing on the rolls.

"I know your game, Gran. You can't fool me." Madison poured coffee for both of them and took her cup to the table.

"You always got me up by banging pots and pans together, but this time," she said, sticking a finger into the icing and licking it, "you're forgiven."

And then she remembered. Everything had changed. She and Ella could no longer have cozy meals in the kitchen, not when her grandmother might have actually killed someone.

For a few moments in the comfort of her grandmother's kitchen, caught up in warm memories from the past, she'd actually managed to forget it. Suddenly her appetite dissolved and she pushed the plate away.

"What's wrong, honey? Aren't you hungry?"

Madison heard the concern in her grandmother's voice and she noticed Ella hadn't touched her roll. She saw again how exhausted Ella looked, the once-bright eyes now sunken and rimmed in a dark purplish color, the veins near the surface of her skin. Whatever was going on would surely kill Ella unless someone put a stop to it.

"Gran, tell me about Adelle. You know, your friend from childhood, you said, the woman who was here that night."

Her grandmother's face suddenly became so ashen that Madison felt a ripple of fear. Was this too dangerous? Might Ella collapse if she pushed too hard?

But if she didn't, Dexter would have to. She had no choice.

"I don't think she's a friend," she continued. "I think

something's going on and you're involved."

"You're tired, honey." Ella's voice trembled. "You've just gone through a terrible experience. Let's just enjoy the day and not worry about Adelle. Just think, Maddy. You're free! Bates is dead. He'll never bother you again."

"You knew, didn't you? All those phone calls yesterday, you knew something was going to happen to him."

Before her grandmother could answer, the doorbell rang.

Madison opened the door to the mailman and received a special delivery envelope. There was no return address.

Back in the kitchen, she slit the envelope with a paring knife. Inside was a sheet of paper with cut-out letters like she'd seen in movies.

Was someone playing a game? She checked the envelope again; it was addressed to her in care of her grandmother's address.

"The rattlesnake was a warning," it read. "You must stop inquiries into things that don't concern you. If you persist, watch out! Next time you won't be so lucky."

"What in the world . . . ?" Madison fell onto a chair and read it again.

"What is it, honey? Let me see." Her grandmother took the page and silently read, and when she glanced up, her lips had thinned to a slash and Madison thought she saw a flash of something in her eyes. Rage? Whatever it was, it was gone in an instant.

"Who would send such a thing?"

Ella swayed as if she were passing out. She touched her forehead. "Oh, my head."

Madison jumped up, grabbed her grandmother, and led her to the sofa.

"I'm all right, Maddy. Don't fuss. I'm out of my new headache medication, so could you pick it up at the drugstore?

The pharmacy's open until nine, and if you hurry, you can just make it."

Madison retrieved the old container from Ella's medicine cabinet and flew out the door, only to realize when she reached the car, that she'd forgotten her handbag. Rushing back into the house, she heard her grandmother's voice. Her old strong, angry voice.

"How dare you send such a thing to Madison," she said. "I can understand your actions against me. After all, *I betrayed the Society* and all that. But—"

There were moments of silence, then, "Yes," Ella continued, "I take full responsibility for my carelessness, but I hadn't counted on Maddy dropping in. When she said she'd been at Jimmy's, it shook me."

Silence again.

"Listen, you want to kill me, there's not much I can do about it, but—" She listened again, then, "Oh please. Don't think I'm an idiot. That snake didn't crawl into my car on its own. We've been friends for over thirty years, but you hear this. If one hair on Maddy's head is injured, I'll ruin you. I'll call Dexter and tell him everything I know about your so secret organization."

CHAPTER THIRTY-FIVE

After a two-hour layover in Atlanta, the plane landed at the Akron-Canton Regional Airport. Dexter had managed to catch some sleep during the last leg of the flight, only waking when the plane began its descent.

Keeping Sosa in sight, Dexter followed him to a car rental counter. Not wanting to be obvious, Dexter approached a different rental.

Comfortably seated in a Yukon thirty minutes later, Dexter tailed Sosa's blue Corolla as it caught I-77 South. His stomach was so empty it felt glued to his backbone, but he didn't dare risk pulling into a fast-food place.

He rolled down the front window and rested his elbow on the sill, savoring the fresh air and open countryside after the stuffy airline cabin. Outside, the temperature was warm, high eighties, a little humid, but not enough to sweat. When, an hour later, the Corolla took U.S. 40 west, Dexter followed him past a sign that read, Welcome to Cambridge.

Was that the golden arches just ahead on the right? Picturing a juicy, fat, Big Mac, his mouth watered. Could he risk a quick run-through?

The gods must've been with him because that little blue car turned into the drive-thru. He followed and had the first sandwich scarfed down before they pulled back to the highway. He hoped Sosa reached his destination damned soon. His stomach couldn't take much more of this shit.

Instead of continuing west, the blue car crossed the highway and pulled into a parking lot across the street from a grocery. A patch of green grass and a few trimmed shrubs rimmed the parking area, and Dexter followed as the car stopped in front of a bar on the far side. Sosa didn't open the car door; instead, he seemed to be waiting. Dexter pulled up next to a closed tire shop and angled around to watch.

What the hell? Was Sosa going to meet someone?

Dusk turned the sky indigo, and stars appeared, more than Dexter had seen in years. At any other time he would have stepped out of the car and enjoyed the evening air.

Just then, the door of the bar opened, throwing a sliver of yellow light onto the parking lot. Even from fifty feet away, Dexter could hear laughter and a blast of twangy Country and Western music before the door banged shut. A man and woman exited, their hands entwined. Dexter tensed. Was that who Sosa was waiting for?

Just then, the door opened again and a long-haired man stumbled toward a blue pickup. Years of investigations alerted every muscle in Dexter's body. Easing out of the Yukon, he cautiously moved forward. The roof light in the Corolla flashed. A man's voice spoke in a heavy Spanish accent.

"Are you David Pacer?"

The long-haired guy stopped and slowly faced Sosa as if used to being stopped.

"What's it to you?"

Before Dexter could stop him, Sosa raised his hand and opened fire, five shots in succession from a handgun, and Pacer went down.

"Who were you talking to, Gran? Who's behind all this?"

Her grandmother hung up the phone and slowly turned to face Madison. "Who's behind what, honey?"

291

"I know you killed Bates, Gran."

"What are you talking about? I was home all day."

"But you made it happen, didn't you? Is that why you killed that guy in Yuma?" Suddenly, as Madison put the pieces together, it was all making sense. "Is that how it works? You kill someone and someone kills for you like some bizarre quid pro quo?"

All the color drained from the older woman's face. "I don't understand," she began, but, as if realizing protest was futile, she said nothing more. Madison had never seen her grandmother look so defeated.

"I knew you'd guessed when you announced that trip to Yuma," Ella said softly, her entire body sagging, "but I hoped, prayed I was wrong."

"Dexter and I talked to a woman in the food bank line while we were there," Madison said gently, "and she identified your photo. We know you killed him. We just don't know why."

"So Dexter knows too?" Ella's voice dropped in resignation.

"I didn't know what else to do."

"God."

"Dexter talked to the Yuma police to see what they had. He loves you too, Gran, and wants to protect you."

"I suppose he'll have to arrest me."

"He mentioned something about clemency, but whatever he does, it'll be in your best interest."

Ella met Madison's eyes. "Do you hate me, Maddy?"

"Hate you? I love you, no matter what. But I want to know why you'd do such a thing."

"Halt! Police!" Dexter shouted, running to the downed victim. Sosa jumped into his car and sped off. Knowing Sosa was due back at the Ohio airport and they could nail him there, Dexter gave his attention to Pacer. He pressed two fingers to his carotid artery and felt nothing.

The Society's latest victim was dead.

Dexter pulled out his phone to call 9-1-1, and he saw a voice mail from Maddy. When he listened to her message about the death threat, he went cold.

"First thing," he told her after getting her on the phone, "is for you and your grandmother to get out of that house. Go to a motel. I know the owner of one in Redlands, and I'll clear it for you. Don't give your name, don't write anything down, just tell him I sent you and go straight to your room. Don't let anyone in, not *anyone,* until I get there. Got it?"

He glanced at the body, torn again between duty and his obligation to the only family he'd had for years. He made a decision, one he hoped he wouldn't regret.

Instead of calling the local cops to give evidence, he got the hell out of there before someone saw him. Once on the interstate, he called the airlines for an immediate flight home.

It was all so incredible to him, but facts were facts, and he knew now that Cora must be the head of the Society. But he still couldn't believe that Ella could have murdered anyone. Arresting her would be like cuffing his own mother.

There had to be a reason, and the only thing he could think of was Maddy. Somehow, there had to be connection.

He'd find out once he got there. Surely if Cora were the head of the organization, she wouldn't go further than to threaten someone who was, after all, her best friend. And then he remembered the Mojave green in Ella's car, alert, ready to strike.

Obviously the Ruby Red Society didn't let anything, even a life-long friendship, stand in its way.

At the stop light before entering the on-ramp to the I-10 west, a gray and black Avalanche pulled beside Maddy's car in the right turn lane. The driver, a silver-haired gentleman, nodded, and smiled. Instead of returning the smile, Madison tightened her grip on the wheel. Then she felt sick.

Was she doomed to be suspicious of every senior person who noticed her? She hated that feeling, hated what was happening to them, but until the Society was brought down and the members exposed, she'd better be suspicious—for her grandmother's sake as well as her own.

A few moments later, they merged onto the freeway, and just to make sure the Avalanche wasn't following them, Madison hung back to let it pull ahead.

Once settled in their room, Madison jammed one of the straight chairs under the doorknob. When she turned to her grandmother, she saw the horrified look in her eyes.

"This wasn't supposed to happen," Ella whispered, her eyes stricken. She seemed to shrivel, and Madison held her and soothed her with soft words as her grandmother had done for her all those years.

"It's going to be all right, Gran. We're safe now. Why don't you get into bed and relax? I'll make us some hot tea."

After helping her grandmother into bed, Madison brought her a cup of tea and sat on the edge of her bed.

"Gran," she said in a low voice, "don't you think it's time to tell me what's going on?"

Her grandmother wrapped her hands around the cup as though she needed to feel the warmth.

"I never wanted you to know anything about any of this, so it's difficult to talk about," she began. "I don't even know where to start."

"Tell me about Adelle, Gran. Did you help her kill Jeff Hawley?"

"Adelle? I didn't know her. I'd never seen her before I picked her up that night at the car rental place. It was all over by then."

"You picked her up after it was over? So you didn't kill Hawley?"

"Of course not. I just provided a safe place for Adelle, or whatever her name was, until her flight at four in the morning."

"I don't understand. If you didn't know her, why did you help her escape?"

"She was assigned to me."

"*Assigned?* Gran, you're not making sense."

"When I joined the Society, I had to perform certain services. I had to . . . eliminate someone, someone in another city or state to avoid a motive. In my case, it was the guy in Yuma."

Although Madison heard the words clearly enough, it was difficult for her to grasp their meaning.

"I still can't quite comprehend you doing something like that, Gran. Not you."

"The other," her grandmother continued in a determined voice, "was to provide assistance and temporary shelter to someone assigned to eliminate someone near me. Look. Do you remember your pre–Civil War history?"

"The Civil War?"

"Don't look at me at if I've taken leave of my senses. Go along with me. Do you remember reading about the Underground Railroad?"

"Something about points of safety along the route to freedom for escaped slaves? Gran, I don't understand the connection."

"People within the organization opened their homes to temporarily hide and shelter the slaves along the way. The Ruby Red Society is based on the same idea, only we're called on to provide assistance one time. More than that could be too risky."

"But what's the point? What do you get out of it?"

"Someone, another 'Adelle' or a 'Bob' from some other city or state, killed Bates for me, and someone else provided temporary aid and shelter to him or her until they managed to make their escape."

"My God," Madison breathed. "If it weren't so sinister, it would be ingenious. Who's behind it all? Cora?"

Ella gave her a sharp look. "What makes you think Cora's involved?"

Madison shrugged. "It fits. After all, she's your closest friend, and she's wealthy enough to fund such an operation. And, she has the personality to command the organization."

But she could tell from the closed expression on her grandmother's face that she was not going to give up her secrets so easily.

"Look. The less you know until everyone's arrested, the better."

CHAPTER THIRTY-SIX

Madison woke at dawn the next morning. Ella was sitting at the round table by the window sipping hot tea.

"How long have you been up?" Madison gave her grandmother a kiss on the cheek, then pulled the drapes to check the parking lot one story below.

Outside, everything appeared normal with no one lurking in a car with binoculars trained on her window—at least from what she could see. The first light of early morning gave the cars and pickups a dull gray cast, and Madison shivered. Closing the drapes, she made coffee.

"I'm so sorry I've put you in such danger, honey." Ella sighed and put down her cup. "I did all of this so you wouldn't be, and now look at us."

"We're safe for now, Gran, and that's the main thing. Once Dexter gets here, we can decide the best thing to do."

Ella nodded. She looked exhausted despite a night's sleep—if she slept at all. "I wonder how long I have until the police arrest me."

"Don't worry about that right now, Gran. Let's just wait for Dexter."

"I need to go to the cemetery."

"The cemetery? Why there, of all places?" Madison wondered if all the stress was causing her grandmother to have a breakdown. "It's too dangerous to leave the motel, Gran. You can do it later. I'll even go with you."

"Don't try to placate me, Madison. I haven't gone off the deep end, at least not yet. I simply have something to do before they arrest me."

"What do you have to do at the cemetery that's so important?"

Her grandmother's eyes filled. "I have to tell your mother that Bates is dead and you're all right. I'll go with the cops afterward, but first, I have to tell Susan."

"Gran," Madison said quietly, "don't you think she already knows?"

"Maybe so, but I need to visit her grave. You might think it's silly, but I always feel better after I've talked to her."

"I don't think it's silly at all." Madison leaned over and slipped her arms around her grandmother, breathing in the familiar scent of Ella's favorite soap and body lotion that had always given her comfort, wondering how she could stand it if Ella really had to go to jail. No matter what she had done, Madison knew Ella had done it for her. She'd find the best lawyer in the country, no matter how much it would cost. She'd do anything to protect her.

Worried about her grandmother's pallid complexion, Madison grabbed Ella's handbag, then with horror, remembered leaving the house last night with the prescription bottle, then rushing back in.

"Oh my God, I didn't get your prescription refilled. I have to go."

"If it's not safe for me to go to the cemetery, it's not safe for you to go to the drugstore. I'll just lie down a while and I'll feel better."

"I'm getting your medicine, Gran. Don't argue. If I remember right, we passed a twenty-four-hour Walgreens not far from here."

After calling in the prescription, Madison kept an eye on Ella and was thankful when she fell asleep. Why hadn't she heard from Dexter? Had his flight been delayed? She called, but again, her message went to voice mail.

An hour later, her grandmother woke, her eyes cloudy, her complexion so pallid that Madison grabbed her keys and handbag.

"Please, honey," Ella said, her voice weak, "don't risk it. We'll wait for Dexter."

"The hell we will."

"Maddy! Watch your mouth, young lady."

Her hand on the doorknob, Madison turned to her grandmother with a smile. "Love you, Gran. And don't worry. I'll be careful."

Dexter nearly went mad when he couldn't book a direct flight into any of the southern California airports near the Inland Empire, but he finally arrived at LA International, almost eighty miles west.

While waiting for his rental car, he called Madison. When he learned she was on her way to the drugstore, he hit the mute button and exploded with obscenities.

"Get back to the room *now*," he told her. "I'll pick up the prescription on my way."

Twenty minutes later, Madison sat at the Walgreens' parking lot exit and waited for a break in traffic, the refilled prescription in the seat next to her. She simply couldn't return to Gran without the needed medicine.

Once the line passed, she spotted a gray and black Avalanche idling on the other side of the street with the same white-haired man behind the wheel. At that moment, he glanced in her direction. Their eyes met, and she knew.

It was the same guy she'd seen before, and, he was waiting for her.

The car behind her honked, so she pulled onto the street and headed for Redlands Boulevard. Her first instinct was to run to the police station, but she'd have to tell them the entire story, and if the police got involved without Dexter's help, they'd treat Ella like a criminal.

What else could she do? Think fast, Madison. Get that brain going. She only knew she had to keep that guy's attention on her and away from Ella.

She hit Dexter's number on her cell, but it went dead. Damn! In her frantic rush to get to the motel last night, she'd forgotten her charger.

Just then, a motorcycle cop, lights silently flashing, exited the mortuary just ahead on the right and stopped traffic directly in front of Madison. Not now, she thought. She couldn't stop now.

From the mortuary's drive, two more motorcycle cops led a funeral procession onto the street.

Come on, come on. Her fingers drummed the steering wheel. She glanced into the rearview mirror, and even though she didn't see the Avalanche, she felt that prickling sensation and knew he was close behind.

Finally, when she could see the last car in the long line, she had an idea. Would it work? It had to; she had no other option.

She pulled up beside the motorcycle cop. "I was held up in traffic," she told him, "but I need to be in that procession!"

He nodded, and when the last of the cars entered the street, he waved her in and pulled in behind her.

Safe for now, she thought as the line of cars headed east. To Desert Lawn? No matter where they were going, at least she had more time. She'd figure out what to do once they got there.

When Dexter arrived at the motel, he had to knock a couple of times before the door, held by the safety chain, cracked open.

"Sorry. We don't want any," Ella said, her eyes pleading with him. She slammed the door in his face.

What the hell? Dexter knew Ella was trying to say something, but what? Before he could sort it out, he heard a click from inside, and to his astonishment, Senator Logan Stone opened the door.

"Come in, Dexter," he said.

"What are you doing here?" Dexter scanned the room. "Where's Maddy, Logan? Did you take her somewhere safe?"

"I'm sorry to see you, my friend," Senator Stone said smoothly, "but I suppose it was inevitable." As usual, he was impeccably dressed in trousers, a pullover, and a sports jacket. "Better still, I'm sorry you saw me."

"I don't understand. Is Maddy all right?"

"That's what I'm trying to find out. You might as well have a seat." The senator spoke as calmly as if they were at a social gathering. "I was just about to make a call."

Once he was on the phone, his voice changed, became the brisk, professional tone that was so well known on Capitol Hill.

"This is Jericho One," he told whoever answered. "Report at once." He clicked off. "It won't be long now," he told Dexter and Ella.

"What won't be long?" Dexter asked, sinking into a chair next to the senator. "What are you doing here? How did you know where I sent Maddy and Ella?"

The senator's phone buzzed. Ignoring Dexter's questions, he answered it, and after listening for a minute, snapped, "Abort! Yes! This is Jericho One, and I'm ordering you to abort your assignment!"

He snapped his phone shut. "Damn," he muttered. "They're instructed not to take calls at the last minute in case of sabotage."

"Sabotage?" Dexter asked, rising from the chair. "What the hell's going on, Logan? Where's Maddy?" His hand slid toward his concealed weapon. "If I don't get some answers damned quick, I'll haul you out of here like a common criminal."

"I don't have time for explanations, so cut the melodrama, Dexter. Right now Maddy's alive, and I'm trying to make sure she stays that way. If you want to help, sit down, shut up, and let me do what I must." He pushed a tab on his phone again.

"Please, Dexter." Ella pleaded. "He's the only one who can save her."

Dexter sat.

"Mr. Chauncey," the senator said into the phone, "I need a GPS on Madison's Saab. Immediately."

"Where is she?" Dexter asked Ella in a low voice. "Why isn't she here with you?"

When Ella explained about her pills, Dexter cursed. Damn, he should've known Maddy would risk anything if she thought Ella was in danger. He should've been here for her, not chasing some idiot in Ohio.

"Wait a minute," he said. "When you said Logan could save her, what did you mean? What does he have to do with it?"

"He ordered the hit, and he's the only one who can stop it."

"What?" Dexter gaped at the senator, trying to make sense of what Ella was saying.

"He's the founder and chairman of the Ruby Red Society."

Stunned, Dexter stared at the senator, who was still on the phone. *"Logan?"*

"When the death threats didn't stop Maddy from investigating, he and his advisor approved the hits on Maddy and me, but Logan said he couldn't go through with it. He came here to get us to safety. He didn't expect to find Maddy gone."

Dexter could scarcely believe what he was hearing.

"What about Cora?" he demanded.

"Cora? What about her? She has nothing to do with the organization."

"But she took someone to the airport, and—"

"She was doing Logan a favor. She had no idea what was going on. I don't have time to talk about it now."

The senator finished his call.

"Did you find her?" Ella asked.

"She's leading my man on a chase to the cemetery," he said admiringly. "She's quite a resourceful young woman, isn't she?"

"Logan," Ella said, a hint of desperation in her voice, "did you stop the hit?"

"I'm about to make one last try." He picked up the phone. "Unfortunately, and to my lasting regret, it may be too late. My people are well-trained."

"You must stop it," Ella told him. "Otherwise, you'll have murdered your own daughter."

"My daughter? What are you prattling about, Ella? Have you taken leave of your senses?"

Dexter's stunned gaze went from Ella to Logan, trying to absorb it all. Logan Stone—the man he'd admired since his early days on the force, who, after winning the senate seat, continued his legislative work on new crime bills—the chairman of a murderous organization? It couldn't be. Now Ella was saying Logan was Maddy's father? Had everyone gone mad?

"You heard me, Logan," Ella said. "Madison is your daughter."

"That's preposterous."

"Do you think for one minute that I didn't know about your affair with my daughter? She told me everything. She was in love with you. She was even going to divorce Daniel for you. But when he was mustered out of the service, she felt she should give her marriage another try. Then she found out she was pregnant—with your child."

"Madison is Daniel's' daughter," Senator Stone insisted, "not mine."

"That's what Susan chose to tell you."

Dexter watched the exchange between Ella and Logan. He'd always known the senator had a special relationship with Madison, but he never once suspected it went beyond simply fondness.

"I don't believe you," the senator said, but Dexter, noticing how pale he'd become, wondered if that was true.

"Check his medical records," Ella said. "Daniel took a hit in the groin during the invasion. After that, he couldn't father children. Madison's yours, Logan. Do a DNA check. And look at this," she added, taking a photograph from her handbag. "It's a recent headshot to update Maddy's column. If you look at it with an open mind, you'll see the truth."

Dexter, watching Logan study the photograph, saw the realization spread across his face.

"My God," the senator breathed, "it could be a photo of my mother taken when she was a young woman. Why didn't I see it? I should have recognized the tilt of the nose, the arch of the brow."

"You've always had a special relationship with her," Ella said, "and I think that inside, you always knew. Stop the hit, Logan. You must save her."

Logan jumped up. "I don't know that I can. But I can try. Come on!"

He flew out the door with Ella and Dexter right behind him.

CHAPTER THIRTY-SEVEN

It wasn't until the funeral procession took the Cherry Valley exit from I-10 that Madison knew for certain they were heading for Desert Lawn Cemetery. With the motorcycle cop behind her, she'd felt safe during the drive from Redlands, but they would soon reach their destination. What would she do then?

At the stop sign, she glanced back at the freeway's exit, hoping the police escort caused the Avalanche to give up the chase. She didn't see it, but she didn't have time to linger; the cop behind her revved his engine. She had to move on.

She sped up slightly to join the procession. When it reached the cemetery, the motorcycle officers took a position near the entrance and sat patiently until the entire line of cars entered. Then they headed back to the freeway.

Her protection was gone! Madison's heart dropped to her toes. She checked the rearview mirror. No sign of him, but how much time did she have?

She pulled out of the line, pausing long enough for the mourners to cross to the grassy lawn. She had to get moving, but the number of people getting out of their cars and crossing the road to the lawn was staggering. If she could just move forward a few feet, she could cut through to that short driveway ahead, circle around, and make her escape. She only managed to inch ahead a few feet before pausing to let more people cross.

She checked her rearview mirror again. The Avalanche was making the turn into the cemetery.

What should she do? Try to leave or take refuge with the group of mourners? She doubted her assassin would take the risk and shoot as long as she was in a crowd.

The Avalanche slowly cruised past the entrance and she knew as soon as he spotted her. He paused and obviously waited to see what she would do.

Should she make a run for the freeway? But Desert Lawn Drive wasn't heavily populated, and he could fire at her from his vehicle or push her off the road. The crowd of mourners didn't provide much safety either, but, she thought, perhaps she could get someone to call 9-1-1.

Making a fast decision, she almost jumped out of the car and hurried to join the people at the gravesite. Behind her, the Avalanche pulled to the curb.

Almost running, she wove through the crowd, hoping to find someone she could ask to call the police. But she had to be careful. She didn't know what the assassin would do and she didn't want to endanger anyone in the crowd.

"Excuse me," she whispered to a young couple standing close to the gravesite. The minister was preparing to begin the service. "I need your help. My cell phone's dead and someone's following me. Call the police." When they looked at her skeptically, her voice rose. "Please. He's here now. I'm in danger, and there's no time to explain."

To her relief, the woman pulled her cell from her handbag and made the call. But at that same moment, Madison heard a slight movement behind her, then felt something pressed against her back.

"Don't move," a man whispered in her ear. "I have a gun. If you make any noise, I'll open fire on everyone here."

Stifling a scream, Madison threw a panicked glance at the couple next to her, but they'd edged away after making the call, and everyone else's attention was focused on the minister.

Oh, God, what could she do?

Taking her arm, he weaved her through the crowd. She stumbled over metal markers and gravesites, kicked over vases of flowers left for loved ones, all polite respect gone as she followed his lead, desperately thinking what to do. She just couldn't go quietly to her death. She had to get her brain working.

"You haven't killed anyone yet," she told him, fear making it difficult to catch her breath. "You could let me go and leave."

"Shut up," he said, pulling her along.

"Don't do it. The police know all about the Society, so save yourself. You could leave right now and not be guilty of anything."

"I have my orders," he muttered.

"But she's going to prison. Don't you understand? Everyone involved will be arrested."

For the first time, he halted and looked directly at her. "Lady, you don't know what you're talking about."

They had nearly reached the edge of the lawn, and Madison knew she wouldn't have a chance if he managed to get her into his car.

She stumbled. When she glanced down she saw they were standing beside her father's grave. A ceramic vase filled with summer flowers stood between it and her mother's.

Her eyes filling with tears, she sank to the ground.

"Get up," the man said fiercely, pulling her to her knees.

"I can't get up," she said, yanking her arm free. "I twisted my ankle," she lied, rubbing the offending ankle, trying to buy time. Where were the police? Why hadn't they come?

Mourners from the open gravesite walked past them toward their cars. The service must be over, Madison realized, and if she didn't think of something fast, she'd be alone with her killer. Help me, she prayed silently. What should I do?

From somewhere in back of the cemetery, a lawnmower cranked up, and suddenly, time seemed to stand still. Long-buried memories burst out of suppression and Madison could once again see her parents.

She was about five and was watching her parents dance funny in the back yard, practicing self-defense moves, she later discovered. When they were over, her father cranked up the lawnmower, and her mother . . . Warm memories washed over Madison as if she were embraced in loving arms, and she could finally see her beautiful mother, feel again the security of her arms as Susan picked up her daughter.

Holding Maddy closely, Susan danced on the soft grass, singing, "You Light Up My Life," and Maddy felt her mother's blonde hair brushing against her cheek, smelled the soft fragrance of strawberries from the shampoo she'd loved. Tears streamed down Madison's cheeks as she drank in every detail in her memory, washing away the burdens of guilt and remorse she'd carried for most of her life, leaving behind only love.

"I love you, Mom," she whispered. "I'll always remember you." A sudden breath of air caressed Madison's cheek.

In that moment, everything seemed to fall into place. Sirens sounded in the distance, and her would-be assassin turned to look.

Madison sprang to her feet, and, remembering what he father had taught her mother, stomped on the assassin's foot and jabbed her elbow into his side. He folded, and the gun tumbled to the ground.

"Get help!" Madison screamed to a woman leaving the service. Frozen, the woman stood watching. Madison grabbed the vase of flowers and smashed them on the assassin's head. He crumpled onto the grass and was still. Grabbing the gun, Madison pointed it at him and waited for the police.

Sirens wailed louder now, and three police cars flew into the cemetery's entrance, screeching to a halt near the downed man. Weapons drawn, several officers slowly approached.

"Drop the weapon, lady!" one uniformed cop yelled at Madison, and she realized he thought she was the armed assailant.

Before she could explain, the senator's car sped into the cemetery and slammed to a halt next to the police cars. Waving off the officers, Senator Stone hurried to Madison's side and took the gun from her hand.

"Thank God I was in time," he said, folding her into his embrace.

Just then, the assassin moaned and tried to get to his feet. Dexter yelled something to one cop and ran after the senator. Ella followed.

"Gran!" Madison shouted. "Stay back!"

At that moment, the assassin staggered to his feet and turned toward the senator. Senator Stone fired, once, twice, a third time, and the man fell to the ground.

"Drop your weapon! Now!" an officer shouted, but the senator didn't comply. Instead, gun still in his hand, he turned toward the officer. Two shots rang out, and the senator went down.

"Cease fire!" Dexter shouted, running to the senator. "That's United States Senator Logan Stone!" In the background, sirens wailed as more emergency vehicles approached the cemetery.

Yanking off his jacket, Dexter crouched down beside the older man and pressed it to the gushing chest wounds. The senator was barely breathing, but he was conscious. Madison crouched down and cradled his head, her stunned gaze raised to Dexter.

"I don't understand. What's he doing here?"

The senator's tried to speak, then ran his tongue over his lips.

"I'm so sorry, my dear," he said in a raspy voice. "Maybe

things would have been different if I had known. Maybe I would have been different. But at least," he said in a voice so low that Madison could scarcely hear, "if I'm lucky enough to see your mother, I can tell her I saved our daughter's life."

With a sigh, he went still.

CHAPTER THIRTY-EIGHT

Three days later, Madison, along with her attorney, emerged from a special room inside the federal building in Riverside, drained after a grueling morning of giving a deposition.

Dexter and Rico greeted them in the hallway.

"Get some rest," her attorney advised Madison. "I'm sure your part in all of this is over." After she thanked him, he took his leave.

"You okay?" Dexter asked, taking her arm to guide her outside.

"Has Gran been excused yet?" she asked, her gaze sweeping the hallway. Even though Madison desperately needed rest, she was more concerned about her grandmother, who'd also been called that morning to give testimony.

"She's still inside, but I'm sure they're keeping watch on her health."

After a thorough search of the senator's home and offices, no records of the Society were found, and no names of the committee members were discovered. It was as if the Ruby Red Society had been a figment of someone's warped imagination. In desperation, Ella had been offered immunity from prosecution in exchange for turning state's evidence.

Madison knew, from talking to her grandmother, that Ella didn't know anything about the organization other than her own part. But still, she worried about the outcome. Once she saw her grandmother's face after the hearing, she'd know.

At the top of the courthouse steps, a crowd of reporters and TV crews were waiting, shouting questions as they converged on her, enclosing her in a tight little knot.

"Did you know you were the senator's daughter?" one heavily made-up blonde shouted, shoving the microphone in Madison's face. Dexter pushed it away and kept clearing a path. "How do you feel knowing your father murdered thousands of people?" another shouted.

Madison tugged Dexter's arm. "Wait. I want to answer that." Immediately the crowd quieted.

"I was always fond of the senator," Madison said, "and in the end, he protected me and I'm thankful for that. But as far as I'm concerned, my father has been buried alongside my mother for twenty years."

"What about your grandmother?" the reporter asked. "She was involved in the deaths of at least two people." Another reporter yelled, "Everyone better steer clear of your family! They're a murderous group." The crowd laughed and Dexter bristled.

"Go fuck yourselves, you baying hyenas." He hustled Madison across Twelfth Street to his Tahoe.

Inside, she leaned back against the headrest.

"God, they're cruel."

"You're fresh fodder," Rico told her.

"The thing is," Madison said thoughtfully, "I don't know how I feel about any of it. I'm shocked about the senator, yet when I think of him, I remember all the wonderful times I spent at his home and how gracious he was. The other side of him doesn't seem real yet."

"Perhaps that's the best way to remember him," Dexter gently told her. "It'll all die down, honey. I'm sure Ella and you will be harassed for a few days, but then something else will come along, something more sensational. And life will go on."

"What's going to happen to Gran now?"

"I don't know, sweetheart. If she can ever come to terms with her part in the Society, she has a chance to live peacefully for the rest of her life."

After another hour, Ella and her attorney appeared on the steps. Madison strained to see her grandmother's face, but the crowd closed in around her.

"Dex—" she began, but Dexter cut her off,

"I'll take care of it." He hustled to Ella's side and, after a brief word with her attorney, escorted her to his car.

Madison gave her a hug and studied her face. She looked tired—exhausted, really, but her color was good. "Are you all right?"

"Quit your fretting, honey. I'm too valuable for them to harm me."

"Her attorney says it's looking good," Dexter said.

"There's Mr. Chauncey," Ella said.

He was walking across the parking lot accompanied by another man. His attorney? Madison wondered. She'd heard the butler had been charged as an accomplice.

After he expressed condolences, Mr. Chauncey took Madison's hand.

"Oh, my dear, how are you? I was informed of the relationship between you and the senator, and I'm honored to shake your hand. Even though some will never understand his actions, Senator Stone was, to me, the greatest man I ever knew."

"Mr. Chauncey, how can you say that after everything he did?"

"If you'll indulge me for a few moments, I'd like to tell you a story. Mr. Stone, as I knew him then, had just passed the bar when his son was born, and he doted on his small family. He worked very hard to provide the best for them.

"On this particular day, Mrs. Stone had taken their seven-week-old son to shop for a baby car carrier, and the senator stayed home to study for his first big case. He and I heard the car pull into the garage, and when she didn't enter the home, he investigated. What he found haunted him the rest of his life.

"Mrs. Stone was lying on the floor of the garage, savagely beaten in the head with a tire iron. The thief, in his haste to get Mrs. Stone's handbag, threw the child into the wall, and he died instantly."

"God," Madison murmured.

"Mrs. Stone lingered on life-support a few days," Chauncey went on, "and when she died, the senator was inconsolable. Fingerprints revealed the perpetrator was an ex-con, paroled after serving only four years of his sentence for murdering his girlfriend. After a short trial, the judge dismissed the charges due to some technicality about the evidence. The senator began plans for his murder, and when your parents were murdered, he formed the Society."

"So you knew about it?" Dexter asked.

"My attorney has instructed me to take the fifth on all questions, but I'll tell you this. The senator had taken me in several years previously when I lost my family in a drunk-driving accident and no longer cared about anything. I'd become a drunk and hit bottom. The senator gave me life again."

"Justice is a precarious thing," Ella mused several minutes later, watching Mr. Chauncey climb the courthouse steps. "I wonder what'll happen to him."

"I can't answer that," Dexter said, opening the car doors. "But one thing I do know is that it's over. The Society has been disbanded."

Ella nodded and took his arm. "I don't know what we would've done without you, you know."

"You'll have to do without me for a couple of weeks. I've asked Pam to go with me to West Virginia. I don't know how she'll like roughing it by a river or taking fresh fish off a hook," he said with a grin, "but she's game to try."

"Dexter! That's wonderful. I'm happy for you."

Before she stepped into the car, Ella raised her face to the cloudless sky. The sun was high overhead and the temperature was nearly a hundred degrees.

"It looks like another scorcher," she said. "I'd say let's get some lunch, but it's almost too hot to think of food."

"Well, I could eat," Dexter said, "and I doubt you've had anything today."

"Who can eat before a court appearance?"

"I know a great place," he said, "a nice cool restaurant in Oak Glen. It so happens that I know the young owner and I bet Greg will give us a good deal." He turned to Madison. "What do you think?"

She smiled. "Let's go."

CHAPTER THIRTY-NINE

Eileen Glass Joyner had just taken her seat at her kitchen table for lunch with her ten-year-old grandson when her doorbell rang.

"Drink your milk, Alex. I'll be right back." She rose from the table and made her way through her Northglenn, Colorado, tri-level home. She opened the door to a UPS man standing beside a large box with a photo of a brand-name sewing machine on the outside. His truck idled in the driveway.

"I see you're getting a new sewing machine, Mrs. Joyner," he said with a smile. "Hope you enjoy it."

"Thanks, Tommy. I'm sure I will." She signed the electronic clipboard and handed it back to him.

After the truck clattered out of her driveway, Eileen scooted the box across the carpeted living room. Alex appeared, a ring of milk on his upper lip. His gaze fastened on the box.

"Is it for me?" he asked, his blue eyes shining with excitement.

"Not this time, honey. It's for me. Help me push it into my sewing room."

He helped her push the box down the hallway and into the back room full of assorted furniture. An ironing board stood next to a window, and clothing patterns were stacked on an end table.

"Go finish your lunch, sweetheart, and I'll be there shortly."

After he left the room, she opened the box and glanced at the assortment of smaller boxes, all neatly labeled and categorized by the year and state. One box held CDs, another, flash drives, and on the bottom was a box of files.

The invoice had her name, address, and the sender, The Ruby Red Society.

With a smile, Eileen rose and returned to lunch with her grandson.

The Society would continue on.

ABOUT THE AUTHOR

Brenda Hill's novels are about women in crisis. She highlights a problem and offers a possible solution while celebrating the inner strength women sometimes forget they possess.

In her first novel, *Ten Times Guilty,* a young single mother struggles for value after a brutal attack. Her second, *Beyond the Quiet,* tells about a new widow who loses everything and fights her way back.

Brenda lives in southern California and is currently working on her next novel. She enjoys hearing from her readers. You can send her an email from her website: http://www.brendahill.com.

For Every
Individual...

Renew by **Phone**
269-5222

Renew on the **Web**
www.imcpl.org

For General Library **Infomation**
please call 275-4100